PRAISE FOR THE SHROUD

"The chilling details are both horrifying and gratifying, delivered in a way that feels entirely fresh and new to the horror genre. Gritzmacher again has seamlessly transported this reader through time and place, completely engrossed and covered in goosebumps."
  - Brenda-Brendabookstack

"... Gritzmacher effortlessly weaves multiple timelines... a fantastic historical horror novel... exquisite world building and diverse characters... like reading a horror version of an Indiana Jones movie..."
  - Lauren-Booksnbeers13

"The Skulldiggery series is phenomenal... overwhelmingly dark, eerie, and atmospheric... gives you goosebumps, has the hair on the back of your neck standing straight up... It's easily become one of my favorite series, and D.M. Gritzmacher has become a favorite author of mine."
  - River Gardner-Horror Author

PRAISE FOR THE LINGERING

"DM Gritzmacher is such a brilliant writer. His ability to infuse historical facts into his stories and make them his own so smoothly while still making it a solid page turner is flawless."
  - Horror Haus Books

"Part National Treasure, part Stand by Me... academic puzzle-solving and coming-of-age adventure. Fast paced, believable likable characters, engaging dialogue, and a gotdamn horrifying monster..."
  - Christine-Amazon

"...being reintroduced to the characters of Secrist and Stander was like meeting up for drinks with old friends. ...strong Stephen King vibes... It really was everything I love in a horror book..."
  - Tersie-Goodreads

"This book was awesome, super creepy, and addictive. ...makes you stay up all night reading... The creative storyline is unpredictable... compelling and thrilling ...reminds me of 'stand by me' with the kids banter and antics, but way more messed up and terrifying..."
  - Karen-Amazon

PRAISE FOR THE QUARRY

"THIS BOOK IS ABSOLUTELY amazing, heart wrenching and is very emotional at times. It was very well written and holds your attention the entire time."
  - Erin S.-Goodreads

"...an extraordinarily disturbing story emanating from a dark subterranean maze... From old wives tales to a real unimaginable evil... combines gods, monsters and myths... an advanced level of scariness."
  - Mike Rankin-Horror Bookworm Reviews

"If (the movie) The Descent was a book, it would be this."
  - Gavin-Amazon

"Dark and terrifying. I loved every minute of the book and felt so many emotions while reading."
  - Brandy-Goodreads

"...edge of your seat reading, so be sure to plan a good stretch of time as you won't want to put it down."
  - Cindy-Amazon

PRAISE FOR THE RELICT

"...A STUNNING READ... KEEPS the reader wanting more and more... beautifully written... If you read the Agent Pendergast series by Preston and Child you will love this."
  - Rhonda-Goodreads

"...powerful occult thriller... a gripping blend of horror, thriller, and investigative mystery..."
  - D. Donovan-Senior Reviewer-Midwest Book Review

"...knows how to write around the action of the story... not just bare bones... expressive quotes throughout the book... adds so much life to the book. Hard to believe this is a debut novel..."
  - Kelly-Review Cat 86

"Mixing Norse mythology/history with Native American folklore was brilliant. Everything was done respectfully... This is definitely a mystery, horror, thriller and I highly recommend reading this!"
  - Erin, Amazon

"This book was quite the page turner, very well written, a bit creepy and a bit gory and I kept trying to guess what was going to happen at the end! I'll definitely continue on with this series..."
  - Christina-Amazon

THE SHROUD
SKULLDIGGERY BOOK 4

DM GRITZMACHER

PIQUED PUBLISHING

First edition 2024

Library of Congress Control Number: 2024903194

The Shroud Print- 979-8-9866387-7-5

The Shroud EPub- 979-8-9866387-8-2

CONTENT WARNING

The Shroud contains graphic depictions of violence, sexual assault, and gore that may not be suitable for some readers.

SHROUD

Shroud-1: a cloth used to wrap a corpse for burial; winding sheet. 2: something that covers, protects, or screens; veil; shelter. 3: any of a set of ropes or wires stretched from a ship's side to a masthead to offset lateral strain on the mast.

PROLOGUE
Egypt, 2600 BC

THE DIGGER GASHED THE soft earth repeatedly. The rise and fall of his tool in the flickering light of the flaming torches nearly as fevered as the one who yielded it. The lone man ignored his sweat drenched brow as he labored beneath the unflinching eyes of the painted figures that dominated the stone walls around him. Continuing to widen the hole he'd only just begun to dig, even as the shifting sands threatened to refill the small trench after each shovelful. The work was tedious, but not nearly as wearisome as all the years it had taken the man to finally reach this hidden and sacred spot. *All that lost time was no longer of consequence to him,* thought the man as he speared the hole again. He alone had discovered the hidden tomb of Nefertem, offspring of the creator god himself, Ptah. If all the archaic writings he'd pieced together were true, the man would have an eternity to make up for any of the time he'd lost.

He alone, Imhotep.

Behind him, the only other living creature in the underground chamber chortled and gurgled contently. The baby, his own son not yet weaned from his mother, reached out and grasped for the simple toys lying around him on the blanket where he lay. A small carving meant to mimic the sacred Ibis bird soon found itself lodged firmly between the toothless, smiling gums of the child. Slobber began to coat the tiny wood statue as the child's pudgy fingers tried desperately to hold it in place. When it finally slipped from the infant's feeble grasp, the intricately etched bird figurine landed between son and mother.

The mother, throat slit and now bloodless, lay unseeing in the chamber.

Imhotep grunted as he finished the last of his digging. He tossed aside the shovel he'd used to open the earth at his feet, then scrambled hurriedly out from the small empty grave. He panted and mopped hastily at his face, eyes, and damp hairline. Barely taking the time to wipe the sting of sweat from his red-rimmed eyes. Struggling to contain his excitement and enthusiasm for what would come next. His lifelong pursuit was about to culminate in the grandest of desires that most men dared not even dream of. But now, as he trembled in excited anticipation, his time was finally at hand. Eternal life beckoned him with warm and inviting arms.

Waiting to embrace only him.

Donning his white ceremonial and sacred robe, Imhotep, an educated and scholarly high priest of Ptah, stepped over the body of his wife to gather up his son. He gently wrapped the child in the blanket underneath and lifted the baby to his chest. Holding him close and kissing his forehead once as he smiled down at his softly cooing son. Then, turning around, Imhotep somberly walked with the baby over to the hole he'd only just finished digging. After softly laying the infant in the shallow pit, he tugged at one corner of the blanket and purposefully covered the child's face with it. His son began to cry. Terror and confusion growing louder in every wail coming out of the earthen pit. The high priest and father worked on seemingly without recognition. Placing the end of his shovel once more into the soft sand and dirt he'd only just turned over. Without looking down at the shrouded form wiggling under the blanket, Imhotep rapidly dumped one shovelful after another back into the shallow pit. It was the fourth pile that finally extinguished the desperate yowls of the infant. Or at least muffled the last sounds it would ever make... But the sudden silence hardly slowed his pace. The high priest worked quickly to replace the soft sand, pebbled gravel, and dirt that he'd dug out. When the last of the displaced earth fell, the man swatted the top of the small rise protruding from the ground with the flat side of his shovel. Imhotep further tamped down the slight rise by stomping both of his feet across the mound until he was satisfied the ground was even, more or less.

Exactly as it had been before.

Using the bladed end of his shovel, the man rolled the dead body of his wife onto her back. Reaching down, he withdrew the lone possession of the still cooling corpse. A glinting rod of gold, nearly as long as his wife had been tall, with an oddly shaped teardrop symbol at the top of it. An unlearned observer might think it merely an oversized scepter and Ankh. The Ankh hieroglyphic character eternally associated with the lands of Pharaohs and said to be the very key of life, or signify the actual cre-ation of life. The man, his revered long ritual robe hanging loosely from his frame, smiled as he withdrew the lengthy, golden rod. Mumbling the sacred prayers of Ptah as he worked, Imhotep dipped the tapered end opposite the oval symbol into the pool of blood that had cascaded down his wife's neck as he'd slit it. Ritualistically, he then glided over to the long-lost sarcophagus that had been secreted away in the eternally shifting sands of his Egyptian homeland – ignoring the glinting, golden treasures that surrounded the stone coffin. With a confident hand, he lined up the tapered end – now greased in the dripping blood of the one he'd loved most just as the ancient writings instructed – with the single small opening on top of the intricately adorned lid. He slid the golden rod inside, turning it slightly to fit the perfectly tailored hole. As it settled in place, a blinding, blue-tinged white light briefly erupted all around the chamber.

Imhotep instantly paralyzed as all around him went black...

CHAPTER ONE
PRESENT DAY

"FOR FUCK'S SAKE, FRAZIER! Would you just find a spot already?" Rolling his eyes, Stander leaned forward on the picnic table bench where he sat and put both hands under his chin. His dog Frazier – a medium sized brown and white pit bull/boxer mix – cocked his head once before pointedly ignoring the pleas of his exasperated owner. "By the time you finally decide where to drop and pop, we could have already been there."

"Excuse me, sir." From behind Stander, a woman's shrill voice cut across the thrum of the interstate traffic rumbling just beyond the rest area where he waited. The background buzz of endless semi-trucks, cars, and motorcycles rushing up and down I-80 towards their intended destinations unrelenting. Without looking, Stander already knew who the speaker was. No matter what she may have been named at birth, she was definitely a Karen. Anyone addressing Stander, with his thickly muscled arms covered in colorful tattoos, bushy white moustache, and long wavy grey hair, as "sir" was always very self-important. Though usually, Stander had learned from his experience with the public as a bar owner, not very important to anyone else.

"Your dog is supposed to be kept on a leash at all times in rest areas." Stander turned and faced the woman. As he did, she looked down at the fearsome skulls populating his black *Mudvayne* concert t-shirt with unshrouded disgust.

Russell Stander, or just Stander as he was known back home, quickly assessed the speaker. The woman, maybe ten years younger than Stander and likely in her mid-forties, was waddling alongside a lanky man with a bad comb-over that kept flapping back and forth in the summer breeze. The couple wore brightly colored matching shirts that screamed "we're on vacation" and the sour facial expressions of deeply depressed morticians. In their hands were loads of overpriced and undersized bags of snacks they'd obviously just purchased from the vending machines inside the rest stop shelter.

Stander, a little over six feet tall, solidly built and at one time a professional prize fighter, stood and stretched languidly. He started to open his mouth in defense of Frazier, but the couple never broke stride or even looked back at him as they continued to their parked vehicle. A smug look of satisfaction on Karen's face. As their car backed out of the parking spot, Stander noted the array of political bumper stickers and the stick-figure-like-fish that dominated the car's back window. As the car sped off, Karen flipped Stander the bird with both hands. Behind Stander, a voice asked, "What was that woman's problem? Did you make a crack about having to see her in those tight leggings?"

"I could have, but I didn't say a word. I swear." Stander looked over at the salt and pepper haired man dumping the last scraps out of a small corn chip bag directly into his mouth as he approached. "No reason to state the obvious. There is nothing more truthful than a pair of yoga pants."

"Or a man's speedo in a cold pool." Thomas Secrist, a retired Michigan state police detective and Stander's best friend, swept a few stray crumbs out of his greying moustache. "Wonder why they left in such a hurry?"

Stander snorted once before making his way over to where Frazier had finally squatted. He pulled a small plastic bag out of his back pocket and scooped up the dog's mess as Frazier sat calmly on his haunches appraising his work. "I don't know. There must be a big book banning meeting they are late for."

Once Stander tossed the bag in the appropriate trash receptacle, Secrist and Frazier jumped into the passenger side of Stander's black Jeep. Their destination was just a little less than an hour away, Stander sped up as the vehicle barreled down the rest area's ramp and rejoined the interstate. Deftly darting in and out of traffic in the late afternoon summer sun. Having to stop for Frazier so close to Relict Mansion, where they were headed, had annoyed Stander. But he knew it was the impending return to his deceased great aunt's home that had him on edge. This was his second trip back to the enormous grounds and manor since he'd inherited the place after his father's death. He felt certain the massive home held secrets. The long-abandoned mansion pulled at him in inexplicable ways.

During his first visit back since he was a kid, just a handful of weeks ago after nearly forty years away, he'd reconnected with a childhood buddy named Chris Bond. Chris had been one of his best friends before adolescence, girls, cars, and music had changed Stander's priorities and conspired to keep him away. He'd also, along with Chris and Secrist, uncovered the identity of a being that, before Stander and Secrist ultimately destroyed it, said it had roamed the earth since the dawn of man. A near eternal creature able to swap the flesh of humans on and off like a suit of clothes to disguise itself. A monster that had preyed on the human race by hiding among gullible religious zealots and exploiting their fears and faith to sate its hunger. The fact that the being had known and feared his Great Aunt Madeleine was perplexing. That, coupled with its choice to live near her home, and Stander's discovery of artifacts and symbols in Relict Mansion that matched what he'd unearthed in an ancient Roman quarry over in France, screamed for further investigation. Now, with his childhood friend Chris safe in a drug rehab back near Stander's home in Marquette, Michigan, it was time to dig into some of the rumors and stories that had always swirled around Relict Mansion. Separate fact from fiction.

Stander's dad, Dr. Timothy Stander, had lived for brief periods of time with his Aunt Madeleine on the grounds. Later in his life, after Stander and his older sister Sherry had been born, their dad still brought them both down for occasional visits. But there was an obvious wedge in the relationship between Stander's dad and Madeleine. Though he had never pressed his father about the reasons, with all that happened over the years, he felt certain her home was the key. The strangeness that had haunted Stander his entire life felt like it was coming to a head. His sister Sherry's fate and body had only recently been discovered after being lost for decades. The fate of his dad's second wife and Stander's mom, Jeanne, who had disappeared when Stander was a boy, had finally been revealed. She'd died in a gruesome accident deep underground in a quarry near her childhood home in France. And the alien being he and Secrist had uncovered, turned out to be the same creature that had chased and killed several of Stander's friends when he was a boy. It was clear to Stander these recent revelations were all connected to his lineage.

And Stander was the last of his family still alive.

An hour later, Stander's Jeep and his two travel companions faced the massive, three-story house that had once been home to his Great Aunt Madeleine. Miles from the nearest town, in a small farming community named Almore. The manor and grounds were also only a few miles away from the Mississippi River on the Illinois side. Though surrounded by bean and cornfields in most directions, the land itself was nestled within a cluster of thick woods that hid the home from the blacktop road that went past its iron gated drive. Above the new arrivals' heads, tall trees swayed back and forth in the warm summer breeze. Lush green grass, neatly clipped and trimmed, surrounded the long driveway and home. Upon exiting the car, Frazier immediately began to investigate the premises. His nose to the ground as Stander and Secrist unpacked their belongings from the back of Stander's vehicle.

The large manor was rimmed with several tall spires that stretched towards the sky. The tops of each adorned with lightning rods from the previous century. A series of tall windows dominated the front of the mostly brick and stone structure. The architecture that inspired the mansion's creation was hard to pin down. Relict Mansion seemed to be a hodge-podge of leftover designs from bygone eras. However, despite the competing styles, the whole of the manor somehow made sense. Strange and different, yet the beauty of the gothic Victorian styling was hard to deny. In a European country, it would likely be called a castle. Only in America, with so many cardboard cut-out homes built nearly identical, did the structure seem out of place.

"Well," Secrist began, "doesn't look like much has changed. The place is still just as intimidating and weird as when we were here last month." He dropped his bags at the double front doors before returning to the car to retrieve some of the tools they'd brought. "Did you get the electricity and water checked out and restored?"

"Yeah. I hired some auctioneer that doubles as the area's real estate agent to get everything working. He said the local handyman spent a couple days here along with his wife getting everything in order. There should be two rooms already made up for us this time. And get this," Stander dropped a large bag of dog food beside the tools Secrist had begun to pile next to their belongings by the doorway. "Each of our bedrooms has their own private bathroom."

"Do we have a working kitchen this time?" Secrist slammed the back of the Jeep shut and carried a sledgehammer and pickaxe in each hand. By the time he'd made it back to the front door, Stander had it unlocked and let it swing open. Black and white tiles and a buzzing, half-lit chandelier greeting them as they stepped inside.

"Yup. We even have a fridge with an icemaker this time." Frazier darted around Stander's feet and raced up one of the two long stairwells that led from the foyer to the second floor. Stander, with a bag in each hand, dropped them at the foot of the stairs.

"Where do you want me to put these?" Secrist gestured towards the sledgehammer and pickaxe in his hands. "And the rest of the tools."

"We are starting in the old library where that big fireplace is. Set them all down in that room."

"You aren't messing around this time, huh? We tackling the mantle with the weird symbol engraved on it first?" Stander nodded as he walked back outside and grabbed the plastic carrying case holding his rechargeable tools. He followed Secrist down a long hallway that led to what was once the home's library. "And you're still positive the symbol matches what Lucas found by that old quarry?" Secrist motioned towards the massive stonework fireplace. Above it, carved deeply into the stone workings that made up the hearth, was an odd symbol carefully etched into the rock. It was rounded and teardrop shaped. Inside the curvature of the circular shape were a series of eleven markings. Each resembled tiny, off-centered swastikas.

"There is no question. You've seen the images Lucas sent us from what he's uncovering in France. That same symbol is carved into the forehead of the monolith buried next to the quarry where I found my mom." Stander felt an involuntary shudder creep up his spine. Neither Lucas, nor the team of archeologists working with him in France, had previously seen the symbol. But they all had been in agreement. It was a bastardized version of the Tree of Life.

"And no one has ever seen that mark anywhere before?" Secrist shook his head. He still expected a reasonable answer to soon be discovered. It was just too much of a weird coincidence. And he hated coincidences.

"Actually..." Stander rolled up one of the sleeves on his black concert t-shirt. Underneath the cloth, the most prevalent image was an elaborately drawn wolf's head done in ink across his bicep. The tattoo had been the very first one Stander ever had done back when he was still in his teens.

"Are you serious? Did you get another tattoo?" Secrist had seen Stander without his shirt enough to know he had full sleeves of color. "Don't tell me. You had that symbol inked on you? Where did you find any blank skin to use?"

Stander shook his head and beckoned Secrist towards him as he walked over to the windows. Outside, the last of the day's sunlight made the tops of the surrounding trees seem to flare like burning matchheads. Stander used his hand to stretch the skin tightly across his bulging muscles. As he did so, he tilted his arm slightly until the light from the window hit it just right. When he did, the birthmark he'd been so ashamed of as a kid came into focus. Though still covered with the faded ink from the old wolf's head tattoo, the shape and features of the birthmark were clear. It was identical to the carving above the fireplace.

"What the hell? You were born with that?" Stander nodded his head. "Did your mom or dad have one?"

Stander shook his head no. "Neither of them did. But," Stander grinned joylessly, "my Great Aunt Madeleine did. On the same arm and in the same place." Secrist's eyes drifted from his birthmark to the fireplace hearth and back again. He didn't have to say a word.

"Exactly." Stander pulled his shirt sleeve back down. "What the fuck..."

For the rest of the evening, as the setting sun bruised the Midwest sky in shades of purples and pinks, Stander and Secrist unpacked their belongings and settled in. Frazier made himself at home, but followed after the two men if left alone for long. When Stander retired to his room for the night, Frazier jumped in the bed and laid down beside him just as the dog did back at home. Stander cracked open a Dan Simmons novel titled The Terror and read uninterrupted until finally turning off the lamp beside his bed. When he rolled over, Frazier nestled in beside him and they both fell asleep.

CHAPTER TWO
CAIRO, EGYPT - 1962

SAQQARA NECROPOLIS

AS HE STEPPED GINGERLY around the discovery, Tim squatted and whisked the worn bristles of his handheld wood brush back and forth carefully across the find. Meticulously removing much of the accumulated grit from one of the funerary statues. Under his feet, loose sand crunched as he shifted his weight back and forth while he worked. All around him a multitude of eyes – beautifully hand painted and unwavering – solemnly observed from the stone walls at his every side. When Tim was satisfied the ornamental figurine was intact and not likely to crumble if moved, he pulled it cautiously from the ground. Using both hands, he delicately handed their latest find up to his father, Professor Emery Stander. The two men, Tim Stander aged 32 and his father, 62-year-old Emery, both dressed in nearly identical khaki-colored shirts and pants, exchanged nervous but happy glances.

"Wait until your Aunt Madeleine sees what you've found, my boy." Emery's wizened eyes animated in the artificial light flooding the small interior dig site. "She will be so proud of you!"

"What *I* found?" Tim beamed up at his father from the shallow trench he stood in. "I only do the grunt work. You are the brains of the operation." He stepped up and out of the sand pit they'd been working in for the last three days. "So let me be the first to congratulate you, dad." He pulled off his leather work glove and extended his deeply tanned hand. "This is a remarkable find, Professor Stander." The two men shook hands enthusiastically. Emery carefully clutching the frail Ibis bird statue to his chest. "I am so proud to be the son of one of the leading archeologists working in Egypt right now."

"Shush, shush, shush all that nonsense." Emery scolded his son good naturedly, "I haven't been leading anything. Unless you count the wild goose chases we've been on the last few years. These," he gestured back at the freshly dug trench at the feet of both men, "are nearly the only tangible objects I've found in these desert fields this entire digging season." Both men looked back across the gouged earth below them. Though the material around the find had barely begun to be removed, parts of similar Ibis funerary statues could be seen rising from the sand. Less colorful and decorative, but infinitely more important, were the mummified remains of once living Ibis birds intermingled with the glazed totems. The feathered animal graves marking a likely place of sacrifice and worship for those who had once deified the mystifying high priest named Imhotep. "Besides," the older Emery Stander continued, "we would have never thought to uncover this area without Madeleine's suggestion. This find is as much hers as it is ours."

"Well, I know she is paying for all of this. But a lucky guess from the banks of the Mississippi River where she lives without lifting a finger hardly qualifies her as the finder." Tim, wiping the back of his perspiring neck with a handkerchief pulled from his back pocket, flashed a crooked grin at his father. His Aunt Madeleine was Emery's much older sister, though one would never guess it. In many ways – physically, her mannerisms, sharp mind, and energy level – she seemed almost younger than Emery. Both with different mothers and born some twenty years apart, there was little family resemblance between the two of them.

"Don't bite the hand that feeds you, boy." Emery winked at his son from behind his thick black rimmed glasses. "She funds every one of my digs without question. And as for you, the newly minted Dr. Stander, soon to start up his very own medical practice, just remember she insisted on paying for your college education as well. Other men should be so lucky as us two."

"I know, I know... I'm not complaining. I just want to be sure you get the recognition once we find Imhotep's tomb." Tim tied the now damp white handkerchief around his suntanned neck like an ascot. "This is the last season I'll be helping you out here in Egypt. I don't want anyone swooping in at the last minute and taking credit for all your work. Especially since Aunt Madeleine is coming to Cairo to visit us early next week. I bet she'll insist on seeing all this and try to tell us where to dig next."

"You mean **IF** we find his tomb, my boy. This," Emery held the Ibis statue slightly aloft, "is merely a breadcrumb we can follow. We'll have to see if, like Hansel and Gretel, this is the beginning of a trail of bread-crumbs that will lead us home or not." Emery, pale and nearly bald, with only a rim of white hair a few inches thick encircling his shiny head, turned to place the delicate find into the hands of a trusted local Egyptian worker helping the professor and his son with the dig. The man, named Abasi, was the lead digger and translator for the father and son team. He bowed as he took the artifact in his hands and walked swiftly over to the table where two other robed workers were busy cataloguing the meager finds of the day. Placing the small sculpture alongside some of the earlier discoveries.

"Hansel and Gretel? I hope we don't have to boil a witch alive before we can return home to the states!" Tim laughed as both father and son walked over to where their water canteens hung. The arid heat of the Egyptian desert keeping this path well-trodden. Both men taking turns drawing long drinks of water from their steel containers as they talked.

"Imhotep certainly did do magical things back in his day. But all his many accomplishments were based in science, math, and architecture.

Not magic." Emery tugged a pack of slim, Turkish-branded cigarettes from out of his front pocket. Placing one in his mouth, he then fished out a personalized steel lighter from the front pocket of his khaki trousers and lit it. He took a deep drag as he looked out across the dig site contently. The exhaled smoke drifted aimlessly above his head. Though the site they worked was not deep underground, the hard-packed earthen walls overhead blocked the desert winds that often swirled across the sands of the Saqqara desert some forty feet above their heads. Eventually, the cigarette smoke nonchalantly trailed alongside the thick, braided rope the small team used to reach their dig site each day. The slowly dissipating smoke finding its way up to the piercing beam of sunlight coming from the shaft that led to the surface. Leaving the small cluster of workers, the two American men and the dim electric light they worked in behind.

"I don't know, dad." Tim stretched and looked down at his white-faced and black-handed watch, the end of the work day now upon them. "He sure must have seemed magical to his followers. A physician, mathematician, astronomer, and a poet... Architect of Djoser's step pyramid, the first pyramid ever built in Egypt."

"Supposedly the first. I have my doubts as you well know... And don't forget, my dear Dr. Stander, he is also considered the writer of the very first Egyptian medical texts. Describing almost fifty different common injuries and their treatments. As well as listing hundreds of different anatomical terms!" Emery bent down and crushed the last of his burning cigarette into the loose sand at his feet. Tucking the spent filter in his pocket to keep the dig site as uncontaminated as possible.

"A remarkable man, for sure. I can understand why you think finding his tomb would be so important." Still standing beside Tim, Emery turned his head and coughed loudly into his hand. "After all, you've spent the last five digging seasons focused solely on unearthing Imhotep's final resting place. It's like you're obsessed with him."

"That is the one thing my sister Madeleine and I have in common. Our united passion for discovering his secrets." Emery turned and coughed once more before reaching again for his canteen. He hastily spun the lid open and drank heavily from the container. Tim watched his father with a clear look of concern on his face.

"And after this digging season, you'll see the specialist in Chicago about that cough. Right, dad?" Emery nodded distractedly as he slid the long cloth strap from the canteen over his shoulder.

"Yes, yes, yes to all that nonsense..." Emery looked down at his own ticking watch before looking back up and addressing the small cluster of men working alongside himself and his son. "Time to call it a day, gentlemen. Let's clean up and head back up to the surface."

Abasi, their translator and head digger, a heavy-set man with dark skin and piercing black eyes, turned and barked orders out in Arabic. The small group of men immediately tossed down their tools, each anxious to return to the surface and to their families. One by one, all the men were pulled to the surface by the series of pulleys above ground. The ingenious design allowed even the heaviest among them to be easily lifted out of the cavity by a single man above. The hand crank, a series of large, leveraged wood wheels, raised and lowered the thick rope each man rode up and down the narrow shaft that led to their latest dig site.

After watching his father raised above his head, Tim placed his foot in the looped and tied end of the long rope when it descended one last time for him. He wiped his wispy brown hair away from his eyes and looked out across the now abandoned work site as he was lifted upwards. Near the surface, just before his head crested the opening at ground level, he saw the hint of something blue poking out from where their dig had left off. Though he only saw it for a moment before he was topside once more, the blue hue matched the distinctive blue painted pottery often associated with the divine in ancient Egypt. Stepping out of the braided loop and back on the solid ground of the surface, Tim shared what he'd seen with his father. Both men excitedly discussing the possibilities as their Jeep weaved its way through the sands of Egypt on its way back to their hotel in Cairo some 20 miles away from their site. Though the next day was Sunday and an "off day" with no work planned, Emery said he would try to contact Abasi and see if he and any other of the men would be willing to meet them tomorrow anyway.

Arriving at their hotel after the bumpy and dusty ride, Emery went to the bustling front desk to check for any messages that may have come in that day. Tim went up to his room and when he opened the door, he was met by the delighted cries of his nearly one-year-old daughter.

Sherry Stander.

CHAPTER THREE

"WHAT DO YOU MEAN you are going back?" Sherry was squirming in her father's arms as he lightly poked and tickled her bulging belly. Dressed only in a saggy cloth diaper, the little girl giggling and dramatically arching her back as father and daughter played together in the bland hotel room.

"I know tomorrow was supposed to be my day off," Tim began. "But we are likely really onto something now. I only have a little over one more week here in Egypt before we head back to the states. Dad only has one more month before this entire digging season is over as well. I want to maximize each and every day."

"But, honey," Lucy, Tim's wife of three years began. "What about our trip together down the Nile? We already paid for the little boat ride." Lucy, her long, jet-black hair tied behind her in a ponytail, looked up at her husband from the edge of their bed where she sat. A brown electric fan perched on the single desk in their hotel room oscillated casually back and forth in front of her. The artificial breeze lifting the edges of the bright yellow dress hanging at her knees. On the bed beside her, the pages of a Life magazine featuring the triumphant astronaut John Glenn – the first American to orbit the earth – flipped nonchalantly back and forth. "Sherry and I are dying to get out of this room. All we do is walk back and forth to the market. I think I may go crazy if I don't get away from this hotel." She stuck her lower lip out to pucker before blowing several long strands of hair away from her mouth. A look of disappointment clouding her otherwise attractive features.

Tim tossed Sherry playfully and gently onto the bed beside her mother. The little girl squealed with delight before scampering on all fours up the mattress and using the headboard to pull herself to her feet. Her light-colored hair filled with electricity and sticking up awkwardly behind her head. She looked back over her shoulder at her parents with big blue eyes before sneezing once and knocking herself off her feet in the process. Landing on her butt beside the pillows with a startled look on her pudgy, cherub face.

"How about this?" Tim kept one protective eye on Sherry. Ready to pounce if she got too close to the edge of the bed. "Why don't you two come along in the morning?" Lucy opened her mouth in protest, but Tim beat her to the punch. Quickly adding, "I know you hate the heat out in the desert, but it would still be cool on the drive out there that early. Plus, underground and away from the sun and wind, it actually is fairly pleasant." Sherry began to crawl back over to her mother who still sat at the edge of the bed scowling. "What do you say? You said you were curious about our new dig site. Here is your chance to see it." Tim smiled down at his wife. Though they'd met in college at 22 years of age, their romance had been a slow one. Dating on and off while he had finished work on his medical degree at the University of Illinois in Champaign. Lucy, her family a middle class one from Chicago, had gotten her teaching degree from nearby Illinois State University, an hour's drive away from Champaign. A chance meeting at a mutual acquaintance's party where they had first met. Ultimately marrying almost eight years later just before they'd both turned thirty.

"But you promised to take me shopping. We need to start thinking about building a house and we both love Egyptian décor. I thought we could start picking some things out and..." A loud knock at the hotel room's door stopped her mid-sentence. With Sherry now sitting safely in her mother's lap, Tim walked over and opened it.

"Good news, my boy! Abasi says he will meet us at the usual time tomorrow." The visitor was his dad, Emery. "He thinks he can get Tata, his foreman and second in command, and maybe his brother as well, if we promise to wrap up before lunchtime. Which I readily agreed to." Behind Tim, Lucy rose from the bed and, with Sherry in her arms, she strolled across the room to the doorway. "Oh! Well, hello there, little one." The distinguished professor's face lit up and softened, dissolving into a grandfatherly look of affection. He stuck one finger out and bounced it lightly off Sherry's nose before she grabbed a hold of it. Pulling it towards her drooling open mouth, unsuccessfully.

"Hi, Emery. I guess you guys found some interesting items today." Lucy looked back and forth once between the two men. "I hope Sherry and I won't be in the way." Tim, relief etched on his face, smiled at his wife before turning back to his father who now had a surprised look on his face.

"We originally had plans for a little boat ride tomorrow, dad. So, I thought they could maybe tag along. Get them out of this stuffy hotel room and see the site before we leave next week." Sherry was reaching for Tim, so he snatched her from Lucy's arms.

"Sure, sure, sure, my boy. The more the merrier." Then, turning towards Lucy, he added. "We'll only be a few hours or maybe even less. Tim may have only seen a shard of broken pottery, anyway. If nothing more of consequence is found, we'll all hightail it out of there. I promise!" He turned his head and coughed once before turning back. "I think," he began before coughing once more, "I think..." This time he turned and coughed loudly four times. Each cough ringing loudly in the hotel hallway and startling an older guest waiting for the elevator a few doors down from him. Tim reached out and slapped his father several times across his back.

"You OK there, dad?" The elder Stander turned back, smiling. Barely getting out that he was fine and he'd see them all in the morning before turning back and walking down the hallway towards his own room. As Tim closed the hotel room door, a dark shadow of concern passed over his features.

Early the next morning, Tim, his young family, and father all made the drive out to the Saqqara dig site where river-fed crops gave way to an unforgiving desert. Located on the Nile River's west bank, some 20 miles south of Cairo, Saqqara was an ancient burial complex marked by crumbling pyramids that emerged from the sand like the monstrous teeth of a massive beast. More than a dozen pyramids are scattered along the five-mile strip of land, which is also dotted with the remains of temples and tombs that span nearly the entire known history of Egypt.

There they were met by the robed Abasi, Tata, and one other man who had been working with Professor Stander the entire digging season. After a few pleasantries, everyone, including Tim with Sherry held safely in his arms, made their way back into the narrow shaft. Only the single man working the manual lift at the surface remained atop the dig site. After landing safely underground, as Lucy and Sherry stood watching, the men all stepped into the shallow pit where they had unearthed the Ibis statues the previous day. As expected, the shiny glinting blue object Tim had seen during his earlier ascent was quickly located. The four men – Tim, Emery, Abasi, and Tata – partnered together to painstakingly reveal the gleaming blue object buried in the sand. In less than thirty minutes, the men had uncovered what turned out to be a sizable find.

"An amazing piece of artistry, isn't it?" Emery gazed in wide-eyed wonder at what the dirt and sands had hidden so completely. The spot of blue Tim had barely glimpsed peeking out from the sand was from a large piece of collapsed stone wall. The toppled barrier, beautifully hand painted with a multitude of images, had likely once been a temple wall. Or, perhaps, another related but previously unknown religious structure. The many offerings of the Ibis bird stacked around where the wall had once stood the most obvious clue. "I never tire of seeing that bright blue color emerge from out of the past."

Lucy, wearing khaki slacks, boots, and a white blouse, stood outside the pit near the edge. She asked, "How did they make such a gorgeous color of blue? The color is so brilliant. It looks like it could have been painted yesterday." In her arms, baby Sherry sucked contently on a pacifier that bobbed in and out of her mouth.

"That is cuprorivaite. It is a calcium copper silicate that we can thank the ancient Egyptians for inventing. It is actually considered the first ever synthetically produced color pigment. Not surprisingly, it is known simply as Egyptian blue. They made it by grinding up limestone mixed with sand and another copper-containing mineral, likely azurite. Which was then heated and baked. The end result was an opaque blue glass which had to be crushed and combined with thickening agents such as egg whites to create that color of glaze. Astonishing, isn't it?" Emery paced around the border of the fallen stone wall, the buckled and broken piece roughly twelve feet across both ways, admiring and trying to make sense of the painted scenes depicted on it.

"The Egyptians held that hue in very high regard and used it to paint ceramics, statues, and even to decorate the tombs of the pharaohs. I think the color remained popular even throughout the Roman era in Egypt." Tim paused before asking his dad, "Didn't the Romans even adopt the Egyptian's technique for creating that color as well back in Rome?"

Distractedly, Emery answered over his shoulder. "Hmmm... uh, yes. At least until newer methods of color production started to evolve." He squatted and ran his fingers across the various images that adorned the fallen piece of stone wall. His hand stopped moving and rested on an image of a feathered bird, another caricature of the Ibis.

Lucy carefully slid down the embankment that circled the pit where the work was ongoing to get a closer look. Sherry spit out her pacifier and Tim bent down to retrieve and clean it before placing it back in her mouth with a smile. Abasi and Tata worked beside the Standers, continuing to remove debris from around the edges of the collapsed portion of wall with the beautiful motif. "Why all the birds? The Ibis statues, the mummified remains, and now all the images of them painted on the wall?"

"Well, in ancient Egyptian society, the sacred Ibis bird was worshiped as the god Thoth and was supposed to preserve the country from plagues and serpents. That was one of the reasons the birds were also often mummified and then buried with pharaohs. Thoth was an extremely important god to them. But I'm not sure the hieroglyphs on this wall reference Thoth." Emery stood once more, his knee popping audibly. He walked over to Abasi and pointed to the ground near where they continued to work. Sand seemed to be sliding down and disappearing under one corner of the wall like a small whirlpool. "What do you make of that, Abasi? Should we be concerned?"

As Abasi leaned over to look at where Emery gestured, Tim noticed it as well and approached. As did Lucy with Sherry still in her arms. As the vanishing sand began to quicken its pace, Tim said, "Just like an hourglass, huh? I hope that doesn't mean our time here is up!" He started to laugh when the end of the wall, and the ground under it, suddenly dipped dramatically. The clustered group glanced back and forth at one another briefly.

A moment later, the entire wall, as well as the six who stood around it, suddenly began rapidly sliding deeper underground. The entire contents of the small digging pit vanished beneath the sands amid the startled screams of the fallen.

The first Ibis statue pulled from the ground by Tim yesterday sat on the table where it had been cleaned and catalogued earlier.

It watched stoically as a single, desperately clutching outstretched hand with a ticking wristwatch and brown leather strap grasped futilely for a handhold. Before it slid silently out of sight.

Its time above ground ran out...

CHAPTER FOUR
IOWA/ILLINOIS BORDER - 1964

THE QUAD CITIES

The rain drummed incessantly along the top of the black umbrella. Normally, the rhythmic pattering of raindrops, and even the blustery wind summer storms often bring, didn't disturb Howard. He liked watching little tempests build before releasing all their pent-up fury like a spoiled child denied a new toy. However, tonight, anything he normally enjoyed was far from the detective's mind. He stepped once more around what was left of the body at his feet, eyes straining for any clear sign of why this carnage had occurred.

"What have we got, Jeffrey? Robbery gone bad?" Howard Davis barely glanced at his new partner. Though he'd bolted out of bed and came as soon as he'd received the call, the younger detective had still beaten him to the scene. Howard hated having to be filled in by the new guy. Especially since Jeffrey had just moved here from Marquette. Hired away from his home state of Michigan just three weeks ago to take the place of Howard's previous partner.

"Tough to tell yet, boss. If the motive was robbery, the assailant sure did a piss-poor job. The old lady's purse is just over there," Detective Jeff Plant motioned towards an oddly shaped lump at the beginning of the alley, "with a little over twenty dollars still inside." Howard nodded nonchalantly, he'd already spied the spilled contents and shiny black bag.

Around them, a small gaggle of uniformed officers were busy combing the immediate area for any potential items of interest or clues. Their dark coats were slick and shiny under the steady volley falling from the sky above, flashlights sweeping back and forth along the ground of the near pitch-black alley. A single policeman stood near the head of the alley questioning a couple of late-night onlookers while artfully keeping them at bay. Next to him rain water briefly pooled before cascading down a large metal storm drain opening near his soaked feet. Across from him, an identical drain practically choking under the unrelenting downpour.

Another cop unsuccessfully hid from the deluge in a recessed doorway. Above his head, the tattered remains of a canvas canopy that once shielded the receiving door of the building where the alley dead ended. Colorful graffiti bordered the single doorway on both sides. The policeman scribbled furiously as he jotted down the statement from the lone sanitation worker who'd stumbled upon the grisly find and first reported it. But, at almost 3:00 AM in a driving rain, it was doubtful any of the tiny crowd gathered had actually seen or heard what happened.

"Murder weapon?" Howard looked up and met Jeff's eyes. He knew the young man was barely in his thirties and likely didn't have much experience with this kind of thing. Not that Howard had either. The corpse of the old woman had been butchered with a savagery Howard had only ever witnessed during his time overseas in the service some twenty odd years ago. Here, in the small town of Rock Island, this kind of brutality was almost unheard of. Even if you factored in the other three towns that made up the "quad cities" as locals called the four bordering towns huddled on either side of the Mississippi river.

"There doesn't appear to be anything left behind by the assailant. With this much rain, most anything we do find most likely won't have much value." Jeffrey Plant didn't have an umbrella or hat, and rainwater streamed down his face and off his pointed nose. His normally frizzy brown hair matted down and dripping. "With the exception of the warehouse on this side," Jeff pointed to where the uniformed officer continued to take the statement of the garbage truck driver under the sagging canopy, "these buildings are all empty and locked up tight. I figure we'll come back sometime tomorrow and see if any of the employees from that Hancock Medical Supply warehouse saw or heard anything suspicious before they left for the day. Other than that, the coroner is already on the way. Hopefully, he'll be able to provide some answers once he is able to examine the remains."

"Yes, agreed. Not much we can do in this rain and with such poor lighting." Howard gestured at the single street light at the beginning of the alley where the old lady's body had been discovered. Though the medical supply building and empty warehouses surrounding the scene were each only a few stories high, with no lights and the moon covered by thick storm clouds, the alleyway was like the darkened tunnel of a spook house. Shrouding the things most feared whether they were there or not. Only the lights brought by the police department cut into the gloom of the stormy night. "Listen, good job getting to the scene and securing the area so quickly. I'll stay until the coroner collects everything and the other officers finish. Why don't you head back home? Get out of those wet clothes before you catch pneumonia."

The younger and much taller detective's face showed surprise. "Are you sure?" He stammered a bit before adding, "I mean, thanks. If you really think that's OK..." Howard nodded, the rain water collected around the bridge of his cap pouring down the front and splashing his leather, wingtip shoes. "I do have someone waiting on me."

Howard, sporting the same flattop crewcut he'd adopted during the second world war, stood just a few inches over five feet and was barely 130 pounds when, like he was now, soaking wet. He looked up at his nearly six-foot-tall new partner. "You should skedaddle, then. I'll see you tomorrow morning when we can review everything in the light of day. And be dry doing it." He reached over and patted Jeffrey encouragingly on his wet shoulder.

"What about your wife? Earlier you mentioned she was having some complications. I feel bad leaving…"

"It's fine. Her mother lives close by and just a phone call away. Believe me, we have everything taken care of at home. Now get out of here. I see the coroner pulling up now." Howard turned before Jeff could reply or argue.

As Howard walked over to meet the coroner at the body, he watched his new partner out of the corner of his eye slowly turn and head to his car. Howard breathed a sigh of relief. He knew he was on a tight leash and needed to show Jeff the ropes, make him feel welcomed and all that. Especially after what had happened between Howard and his last partner. But this was not the night for that. There was something nagging the veteran detective about this murder victim, and he couldn't quite put his finger on it. Howard needed to mull everything over and figure out what was bothering him about this. It was just easier to do without explaining himself to the new guy.

"Howard." The coroner reached across the sprawled body lying torn apart on the wet pavement of the alley.

"Jim." Howard shook the outstretched hand. "What a night for a call like this." He gestured at the rain continuing to soak the alley around them. The county coroner, Jim Stearns, just grunted. "Hope you weren't planning on having a big breakfast later."

The coroner kneeled and pulled off the tarp covering the body lying in the puddle where it had been found. He quickly shot a look of surprise up at the diminutive detective. His face revealing nothing, but his eyes reflecting the same shock that had nearly buckled Howard's knees when he'd first seen the remains.

Remains, as in much was missing…

The old lady was likely at least in her sixties, if not early seventies. She'd been wearing house slippers although they, and her feet, were barely still attached. Each foot had been almost completely severed from the body. The rest of her varicose-lined legs appeared untouched until they met at the "Y" between her hips. Starting at the steel wool patch that covered her sex, she'd been butchered in a sloppy and, perhaps, hurried manner. A jagged cut running the length of her body until it ended just below her neck. The torn skin on either side of the serrated opening pulled wide. Exposing white ribs now washed clean of the gore and blood that would have first poured from the frenzied butchery. Each of her heavy breasts lay on either side of the body. They, like the rest of the victim and the gaping opening she sported, were now nearly bloodless in the continuous downpour. The light blue nightgown and pink robe she'd been wearing had been torn or cut in half the same way her sternum, chest, and stomach had been.

Ferociously.

"Where are the rest of the organs?" The coroner stood and seemed more comfortable looking all around the eviscerated corpse versus directly at it. Howard had worked a lot of years with Jim. He'd never seen him so clearly avoiding the answers the dead whispered at him from beyond.

"I was hoping you'd be able to tell us." Howard found himself also looking away. He'd seen the twin bands of gold on her left hand. This woman was somebody's wife, a mother, and likely at her age, a grandmother. The ruthlessness of her premature death was hard to look at. "They aren't in the alley as best we can tell. But, with all this rain, we can't even be sure she was murdered here or someplace else and then dumped." But Howard wasn't sure Jim was listening to him or not. Both men stood silently in the rain.

Shivering.

Finally, Jim spoke. "I'll know more once I get a closer look. Kind of hard to work in this torrent and without proper lighting." He gazed down once more at the wreck of the woman sprawled along the black pavement. "You, uh… you noticed her ankles, right?"

"No…" Howard started to say, but then it hit him. That was what kept bothering him!

"You remember the girl who got pulled out of the river a few weeks back? That was on the Iowa side of the Mississippi, and the Davenport Police Department handled the investigation. But I'm friendly with my counterpart in the coroner's office over there and he was telling me about it last weekend."

Howard shrugged. It was hard enough keeping everything straight that he was responsible for. Much less be poking his nose in another department's work. "Vaguely, I guess. Just from what I read in the papers. Didn't they decide the girl's body had been hit by a motorboat or something like that? She was all chewed up, wasn't she?"

"The little girl had been in the water so long most of what they determined happened was just guess work by the time she was found. All the wildlife in the Mississippi River had their turn at her first. You know how big the snapping turtles and turkey vultures get around here. My peer said he'd actually suspected a lot of the original damage done was with a single blade. But he said there was just no way to be certain after all that time in the water. Since the girl had never learned to swim, and was last seen throwing rocks off a dock on the river, they determined she'd somehow fell in." Howard nodded; it was coming back to him now. "At some point, they figured her body must have been hit by a speed boat or two to cause all the damage her corpse showed when it was pulled out of the Mississippi."

"Isn't drowning easy to determine? The lungs full of water and all that?" Howard was cold, wet, and without sleep. Why Jim was reciting this story about a drowned little girl from a month ago was beyond him.

"Little tougher when the lungs are gone..." Jim paused before continuing. "My counterpart said without any other plausible scenario, he went along with the consensus. That it was just a terrible accident and tragedy. She'd somehow fallen in, drowned and lost most of her innards after a motorboat's propeller sliced her open. The local wildlife taking all her soft parts. But, besides the girl missing most of her organs just like grandma here, both her feet were missing. Sliced off cleanly at the ankles. Just like hers nearly were." Jim pointed at the disemboweled senior citizen at his feet. "Both Achilles tendons had been cleanly sliced. Since the wounds hadn't been the cause of death, it was hard to justify spending a lot of time exploring different scenarios about how that could have happened. So, the coroner over there didn't push it at the time. But he said it has bothered him ever since." The coroner's face grew grim. "And now I see this."

Howard watched contemplatively as the coroner and the rest of the policemen finished their work at the scene. Just as they wrapped up, the rain began to subside. Howard drove back home under the bright sun of the emerging morning. Could these two deaths somehow actually be related? Both brutal murders just weeks apart in this community? If so, what tied the young girl found in the river to the old woman found butchered in this desolate alley?

CHAPTER FIVE

"Were you good while I was away? Did you miss me?" Jeff Plant locked the door behind him and slipped off his wet shoes beside the front door. He tossed his soaked jacket across the top of the free-standing coatrack in the near corner before unhooking his gun holster and draping it over one of the empty hooks on the same wooden rack. He could see down the hallway of his small, two-bedroom home and he smiled. At the end of it, the doorway that led to his spare bedroom was wide open. Only a yellowish dim light visible. "You didn't soil yourself while I was gone, did you? That would make me very upset."

The young detective peeled his sopping clothes off as he slowly made his way down the hallway. Dropping his tie, shirt, and t-shirt on the beige carpet that covered nearly the entire floor of his rented house. The only exceptions being the kitchen and bathroom lined with new, but cheap linoleum. Halfway to the bedroom, he stopped and leaned against the newly painted white wall. He reached down and pulled off his drenched socks one by one before unbuckling the belt around his waist. "I know you really liked it when I started to get rough with you just before I left. Time to finish it."

Jeff looked up at the bland pictures hanging along the hallway as he unbuttoned and unzipped his pants. Each were reproductions of art he'd purchased at the local Sears store. Serene scenes of nature, boats with puffy sails and tangled shrouds, or beaches speckled with colorful umbrellas. He hated the uninspired scenes depicted, but they served their purpose. With the exception of the room he was about to enter, the décor he'd picked out after moving into the rental property was all equally unassuming and plain. As he took the last steps before he reached the doorway, he stripped off his brown pants. Without underwear beneath, Jeff strolled nude and unhurriedly across the threshold of the tiny bedroom, his brown belt still in hand. Though shivering slightly, his heated anticipation began to get the better of him. The familiar ache in his loins returning.

Stiffening and inflaming him.

"Oh, no. Don't get up." Jeff snickered as he looked down at the lone figure occupying the bedroom. The woman was gagged and bound, the dark makeup once circling her eyes left in long lines that streaked down both cheeks. Her black hair was tussled about her head in a crown of disarray. Almost completely unclothed, she was stretched across the mattress face down on her stomach. Tied to the bedposts on all four corners. Her wrists were pink and raw, ankles rubbed red and bleeding. On her feet she wore a pair of black high heels that you usually only see Hollywood starlets, streetwalkers, and strippers wear. The woman looked up as Detective Jeff Plant entered and shut the door behind him. Her eyes grew wide and she struggled to speak.

"Hush now, little girl." The woman, decades removed from being a little girl, pulled at her restraints. Jeff slipped behind her, standing at the back of the bed, enjoying her struggles. He bent and took one bleeding ankle in his hands, his breath now rushed and visibly excited. He wrapped the belt around her calf and pulled it tight before reaching under the bed and retrieving a long blade from beneath the plastic covered mattrass. With his other hand, he slipped the black high-heel off her foot and raised it to his face. He inhaled deeply before dropping the leather shoe to the floor like a man drunk on wine. Dipping one finger in the line of blood around her ankle, he raised the gore-streaked digit to his mouth and licked it clean. "Damn you taste good, Kate. I wonder how long you'll last…"

***

Howard unlocked the backdoor of his modest house and tossed his keys into the empty bowl on the kitchen counter. In one hand he held a dripping bouquet of wildflowers freshly yanked from a ditch he'd passed on his way back home. "I'm back, Gloria. Anything happen while I was out?" He tugged his wet hat and coat off before hanging both neatly from the double-hook screwed to the inside of the door. Careful that any of the dripping water would be caught by the black rubber floormat beneath the doorway. He ran one hand over the white hair of his sharply trimmed crewcut as he sat at the wooden dining table that crowded the modest kitchen of the house. Bending over, he slowly untied the laces of his shoes. Pulling each off before turning them upside down over the metal floor vent to dry. With no reply to his question, he moved to the white stove and flicked off the stovetop light shining down from the hood above. He grabbed the flowers he'd liberated and crossed the blue-patterned kitchen floor. Making his way to the back bedroom where his wife was sleeping.

The brown door creaked slightly as Howard opened it just enough to squeeze himself inside the room. On the bed, his wife Gale was sleeping contently; her breath normal and regular. Beside her, curled up like a cat, arms and legs tucked in a ball, Gloria was fast asleep in the rooms' only soft chair. The soon-to-be retired nurse, whom Howard had hired part-time to help with his wife, was snoring loudly, as usual. Gloria's short grey hair poking out from under the striped Afghan blanket of browns, yellows, and oranges she'd covered herself with. Her Hancock Hospital name badge, a pair of glasses and a book by Dennis Wheatly, all the nurses' belongings, lying together on the small round table beside her. The soft glow of the lamp she lay under the only light in the room.

Howard tiptoed over to the bed where his wife slept. He pulled the wilted flowers he'd purchased for her a few days before out of their glass vase and tossed them into the wastebasket beside the bed. Replacing them with the fresh, wild, colorful ones in his hand. He smiled as he imagined Gale's startled joy when she woke and saw them in the morning. He never tired of sneaking impromptu gifts and messages, no matter how little, into the house and surprising her. It was a game Howard started playing back when he first began courting the raven-haired beauty. He never forgot how she had looked at him the time he'd pulled out the tiny stained glass heart ornament that he'd seen her looking at in the Woolworth store downtown. The shocked twinkling in her eyes, and the dimples in her cheeks, as she'd smiled grandly at the small gesture. From that point on, he'd lived only to see her happy.

Howard exhaled contently as he watched her sleeping. Wondering if her dreams still included him as he eyed the rise and fall of her chest. After a few moments, he moved down to the end of the bed and lifted the corner of the blankets where her feet should be. He verified the bandages were still in place and dry. His wife, Gale, was a diabetic slowly losing her battle with the insidious disease. And, as of three months ago, a double amputee. His wife's once beautiful body being eaten alive by the sickness. Years ago, it had invaded. First, stealing their dreams of having children together. Then torpedoing their opportunities to travel the world before ruthlessly poaching her self-esteem.

And both her feet.

It was all so cruel and unfair. Gale had been the love of Howard's life. They'd found each other just after the Second World War ended. Howard had been a promising young pilot proudly serving in the Air Force before his experiences during the D-Day invasion grounded him forever. The bombs he'd dropped over France that fateful day being the last time he'd ever left the ground. During his recovery, he'd met Gale. At the time, she had been a volunteer helping returning veterans. Though years younger than Howard, she would often read softly beside him when reality became too confused for the ex-pilot. Howard's only war wounds were festering between his ears and hard for most people to understand. But Gale had stuck with him. Believed in him and helped him heal. Her faith, the one constant his sometimes fractured mind could count on.

Once he'd fully recovered, they had quickly been married. Excited to move to Gale's hometown on the border of Iowa and Illinois where Howard, with the help of his new father-in-law, had joined the fledgling police force of Rock Island. Over the next fifteen years, Howard had found the steady routine of police work to be very gratifying. Garnering several promotions along the way, he'd become a detective a decade ago and never looked back. Somehow, he'd found his way out of the darkness of the war, met and married his true love, and built himself a life. He tried not to think what would happen when Gale finally lost her battle with diabetes. He just refused to let his mind go there. Maybe they'll find a cure. Or improve the treatments. Seems like there is a pill for everything nowadays.

Howard skirted past his wife's wheelchair, brushing against the Hancock Medical Supply tag that hung from the side, as he snuck out of the room. He re-latched the bedroom door before walking the few steps over to the living room and his favorite piece of furniture. The couch. He sat down heavily, the near sleepless night starting to catch up with him. He fought against the drowsiness that washed over him before glancing across at the cuckoo clock ticking noisily on the far wall. Six AM. Knowing Gloria would be leaving at 7:00 when Gale's mom arrived to take her place, Howard shut his eyes. He had an hour before then. Maybe just a quick little nap before he had to return to the station.

And deal with the slaughtered dead fate had tossed his way...

CHAPTER SIX
Cairo, Egypt - 1962

SAQQARA NECROPOLIS

THE BLACK WAS ABSOLUTE and terrifying. The only sound came from the cascade of sand still rushing urgently down from above. At first, Tim, rattled by the fall, confused and unseeing, questioned if his eyes were open or shut. When he spied a slowly shrinking beam of light above his head, the question had been answered. He quickly tried to rise, but felt his feet sinking underneath him in the loose sand that had buffered his bewildering descent. The trickle of the tiny grains slowly filling his boots as he wavered briefly on his feet before falling once more onto his back. He was about to holler out when he was robbed of his sight a second time.

"Dr. Stander?" The voice came from behind the light that blinded him, raspy and accent-filled. "Are you hurt, sir?" The question and flash of illumination were from Abasi. Tim raised his hand to block the beam of the flashlight as the portly outline of Abasi slowly came into focus.

"Yes, I'm fine, Abasi. How about..." Tim stopped. His child, his wife, and his father had fallen with him. "Oh my god! Lucy! Lucy! Where are you? Where is Sherry? Do you see her! Lucy!" The single beam of light moved away and lit up Lucy's gagging face just a few feet away from him. She was spitting sand out of her mouth and her hair was blanketed with it, but she appeared to have landed unhurt. Sherry, clutched to

Lucy's chest, the pacifier still somehow lodged firmly in her mouth, was staring up at her with wide eyes. "Oh my, thank god. Honey, honey, are you alright?" Once again Tim attempted to stand and, though more successful than his first try, discovered he could barely maintain his balance. He found himself standing unsteadily on a mound of shifting and sliding sand with an awkward slope. It took all his strength to keep from pitching face forward and falling down the eroding hill where he'd landed.

Flick.

The lighter blazed and a small, dull flame exposed the shadowed features of Professor Emery Stander behind it. Though his glasses were now missing, and his khaki-colored shirt had rolled up and exposed his soft pale belly, Tim's dad appeared to be unharmed. Beside him was Tata, the other Egyptian worker, who slowly stood and precariously peddled his sandaled feet as he half jogged, half fell the rest of the way down from the pile of earthen debris they all had slid down and landed on top of. Moments later, he was standing beside Abasi who panned a flashlight back and forth among the small group. Tim looked above him once again just in time to see the last of the light from where they had fallen disappear completely. The dirt, sand, and debris still above their heads refilling the gap they had tumbled down completely.

"Abasi, can you help my father down?" Abasi nodded in understanding. He elbowed Tata at his side and gestured that he should help Emery down from where he had been planted behind the flickering flame of his lighter. Abasi then shined his flashlight over to where Lucy and Sherry were huddled together. Tim methodically stumbled his way over to his wife and child with the help of the light. Soon, all six of the unlucky party were gathered together around Abasi and the single battery-powered flashlight he held in his hand. Piles of sand, rubble, and rocky material all around them, obscuring much of the four walls that made up the chamber they'd fallen into.

"Stupid, stupid, stupid..." Emery was muttering to himself and shaking as much of the sand free from his hair, face, and clothes as he could. "Why did I allow us to excavate so unsafely? We could have been killed!" He looked over at his son. The regret and anguish on his features easily read.

"But we weren't, dad. Everyone is fine. Right? Anybody hurt at all? Are we all OK?" All around him, the four adults affirmed they were uninjured. Abasi translating and speaking to Tata at his side to get his confirmation.

"But what happened? Where are we?" Lucy's eyes followed the flashlight beam in Abasi's hand as he played it around the room they'd fallen into. They were in a small square cavity of sorts barely twenty feet wide both ways. Crowded in on all sides by sloping sand and at their feet lay the decorated and blue-hued wall they'd uncovered. It sat atop the mound of sand that had buffered their fall as it had sunk down from above. The striking partition now split in several places as it had plummeted down with them. Some thirty feet above their heads, the opening that had briefly cracked wide and swallowed them whole had now filled back in completely. It appeared they'd ridden the collapsed wall like a giant surfboard down the side of a sandy embankment into the hollow space where they now found themselves. The loose and soft sand saving them from any serious injuries beyond some bumps, bruises, and mouthfuls of the desert dirt. The short distance they'd skated down was a mound of sand that resembled a large sand dune. Most of it having just come down from above in a rush like the chamber's newest arrivals.

Abasi, his gruff voice thickly accented, answered in near perfect English. "The foundation around the temple wall above must have given way. Perhaps that weakness in the original construction was what caused the wall to collapse years earlier. The loose sand of Saqqara is much like still water, yes? And still waters can run deep and hide many things."

"Can we get topside again from here? Perhaps climb the sand hill we all slid down to reach the surface?" Emery spoke quickly, the entire time eyeing the top of the sandbank some thirty feet above their heads. Abasi nodded and, like a magician, began to pull what seemed like an inexhaustible coil of rope out from around his belly. The cloth of his long robes hiding the weaved line under them. He handed one end to Tata and directed him in their native Arabic tongue. But, after just five or six long strides up the sand mound, Tata's feet would sink deeply into the loose material. Each time nearly buried up to his waist before retreating and trying again. After half a dozen failed attempts on his part to scale the sand mound, Emery and Tim joined in to help as well. Each man working together and making repeated attempts to scale the loose sand that made up the sloping hill they'd slid down.

Unsuccessfully.

Worse yet, at first unnoticed with only the light from one flashlight and occasionally Emery's stainless steel lighter, it became clear the small enclosure they'd landed in was continuing to fill with sand from some-where above. In the fifteen or so minutes since the group of five adults and baby Sherry had landed in a huff deep underground, nearly a fourth of the small chamber they were in had filled with sand. As more loose, earthen-material slid down around them, the threat of the entire dig site above collapsing on top of them increased. It was the experienced digger and foreman Abasi who noted the danger first. His fear of being buried alive growing more obvious with each passing minute.

"What if we just wait patiently for the room to slowly fill? If we lay flat, so our feet don't sink in the loose sand, wouldn't we slowly rise along with the sand filling this room up? Couldn't we, once we are right near the top, just pull ourselves up to safety?" Tim, his daughter Sherry now in his arms, spewed out one question after another. Desperate to find a way to get his family back to the safety of the surface as soon as possible.

"That strategy would be unwise," explained Abasi who, at times, conferred with Tata in their language before answering. "Tata and I have been digging the lands of our ancestral home nearly all of our lives. We have lost many friends and brothers over the years to collapses like this one. As well as having some close calls in the past ourselves. We cannot wait. It is exceedingly likely we will all be smothered in these rising sands if we don't leave this place very soon." He paused contemplatively as he gazed at the ceiling above. "That is if the entire chamber above us doesn't come crashing down first. I am certain our meddling up there has shifted and weakened everything above us. We must find a way to leave this room as quickly as possible."

"Leave?" Lucy fairly screeched in response. "What are we gonna do? Do you have a magic carpet or genie lamp tucked away under that robe where you had the flashlight and rope hidden?" Tim winced at her unpleasant tone and subtle racism. He shushed the baby in his arms who had begun to cry when her mother started speaking. To his credit, Abasi ignored her accusatory questions and turned to Emery.

"Professor, sir, did you notice the markings there along the very top of the opposite wall?" Abasi trained the beam of his flashlight on a series of hieroglyphs etched into the stone a few feet away. Most of the wall was hidden behind the ever-increasing sand slowly filling the room. Only the top few feet near the ceiling of the room was still uncovered. "I believe they are possibly referring to a burial chamber just beyond this room."

"Well, well, well. Let's see what they say, shall we?" Emery made his way unsteadily to the decorated wall, squinting up at the painted figures and markings still visible along the top. But shaking his head, he said, "I can't really make them out clearly without my glasses. I seem to have lost them in the fall. What do you think it says, Abasi?"

"I do not read the ancient writings as well as you, professor sir. But I believe it indicates there is a passageway leading to the next room on the other side of this wall. With your permission, Tata and I would like to see if we can locate it before the room fills up any further." Though he was polite in his speech and mannerisms, Tim thought he detected a desperation in his tone.

And a beaded line of sweat above his worried brow.

"I'll give you two a hand." Tim handed Sherry back to Lucy, and all four men scrambled partway up the sandy slope that obscured much of the wall below the hieroglyphs. Working together, they began sweeping away the loose material where Abasi indicated he thought the passage might be. Each using their hands to part the sea of sand. Soon, what was likely the very top of a passage or a doorway of some sort, emerged from its hiding place beneath. Abasi scrambled forward and higher up the hill. Lying on his belly to keep from sinking in the soft sand near the top and shining his light into the tight entryway.

"I can't tell for sure where it goes, but it does appear to lead into another room." Abasi continued to dig with his hands, the opening not yet wide enough for his broad belly and backside to enter. "The ceiling above the passage is rock and seems secure." He pulled his head back out and spoke briefly with Tata who, after being handed the wound rope and throwing it over his shoulder, quickly took his place. The much smaller man digging with a hurried frenzy that frightened Tim.

Abasi was looking back at the ceiling above their heads periodically as he helped clear the sand shoveled out of the narrow opening by Tata. Tim and Emery worked as well, all four tunneling like desperate moles escaping a snarling dog hot on their heels. When Tata got ten feet inside the narrow tunnel they'd created, Abasi gestured to Tim. "I think it would be wise for your wife and child to enter after Tata. I do not think we can remain safely where we are for very much longer."

"What? I am not going inside that! The channel is no wider than a coffin." Lucy was pointing and about to say more when behind her the ceiling above began to sag and slowly cave-in once again. Mind changed; she darted up the incline with the help of Emery. Near the top, Tim grabbed her by the shoulders and practically threw her, and the baby in her arms, at the constricted crawl space's opening.

"GO!! Hustle in as fast as you can. I'm right behind you!" No longer protesting, Lucy dove inside, Sherry clutched desperately to her chest. Ahead of her, Tata redoubled his digging efforts, tunneling as fast as he could and foot by foot getting deeper inside the skinny passage. Tim motioned for his father who quickly dropped to his hands and knees, before lying flat on his stomach to scuttle in behind them. Once his father was out of sight and inside, Tim locked eyes with Abasi. Though his eyes reflected fear, Abasi smiled at Tim and patted his rotund belly as he shrugged.

"I, perhaps, lived too full of a life. No room for me yet. You go first." Above Abasi, the torrent of sand and debris began to devour the empty space in the room behind him. Soon everything above him, just as he had predicted, came down in a mad rush of swirling sand and dust. The roar of loosening material not unlike the rumble of terrible ocean waves stirred by a terrific storm. At the last moment, Abasi tossed his flashlight into the claustrophobic opening and shoved Tim in after it. Tim scrambled inside, his shoulders barely squeezing in the channel as he wiggled back and forth like a frantic worm squirming on a hot sidewalk. Just as his feet were tucked inside, a cascade of sand began to pour in and fill the narrow opening behind him. The material instantly enveloping Abasi in its crushing force. Tim, all but climbing up the backs of his father's legs screamed desperately in the black, constricted channel.

"Go! Go! Faster! Faster!" Tim could feel his feet being buried behind him. The sand pouring in the opening threatening to engulf him in their smothering grains. But, though he could not see it, two body lengths ahead of him Tata had stopped digging. He had run into a solid stone wall at the other end and could go no farther. The four adults and baby Sherry were trapped in a narrow tunnel not even twenty feet long and barely two feet in circumference that pressed in on them at every side. They were entombed some 60 feet below the Saqqara desert above them.

Buried alive.

CHAPTER SEVEN

Tim could feel the bulge of the flashlight under his stomach. He twisted in the tightly constrained passage and was just able to squeeze one hand underneath him to pull it out. Quickly flicking the torch's switch and lighting up the cramped passage. Behind him, the sand that had engulfed his feet up to his knees was no longer pouring inside the small opening. Tim thought that was a good sign until he realized it likely meant the entire room they'd barely escaped from was now filled to the top with debris higher than the opening they'd all dove inside of. Going back that way was clearly not an option.

"Dad? Are you OK?" All Tim could see ahead of him were the ribbed soles of his dad's boots and the back of his near bald head. Sand particles dancing unhurriedly in the meager light.

"Fine, fine, fine... You?" He twisted his neck slightly, just enough to briefly make eye contact with his son before turning back and coughing loudly several times. Ahead of Emery in the claustrophobic passageway, Sherry was wailing, and her scared cries tugged at Tim's heart. He could neither see nor comfort her. He flashed back to the exciting day Lucy had first told him she was pregnant. The first time he'd heard Sherry's tiny, rapid heartbeat in his stethoscope, thumping like a camshaft from one of the hotrods he'd driven in high school and college. In his mind, he replayed her birth, the trip home from the hospital, the day his own father first held his perfect baby girl in his arms, and all the hopes he had for her life ahead. The flood of images and feelings filled his eyes with tears. Tim choked back the sob threatening to force itself out of him. He had to get his baby girl to safety. If anything bad ever happened to her, he didn't know how he could live with himself.

"Lucy?" He raised his voice in the cramped interior of the tunnel. "Are you and Sherry okay, honey?" Tim wished he could lay eyes on them, hold and comfort both. But right now, what he needed most was to hold himself together. He thought to himself, *think Tim, think!*

"Okay? We're still alive if that counts as okay." Lucy shushed and soothed Sherry, the baby's cries and shuddering breaths slowed but didn't stop completely. Echoing loudly in the narrow tunnel. "What are we going to do now? I can hardly breathe in here."

"I know. Me neither. Try to conserve as much air as you can. We need to move quickly before all the oxygen in this confined space is exhausted." Tim stopped talking. Lucy was right. Already it was getting difficult for him to catch his breath. *Think Tim, think!* "Dad, can you talk with Tata? Does he see a way forward at all?"

"I only know a handful of Arabic words. But, let me give it a try..." Emery addressed Tata, spewing a few words unconfidently and getting a torrent back in return from him. Emery repeated some of the same words. The only word Tim recognized was the command most often uttered by Abasi at their work site. Dig. Ahead of them there was a shuffling and movement. Tata struggling to part more of the constricting sand blocking their way forward. After a few long minutes, Tata began to speak rapidly, an excitement plain in his tone.

"I think Tata feels an opening parting the sand below him. At least I think that is what he is saying. He is... ah... pushing. I think he means... Yes, pushing the sand out of this opening below him. He seems to think he may have found the entrance to the next room." Moments later, a slight, stale-tasting breeze rippled in. In unison, the trapped Stander family gasped hungrily in and out, greedily filling their starved lungs.

"Oh my!" Lucy exclaimed loudly. "He just sunk down. Tata is moving forward again and his... he just disappeared!"

"Climb after him quickly, my dear. I'll be right behind you." Ahead of Tim, Emery's feet began to inch forward. Soon there was enough space ahead of him that Tim was able to follow. Ten feet farther and the sand and debris he crawled on top of began to slope down. A minute later both father and son were spilled out of the claustrophobic passage nearly on top of one another. Scrambling down the mound of sand that Tata had managed to push into the next room and gain access. Tim clamored to his feet after being deposited head first into this newest chamber. Not bothering to wipe the loose sand from his clothes and hair, he handed his father the flashlight and rushed to embrace Lucy and Sherry in the near darkness. Freedom, something he wasn't certain he would ever feel again, washed over him. They had managed to escape certain death and make it into a neighboring room just as Abasi had predicted. Abasi had saved everyone's lives!

Except his own...

The reunion of husband, wife, and child was joyous yet brief. Emery began hastily pointing the beam from the flashlight all around the new room. At the end of the beam, wondrous things began to show themselves. A mountain of glittering gold artifacts. Small painted statues with gleaming eyes, larger carved images with golden faces and plumed crowns. Heaps of funerary figurines guarding a chamber of significant size and grandeur. Beautifully painted boxes still stacked in an orderly fashion, gilded masks, a finely carved falcon, and piles of linen now blackened with age. Niches carved into the walls themselves bulging with other ornamental treasures. On one wall the painted image of a scarab beetle rolling the sun across the sky. On the other walls, more stunning and ancient Egyptian hieroglyphs. The entire chamber a vast and extraordinary netherworld of treasure and art.

In the very middle of the stone walled expanse, clearly the focal point of the room, a heavy limestone sarcophagus dominated the chamber. Though the lid of it likely weighed several tons, it lay cracked on the sandy ground several feet away from the box-like, stone funeral vessel. As if it had been hastily ripped off and tossed from the top of the sarcophagus.

Father and son glanced at one another. Without uttering a word between them, they both grinned before beginning to walk over to the massive stone coffin. "Imhotep," whispered Emery. As if saying his name loudly would wake the dead interred within.

Both men reached the edge of the thickly walled casket at the same time. The top of it was too high to see down inside. Silently, Tim locked the fingers on both his hands together and bent over. Reverently offering to hoist his father up high enough to steal the first glance inside. Wordlessly, Emery stepped up, placing one foot in the outstretched hands of his son, and reaching out to grasp the ledge at the top. With a grunt, Emery pulled himself up and breathlessly looked down. Ten long seconds of silence filled the ancient tomb with only anticipation before Tim could no longer take it. "What do you see, dad? Is it empty? If not, can you tell if it is Imhotep?"

Emery stepped back down to the ground level of the new chamber. His boots sinking in the deep sand that made up this chamber's floor and faced his son. Tears were carving tracks down his dusty and sandy cheeks. "He is still inside, Timothy. My boy, my boy, my boy... He is still inside." Emery's face broke then. His smile so broad that more flakes of debris fluttered from the lines cracking wide across his joyous face. Emery looked back at the huge stone coffin. "He is still inside," he said mostly to himself.

Tim reached over and hugged at his father who stood unmoving beside him. Finding Imhotep's tomb and final resting place, if that is truly what this was, the culmination of a lifelong dream. Professor Emery

W. Stander had trekked miles of unforgiving Egyptian landscape, dug back in history countless times, and uncovered a revered amount of knowledge, artifacts, and, in some cases, treasure throughout the 1950s. He'd spent nearly thirty years reading about and searching for the body of the man credited with some of ancient Egypt's greatest wonders. For Tim, having lived his entire life in the shadow of his father's quest, the moment was profound. By proxy, nearly the entirety of his own dreams up to this point had come to an end.

They had found Imhotep.

"Bravo, Emery." Lucy, with Sherry held in her arms, said this flatly. "I know this is a really big deal for you guys. But no one is ever going to know if we don't get out of here. Without any water, we'll only last a few days. Shouldn't you be saving your celebratory tears?" Lucy looked away as Tim shot her a look of shock. "How long before the worker up top can get help and dig down to us?"

"Lucy!" Flushing, Tim screwed up his face in anger before he felt his father's hand land on his shoulder.

"She is right, of course." Emery handed Tim the flashlight and pulled a handkerchief from his pocket. He used it to wipe the dampness from his face, leaving smudges of dirt at the crow's feet near his eyes and corners of his mouth. "Both water and oxygen are far more valuable to us than all this." He waved his arms around him, gesturing at the endless array of treasures crowding the burial chamber. Tata stood staring at the glittering bounty. He'd barely moved or uttered a word since they'd entered their temporary sanctuary.

"Yes, of course." Tim shot Lucy another scowl before turning back to his father. "How long do you think it will take him to drive back and get help? Especially on a weekend?"

"Hard to say, but…" Emery's face suddenly fell. He turned and spoke broken Arabic to Tata who finally tore his eyes from the riches piled all around them. There were short words spoken, confusion plain on both men's faces as they tried to bridge the language barrier between them. Each only knew a handful of words in each other's dialect. But the steady shake of Tata's head was clearly communicated. As was the dejected look now darkening Emery's face.

"Tata says Abasi had the truck keys..." It took Tim a few moments for the gravity of the revelation to sink in. "Even once the worker up top realizes we are in trouble." Lucy started to interject, but Emery held up a hand to pause her words. "And by now I would think he realizes something went wrong. But even once he does, he can't make it back to Cairo on his own if the truck keys are buried over there." Without looking, he gestured at the small entrance that had spilled them out of that room and into this one. The room behind them now a tomb as well. One where Abasi had likely been buried alive.

"What about the Jeep we drove?" Lucy, her eyes barely slits, threw out the possibility of the worker taking their vehicle. Tim raised his head briefly, hope sparking his eyes, before he let it fall back down to his chest. He reached inside the front pocket of his pants and brought out a keyring that he held in the air in front of him. Tim, his habit one Lucy already knew, had pocketed the car key after turning off the ignition when their ride to the site that morning had ended.

"No luck," Tim shook his head dejectedly, "I still have them on me." Lucy turned away and exhaled deeply.

For the next hour, the three men and Lucy scoured the stone chamber. Painstakingly looking for another exit or any secrets that might help them discover a way out. In one corner, they found three unused reed torches that had never been lit. The pithy ends of them still wrapped tightly in a material likely once dipped into melted animal fat to help make them burn brighter and last longer. Though, after all the time they'd sat unused in the tomb, much of that effort would likely no longer be very effective. But, except for the torches, and the array of marvelously gilded gold objects they'd first seen upon entering the chamber, nothing else of importance was discovered. As the last of the options seemed to dwindle, they gathered together and sat at the foot of the sarcophagus. The base of the massive stone casket was the only place all four could sit together off of the sand-laden floor itself. Emery placed the steel end of the flashlight on the ground so the lit bulb faced the ceiling, broadly but dimly lighting some of the room around them.

As Sherry began to fuss, Tim rose and took her off Lucy's hands. Walking and shushing the child who had already missed her first nap of the day and was likely thirsty and hungry. As he swayed with the baby in his arms, he stepped over to the cracked sarcophagus lid lying busted apart on the ground. "I don't get it. Why is this here? Any grave robbers or tomb raiders would have taken all the treasure long before trying to move that massive thing. Why would they have opened the sarcophagus?" Tim turned to his father. "Could the mummy inside have been adorned with something more valuable than all this?" He gestured to the piles of glittering gold objects untouched all around the room.

"For goodness sake, Tim. What does it matter now?" Lucy looked over at him with a face darker than the barely lit chamber. "We are all going to die here."

Emery, ignoring Lucy's bleak prophecy, rose to his feet and, as he did, his knee popped loud enough for Tata to briefly look over at him in concern. "I don't... come to think of it, I don't think the mummy inside was decorated at all." Emery frowned. How could ancient Egyptians have buried Imhotep without the usual array of jewels? And without a golden death mask? "It didn't occur to me, but all I saw was a burial shroud covering the body."

Tim walked over and handed Sherry down to Lucy who wordlessly took her. Standing beside his father, Tim reached up and pulled himself over the edge of the stone sarcophagus and looked down inside. His father was wrong. Lying beside Imhotep, or whoever the ancient Egyptian entombed within was, lay a long golden scepter. Tim reached in and pulled it out, handing it to his father before sliding back down to the floor. Both men inspected the rod of gold measuring about five feet in length. At the top of the shiny staff was an Ankh, the most widely recognized Egyptian symbol in the world besides the pyramids themselves.

"What is with all the weird symbols inside the Ankh? I'm not familiar with symbolism of an Ankh decorated in that way. What does it signify?" Tim had fired questions about Egypt at his dad all of his life. He couldn't recall the famed professor of Egyptology ever not having an answer for him.

Until now.

"I have never seen this symbol before." Emery, his glasses buried somewhere in the avalanche of sand, squinted in the weak light of the flashlight. "From the feel of it, the pole itself is likely pure gold. Obviously, the symbol on the top is an Ankh, but very, very different. See how inside the oval teardrop is filled in? Every Ankh I've seen, the space inside the design is hollow. But inside this one it almost looks like, well surely this is my bad eyesight..." Emery started to lay the gold staff at his feet. He no longer felt comfortable holding it in his hands.

Tim grabbed the golden rod from his father. "What? What does it look like?" He peered intently at the strange markings that filled the inside of the Ankh symbol.

"Doesn't that pattern resemble the Tree of Life?"

"From the Bible? Seriously?" Tim lowered the rod until the design at the top was bathed in the full illumination of the flashlight. "Wow, I see what you mean." Silently, Tim counted each mark inside as he touched them with his finger. "There are eleven of these. Does the Tree of Life have eleven points?"

"Yes, eleven." Emery shook his head as he answered. "But how can that..."

"Swastikas! Look closely at the eleven markings. They are tiny, off-centered swastikas. This must be a fake." Tim scowled and rolled his eyes. Fake Egyptian antiquities showed up all the time in the local markets. Gullible tourists unwittingly snatching them up as souvenirs from their trip to the land of pharaohs. It took a keen eye to separate the Real McCoy from the manufactured ones. "But, wait a minute, we have to be the first people in this hidden burial chamber. Anyone else would have taken all the gold. I don't get it?"

"The swastika is an ancient symbol, Tim. We do not really know where, or when, it first originated. Forget about the Nazis. They were just soulless thugs who stole it like they did everything else they could get their hands on. The symbol itself has a long, complex history likely dating back to even prehistoric times. That emblem was said to be a sign of well-being and long life, and has been discovered in antiquity in nearly every corner of the globe. From the tombs of early Christians to the catacombs of Roman Mithraism, it was found to be used at least as far back as 7,000 years ago. Some scholars believe it was meant to represent the movement of the sun through the sky. Others believe the meaning of the symbol is wellbeing, prosperity, or good fortune. It was even used in the prayers of the Rig Veda, the oldest of Hindu scriptures. In Hindu philosophy, it is said to represent various things that come in fours. The four aims, stages, or objectives of life. The number four being cyclical in the balance of life."

Lucy, who hadn't appeared to be listening, suddenly spoke up. "I thought three was the important number. You know, the holy trinity. The Father, Son, and the Holy Ghost."

"That's just your Catholic upbringing, my dear." Emery, now in full lecture mode, though Tim doubted he realized it, went on. "You have to remember; Catholicism is a pretty new religion that only started well after Jesus walked the earth. These symbols here," Emery pointed again to the Ankh topped golden staff with the strange emblems, "easily predate even the oldest of the Dead Sea scrolls. They certainly are far older and likely harken back to the very dawn of man."

"So, we have a long rod made of pure gold topped with the Ankh symbol. Inside the Ankh symbol are eleven points spaced out to form the Tree of Life. Each point marked by a swastika." Tim stopped; brow furrowed in concentration. "The rod was buried with Imhotep..."

"I'm not sure this is Imhotep anymore." Emery interrupted and jabbed a thumb over his shoulder at the stone sarcophagus at his back.

"Well, while we sit here for a rescue that may or may not come, let's see if we can unravel that mystery. Give us something to focus on and take our minds off the predicament we are in." Tim paused; he looked up at the wall closest to them. "The hieroglyph writings all along the walls would likely give us the answer. But, since you lost your glasses, they may be hard to read and decipher. So, let's start with our John Doe mummy-in-the-box instead."

Tim started to set the gold rod down when Tata reached up to take it from him. He walked a few feet away with it in his hands, scrutinizing the bizarre design on the end as Tim continued talking. "I just hope it's not Boris Karloff or Christopher Lee under that shroud." Tim smiled wanly and chuckled once softly. Then pulled himself up and over the top of the stone cavity for a second time. Balanced precariously on the ledge, he reached down with one hand and tugged off the burial shroud that loosely covered the interred body. Turning and draping the long, oddly textured cloth off the side of the sarcophagus. Tim then leaned back over farther, his face merely a foot away from the shriveled features of the occupant as he scrutinized it.

The mummy took in one raspy breath. Then opened its eyes.

CHAPTER EIGHT
IOWA/ILLINOIS BORDER - 1964

THE QUAD CITIES

"The coroner reminded me of something that happened across the river a few weeks ago. Right before you started." Howard slurped at the steaming cup of coffee in his hand. Across the desk, his new partner, Jeff Plant, chewed on one of the stale doughnuts another early rising cop had brought in that morning. Both men were bleary-eyed and clearly missing sleep the night before. "Might not be related. But I think we should pull the file and see if anything jumps out at us."

"You mean from last night's scene? The old lady in her bathrobe?" Jeff tossed the half-eaten pastry into the metal trashcan beside Howard's chair with a frown on his face. "I'm surprised we have his report already."

"We don't. I imagine it will be another day or two depending on his backlog and what he finds before we officially hear anything from him. But he pointed out the wounds on the backs of the victim's ankles. For whatever reason, the killer almost sawed her feet off." Howard tilted back in his creaking chair; brow furrowed in concentration. "Or someone did anyway."

Jeff shook his head as he replied. "Considering all the damage to the rest of the body, that seems pretty minor by comparison. The old coot was disemboweled! Shouldn't we be focused on her recent whereabouts?

Who she knows? Why she was found in that alley dressed only in her pajamas in the middle of the night. See if someone is aware of a possible motive."

"Sure, of course. We need to check all the boxes and follow department protocol. Interview family and friends, see if anything recent or from her past might account for the way she was found." Howard lifted the cup to his lips again and blew once before taking another sip. "I dropped by the scene again before I came into the station this morning. The address listed for her is just across the street from where she was found. She lived in an old house that had been converted into four separate little apartments. The front door to her apartment was locked and no one came to answer when I knocked on it."

"Geez, did you sleep at all? How early did you get here?"

"Didn't really get much sleep. Bad dreams..." Howard turned away and Jeff let the topic drop. He'd been told when first hired and assigned that Howard had some quirky behaviors. Rumors around the small Rock Island police force already beginning to reach him despite his status as the new guy. Bits of gossip and more than a few sympathetic looks when those officers learned Jeff was going to be Howard's new partner.

"I also verified the buildings on either side of the alley where the victim was found are empty and all but abandoned. The only exception being a medical supply warehouse on the corner operated by Hancock Hospital. The rest of the businesses that once occupied those old buildings have all been closed for several years now. So, I'm not very optimistic anyone saw anything. I really think, unless someone was looking straight down the alley from the street, the only other view of what happened would have been from the empty warehouse windows." Howard suddenly stood and stretched. "But we need to verify all this. Maybe get with someone over at Hancock and see who they employ onsite. Could still be important."

"Sounds good. We going to head back downtown then?" Jeff stood as well and walked over to his desk which sat directly to the left of

Howard's. Both desks, like the other ten crammed into the dreary back-room of the Rock Island Police Department Headquarters, were metal behemoths of dull grey. The only difference between Jeff's and Howard's were the tops. Howard's was clean, neat, and orderly. Meticulously spaced photos of his wife dotting two of the corners. Jeff's, on the other hand, was cluttered with old file folders he was reviewing and an array of half-eaten candy and wadded-up gum wrappers. A small clay pot holding an African Violet flower devoid of color – the only adornment.

It was dead.

Around them, several uniformed officers milled about, most having just arrived and their workday only beginning. Jeff pulled his suit jacket from the back of his chair and slid aside the gun hanging from his belt. When he turned back to Howard, his partner hadn't moved.

"You know what you are doing. Just stick to the basics and we'll regroup after lunch. Patrolman Henry is still nursing his bruised ribs and playing department chauffer until he fully recovers from his car accident. He'll go with you since you are still learning the area." Hearing his name, the older cop winced slightly as he rose from his desk before walking gingerly towards the two detectives.

"What are you going to be doing while I'm out running around?" Jeff could hear the annoyance in his own voice but he didn't try to hide it. Was Howard ditching him? Or was this his way of showing Jeff that Howard was the "lead" detective? Make the new guy do the grunt work?

"I'm going to drive across the river and see if I can convince someone in the Davenport PD to let me take a quick look at a file. It's likely a waste of my time. But Jim, the coroner, seems to think there could be a connection." Howard nodded at the uniformed cop waiting on Jeff, "With Henry driving you while I run over there means we can kill two birds with one stone. I doubt neither you or I will learn much of use this morning. But maybe we'll get lucky and Jim will have his report done by the time we get back. Then we can start the real investigation. Together."

Jeff nodded as he trailed behind the slow-moving Henry. What Howard was saying made sense. However, he still felt like his partner was somehow shutting him out. This was the first murder case since Jeff had arrived here in Rock Island. He wanted to make a good impression. But could he trust Howard? Maybe he'd grill Henry about Howard during the short drive back downtown. Find out what really had happened to Howard's previous partner.

The blaze began to build. The fire had started somewhere unseen behind Howard. Perhaps even in the bay area where the bombs his plane carried still laid in wait. Howard understood he needed to reach the target and drop his cargo. Soon! The urgency he felt was both desperate and panicked. Yet seeming unavoidable, like a fate already determined and merely impatient for what it knew was to come. Beside him sat Andy, Howard's copilot, slumped forward in his seat. The only thing holding him in place was the buckled strap across his chest. Andy stared at him with one dead eye. The pupil was so wide it made his entire eyeball seem black as coal. Piercing, almost shiny and iridescent, despite the smoke now gradually filling the cockpit where they both sat.

"Ready to fight fire with fire? Betcha we is gonna blow a hole in the ground so deep that all hell could finally break loose!" Howard recognized the voice before the figure casually limped into the tiny cockpit. It was Finn, the lone southerner of Howard's ten-man crew. A hulking man who'd seemed chiseled from the very steel mills he'd escaped out of his home state of Alabama from when he had enlisted.

Finn was on fire.

The sizzle of his cooked flesh as it fell in clumps around him sounded like bacon in a frying pan. Yet the smell in the cabin was anything but appetizing. Clearly sulfur. Howard tore his eyes away from the cockpit's windows just in time to see Finn unbuckle and toss Andy from his seat. The man on fire plopped himself down into the freshly vacated copilot's chair with a weary sigh. Finn was so close to Howard that the heat from his fiery skin began to singe the hairs on Howard's arm. Yet he couldn't move or tear his eyes from the burning man seated beside him. Dimly, Howard recognized the cushioned seat under the man had begun to melt and drip black plastic.

"Want me take over there, mister northerner? I always wanted to fly one of these big ol' birds..." Finn smiled over at Howard. When he did, his lips curled away from his face like melted wax from a candle shrinking from the flame. In seconds, almost all the flesh on his head had dissolved, leaving a grinning skull of fire with blackened nubs for teeth. "You know what they say. 'When in Rome!'" Finn winked knowingly once before the last of his eyelid peeled away from his eye. Two flaming hands shot out and gripped both sides of the tiny steering wheel of the bomber. Howard opened his mouth to scream, but no sound escaped.

He'd forgotten to breathe...

"Here we go!! Geronimo!!" Finn, or the human torch he'd become, leaned forward and sent the big bomber hurdling towards the ground below. The groan from the craft and its engines bellowing in protest. Howard was thrown forward in his seat. The belts holding him biting into the flesh around each of his straps. He fought against the gravity gripping the plane in its death spiral, instantly pulling back on his controls as hard as he could and desperately trying to level the big bomber out. But the half-steering wheel refused to budge in his hands. As Finn cackled madly beside him, Andy's body rolled forward in the cockpit, coming to rest at Howard's feet.

His lone black eye unblinking.

The smoke-filled plane was in a deep dive. The roaring sound deafening as Howard, knowing he was about to die, stole a final glance out the front window of the bomber. A leering face of flaming stone, erupting up from out of the green forested earth below to meet the plane midair, gaped hungrily. As the plane plummeted towards the enormous face, the jaw opened and yawned widely. Swallowing the big bomber in a single gulp.

Finn, now only a skeleton of dancing flames, said simply as the massive mouth closed around them, "It may take a while to digest all this..." Before bursting into laughter as Finn, Howard, and the entire plane dissolved into darkness.

It was his own screams that awakened Howard. He shot straight up in his seat and banged his head on the hard plastic steering wheel of his car. Instinctively, he yanked at the latch of his car door and leaned his shoulder into the side of it to make an escape. The driver's side door sprung open quickly, but Howard was rudely forced back into his seat. When he screamed again, now with his door wide open, he startled an older black man nearby walking a white dog along the river. It took Howard only a moment to realize he was still wearing his seatbelt. The new habit one his wife Gale had insisted he begin, sure that otherwise Howard would die in a car wreck.

"You doing alright there, friend?" Howard looked up at the concerned face of the man walking his dog. "Did you hurt yourself? Can I get someone for you?"

"No, no I'm... I'm sorry. I uh..." Howard, just wakened, struggled to put words together. The flaming cackle of Finn's taunting southern drawl still resonating in his ears.

"Looks like you hit your head trying to get out of the car." The friendly man waved a finger in the general direction of Howard's forehead. Howard turned and glanced at himself in the rearview mirror. He looked terrible. An angry red stripe a few inches long now visible just below his bone-white crewcut. "Bet that seatbelt surprised you. You won't catch me ever wearing one of those. What if your car goes into the water?" The older black man smiled as he shook his head back and forth. "You be safe now." The man added, "God bless you," as he shuffled after the dog now chasing a yellow butterfly along the shoreline of the Mississippi River.

"Thank you. You too!" Howard rubbed at the mark on his forehead. He reached out and quietly shut his car door. "God bless me..." he muttered with a joyless smile. He turned and laid a hand contemplatively on the notebook lying in the seat beside him. "God, just help me figure out what this means." He withdrew his hand and started the car engine.

Howard pulled out of the white gravel parking lot bordering the river and flipped his turn signal on while he waited for a break in traffic. He had parked at the small riverside park with its lone picnic shelter to get an up-close look at the last place the little girl, Susan Hopper, was seen playing before her mutilated corpse was eventually pulled from the muddy waters of the Mississippi days later. The tiny park and playground had been nearly without visitors as Howard sat in his car. The serene setting under the warmth of the early spring sun as it streamed through his car windows had lulled Howard to sleep before the nightmare had woken him.

As he nosed his car into traffic and headed the few short blocks back to the Rock Island police station, he cast one last look back at the riverside park. It was still nearly vacant and fairly unremarkable. A weathered wood dock stretched out across the river some ten feet from the grassy shore of the park. On either side of it, two oversized drainage tunnels spewed mossy colored sludge into the river. Howard had read the entirety of the short police report on Susan's death. The white painted dock, now peeling and water logged, was where the investigating officers theorized the ten-year-old had fallen in and drowned. Before later, the investigators again decided, her body had been torn open by the propeller of a passing motorboat or two. Howard supposed it was possible. But now, with the similarly mutilated body and murder of the old lady in his jurisdiction, he doubted that was what had happened. Especially after discovering the hastily scribbled note an unknown officer had made at the bottom of the Davenport's police report on Susan Hopper's "accident."

He needed to share that tidbit with Jeff ASAP.

Pulling into his usual parking space, Howard hurried in and found his new partner at his desk typing. Howard sat on the corner of Jeff's desk until he finished pounding on the typewriter and looked up at him. Jeff said, "Well, I hope you found out something. My trip back downtown proved fruitless. Our murdered grandma was very well liked with no obvious acquaintance fitting the bill as her murderer. One of her neighbors said she sometimes went out in the middle of the night looking for her cat if it didn't come home. It sure sounds like she was just in the wrong place at the wrong time. At her age, in the dark and rain that late at night, she was likely easy prey for whatever psycho savaged her." Jeff paused and flicked his hand at the sheet of paper sticking out of the top of his typewriter. "I just finished writing it all up. All the details are here in the report. How about you? Any luck over in Davenport?"

Howard nodded before tossing his notepad on Jeff's desk. On it, one name and one date. "Everything I read was pretty much what our local coroner, Jim, had already told me last night. The girl, her name was Susan, officially drowned before being hit by an unknown watercraft that caused severe lacerations, dismemberment, and cuts up and down her entire torso. Like our grandma, all of her innards were pretty much gone by the time she was fished out of the water."

"Right. But what about her ankles and feet? Isn't that what caught Jim's eye?" Jeff leaned back in his chair, "Did the report mention that?"

"Yes, but only in passing. It was described along with all her other injuries which, I suppose, all could have been made by the propeller of a boat..." Howard frowned, the downcast expression only amplified the dark bags under his eyes.

"I sense a 'but' somewhere in there. You aren't convinced?" Jeff pointed at the name scrawled on Howard's notebook still laying open on his desk. "This a possible suspect?"

"No. Someone – must have been one of the investigating cops – had written down this guy's name as possibly being connected. But when I asked if anyone had followed up, I got a lot of blank stares. I think our peers over in Davenport were satisfied with their explanation and investigation into little Susan's death. No one gave this name a second look."

"Then why should we? A sicko got the grandma and sliced her ankles up in the middle of his frenzy, a little girl drowned who happened to have both feet taken off by a passing speedboat. Are you saying this guy had his feet taken off, too?"

"No." Howard met Jeff's eyes, "his feet and ankles were untouched." Jeff sat forward in his seat once again, his face drawn and tired as he threw both of his hands in the air. The classic exasperated expression of "what" without having to say a word. "But he was found gutted, all his innards missing and never recovered. He worked for Hancock Hospital and delivered equipment to some of their local offices and doctors. And, occasionally I guess, even to patient's homes."

"Are you kidding me? When did this happen? I didn't read about it in any of our old case files." Jeff nodded at the teetering pile of unorganized folders on his desk. "I'm surprised you didn't make the connection yourself last night."

"I wasn't aware of this murder because, just like little Susan Hopper, it happened on the Iowa side of the river. In Bettendorf. Whichever cop made that note must have recognized the similarities between Susan and that guy. Disemboweled and missing all the juicy parts."

"Just like our grandma."

"Exactly. Three deaths in three different jurisdictions and all three victims are as different as can be. An old woman, a little girl, and this guy. A middleclass working man who had his heart torn right out of his chest. Along with a lot of his other parts." Howard scowled as he reached up and rubbed at the tired muscles in his neck. He knew he needed to catch up on his sleep.

"Just like our grandma..." Jeff repeated before tearing the report he'd just finished out of the top of his typewriter.

CHAPTER NINE

Howard helped Gale ease herself down into the warm bathwater he'd run for her in their tub. He kept his brightest smile plastered across his face and his eyes locked on his wife's hazel orbs. Howard avoided looking down at Gale's legs as he lovingly began washing her long black hair. Dry and kneeling on the bathroom floor behind his wife on his knees, Howard poured water out of the small plastic pitcher he borrowed from their kitchen each time Gale took her baths. It made rinsing the soap from her hair much easier.

"Are you still thinking of letting your hair grow out more? I know Kay and all the regulars down at the beauty shop miss seeing you. I could make you an appointment for next week if you wanted." Howard again dipped the blue pitcher in the mostly clear water beside his wife, then poured it slowly over her head. Careful to not let any of it splash down her face, or into her eyes, as a cascade of white bubbles streamed down her long hair and back. "Maybe Gloria could bring over some of those new fashion magazines you like so much. You might get an idea for a new hairdo or permanent wave." Using his hands, he squeezed the last of the shampoo from her hair.

"I'm just not ready for that. Besides, don't you like long hair? You always used to pester me to let it grow out." Gale turned slightly in the white enameled tub, when she did the movement of her hip on the slippery surface made a loud sound not unlike passing gas. She giggled and playfully added, "Oh! Excuse me! Better pinch your nose."

"No big bubbles, I think I'm safe." Howard chuckled as he began washing Gale's back with a soft pink washcloth. As he gently washed the pale, freckled skin of her shoulders from behind, his eyes kept drifting on their own down to her legs. Specifically, where the abbreviated limbs dissolved into soapy water. Though he kept his voice and tone normal as they spoke about the day, tears sprung occasionally that Howard quickly wiped away. As Gale finished washing herself, shooing Howard from the bathroom to wash her "private parts" as she called them, Howard retrieved her wheelchair from the hallway.

Later, after Howard helped Gale dry off and then dress for bed, he slipped out of their bedroom. Gale had fallen asleep almost immediately. Howard, as usual, couldn't keep his eyes shut for long. Sleep still seeming to avoid him like the plague despite his almost perpetual exhaustion. Howard stayed curled up beside Gale as long as he could. The couple spooning together dressed in their flannel pajamas. Before he carefully exited the bed, Howard pulled back the bedcovers. Though he abhorred the sight, he stared for long minutes at where his beautiful wife's feet should have been. Each stump, crisscrossed in angry scars where her stitches had been, an abrupt reminder of what she was being reduced to. He couldn't help wondering what pieces of his wife would be butchered next. How much more he would have to watch her lose.

Later, tossing and turning on the couch where he at least tried to sleep most nights, visions of dismembered feet marching madly back and forth filled his head. The pace gradually quickening until the thundering sound dissolved into the spin of an airplane's propeller. Or more precisely, four of them...

When the official copy of the report on the slaughtered Hancock Hospital worker arrived on Howard's desk a few days later, he was disappointed to see how thin the manilla folder was. Calling his contact in the neighboring police department of Bettendorf where the body was found – a younger officer who had first worked for the Rock Island PD before transferring – he quickly found out why. The Iowa State Police had swooped in and taken over the investigation from the fledgling, and tiny, Bettendorf group of lawmen shortly after the murder had first been discovered.

Frustrated, Howard and Jeff immediately reported their reasons and requested any information the Iowa State Police investigators had on the killing. Unsure how soon, or even if the bordering state investigating detectives would actually cooperate, was an unexpected and frustrating hurdle. With nothing else to go on, Howard and Jeff tried to piece together what had happened from the abbreviated copy of the original investigator's file. Trying to see what might compare favorably with the scant information from little Susan's accident and the butchered senior citizen found in their jurisdiction.

"Let's start with what we know," Howard began. He and Jeff had commandeered the unoccupied room just outside the locked evidence storage closet in the basement of the Rock Island Police Department. Though the bits gathered from the evidence closet were negligible, Howard liked the solitude when he was trying to puzzle something out.

"We have the hollowed-out shell of one Mary Fitzgerald, aged 69, found in an empty alley near downtown Rock Island." Howard tossed a few of the pictures and the official report across the long wooden table that took up the majority of the small room. "No probable cause, no history of violence from her past, and robbery was not the motive."

Jeff nodded before adding, "And the initial examination ruled out rape, although in the driving rain her killer could have initially left evidence of any...uh... enjoyment he may have had." A fleeting smile crossed his lips before quickly dissolving. "I mean, assuming her killer was a man."

"I think that is a fair assumption considering she was gutted from crotch to clavicle. That takes a lot of power even with the sharpest of blades." Howard paused, "Once we get the coroner's report, we should have a clearer idea of the implement her killer used. When I last spoke to Jim, he expected to have everything pulled together by the end of the week. I think because of what we've learned about the M.O. used on the other potential victims, he is taking his time and making sure nothing is missed."

"Then we still don't know anything regarding the injuries to her ankles and feet, right? Only that they'd been sliced cleanly unlike the savagery of the wounds where her chest cavity was opened." Jeff, standing, but not pacing the room like Howard, placed both hands on the table in front of him. His head nearly bonking the single, low hanging light fixture above the table. His silver tie was pulled down from his neck in a haphazard fashion, and his frizzy brown hair lit up under the bright bulb. Behind him, in one corner, a dark brown oscillating fan turned casually back and forth, slightly lifting the corners of the reports and glossy pictures on the table. "And those wounds to the backs of both her feet matched the little girl dumped in the river?"

"Susan, the girl's name was Susan." Howard circled the long table like a stalking panther; his eyes never leaving the paperwork he'd spread out before them. Though both the sleeves of his button-up dress shirt were rolled to his elbows, his black tie was still tight against his throat. The tips of the white hair of his crewcut flicking back and forth when the fan's air reached him. "Our coroner, Jim, spoke with and saw the pictures of Susan his counterpart over in Davenport took. They both agree the placement and degree of the cuts and wounds are a match. For the sake of this little brainstorming session, let's agree with those experts."

"What is the significance? Does the killer have a vendetta against feet and ankles? Maybe he had some trauma like that in his own life? An injury that never healed?" Jeff pulled the close-up pictures of the backs of both victim's ankles where they'd been cut to his face, scrutinizing both closely. "Or maybe he has a grudge against some doctor who botched a surgery. A foot doctor? Maybe an amputation that went wrong and..."

"Stop going down that rabbit hole. What are you trying to say, Lewis Carroll?" Howard's voice was sharp, though he forced a smile when he tried to lightly add the Alice in Wonderland's author's name as if in jest. His face colored slightly and he turned away.

"Sorry, just trying to think of every possible angle. The wounds on the backs of their ankles are all we have tying these two deaths together. Might be a motive of some sort." Jeff watched Howard closely as he continued walking around the table. His pace slightly quickened.

"If anything, it might be some sexual sicko with a foot fetish. Have you ever heard how some people really get off on feet? I don't understand it myself. But maybe the killer tried taking the victim's feet as souvenirs or something." Howard stopped and took the blown-up, black and white photos of the two victim's feet from his partner.

Jeff turned quickly, his face now shaded in reds and pinks. "I thought stuff like that only happened in New York City, or maybe out in California. Isn't that where all those kinds go for their kicks?" He moved away from Howard who was still eyeballing the pictures.

"What if the cuts were the first wounds? You know the story of Achilles, right? The mother holding the baby Achilles by his ankles in the river Styx. The back part of his ankles, where she held him, the only part of his body left vulnerable. The girl was found in the Mississippi River. The old woman not more than a stone's throw from those muddy waters as well..." But Howard trailed off, the idea fizzling in his head even as he first spoke it aloud.

"What are you saying? The killer attacks their ankles first? What a stupid way to try and commit a murder. One slice and anyone would be screaming at the top of their lungs. If you were going to attack some-one, the hardest place to reach would be the backs of their ankles." Jeff shook his head dismissively, the color of his face returning to normal.

"What if the killer was hiding under a bed? Or underneath some stairs? A quick cut would cripple the victim, they'd be instantly immo-bilized and easy prey." This time Howard didn't let his words trail off. His eyebrows bunched together in thought. "Still kind of farfetched though, huh?"

"I don't know. I think we are grasping at straws here. Even if we do have some whacko cutting at people from out of a sewer grate or something as they walk by, the third victim didn't have any wounds on the backs of his ankles. So that alone..."

"Wait a minute. What did you just say? The sewers?" For the first time, Howard stopped pacing the room. "There are a couple of those big sewer grates in the alley." He looked over at Jeff.

"That is the most ridiculous thing I've ever heard. What do you think we have here? Some creature, some 'It' living down in the sewers and hunting unsuspecting victims? Little kids like Susan 'It' can terrify?" Jeff chuckled as he shook his head. "That would be the stupidest explanation I've ever heard. Quit clowning around. Believe me, NO ONE would ever buy that story. Even if some famous horror writer like HP Lovecraft dreamed it up in a drugged reverie."

Howard nodded, briefly acknowledging the ridiculousness of the unlikely scenario before adding. "Maybe. But have you ever been down in an underground city sewer? Seen for yourself what floats down there?"

Jeff shook his head as he waved a hand dismissively. "What? What floats down there?"

"Everything, Jeffrey. Everything floats down there..."

"Let's quit talking about fictional worlds created by the likes of Poe, Lewis Carroll, and all that Greek mythology. We came down here to compare the similarities between our victim, the girl pulled from the river, and the guy who worked for the hospital." Jeff stood and arched his back, twisting once both ways as his spine popped audibly. "All three were disemboweled, their insides missing, and never found. I can buy into that connection. Not the whole 'people under the stairs' or some unknown 'It' living down in the sewers waiting for victims. What ties the hospital guy to the old lady and the little girl? I know the Iowa State Police didn't leave much in that guy's file. But what do we have?"

Howard flipped open the last, thinnest file on the table. "Elmer Denbrough, aged 51, widowed, lived alone and suffered from asthma according to what is written here. Let's see, worked for Hancock Hospital for the last 12 years." Howard paused; had he ever met the man before? Hancock Hospital occasionally delivered diabetic supplies for his wife. Gloria, the nurse he'd hired to watch Gale after her surgery, also worked for Hancock. Had she been the one who recommended Howard and Gale use their new pilot home service program?

"Says here he was a delivery driver for them. But he was based out of Hancock's warehouse, which is," Howard flipped to the next page and blanched noticeably. He looked up at Jeff before adding, "He worked at the warehouse that borders the alleyway where we found Mary, our butchered grandma!"

"Sounds like it is time we went down there and got into that warehouse." Jeff didn't wait for Howard to agree. He began to gather the papers and photos from the files spread out on the table. "Hopefully someone is working there and will let us look around without having to get a search warrant."

Howard looked down at his watch. "Close to lunchtime. We'll grab a bite ourselves in case they lock everything up over the noon hour. Maybe we'll get lucky and find a loose lipped co-worker of the victim. I also want to take a look at those sewer grates in the alley."

Howard didn't see the eyeball roll of Jeff's as he slid the last of the paperwork back into the file folders.

CHAPTER TEN
PRESENT DAY

"No internet service way out here, huh?" Secrist asked while watching Stander stretch the electric cord from a battered old compact disc player over to a wall socket in the library. He plugged it in and hit the power button before pulling out a sleeve of CDs he'd obviously gathered from his personal collection back in Michigan.

"You kidding? I can barely even get a cell signal for my phone this far out in the sticks. I bet around here they use dial-up and still have AOL email accounts." Stander, dressed in jeans splashed with old paint stains, work boots, and a tattered black shirt with *Kiss* and their four painted faces printed across the front, snickered at his own joke. "This old CD player has just been collecting dust back home anyway. Assuming it still works, I figured we might as well use it. Some of these," he flipped past several, "I haven't listened to in years."

"Why do you even still have all those? You can stream just about anything nowadays. You and that know-it-all electronic bitch Alexa are always blaring your shitty music back home." Secrist was dressed similarly to Stander. His old clothes also stained and torn from doing his own home improvement projects as well as helping Stander with minor renovations from time to time at his bar back in Michigan. Around his neck hung an industrial facemask to keep out all the dirt and dust particles they'd likely be kicking up. Both men knew they would be tearing down a wall in the library of Relict Mansion this morning and had dressed appropriately for the task. Frazier sat passively on his stomach under the room's doorway with his paws stretched out in front of him like an attentive Egyptian Sphinx.

"Shitty music? That's harsh. But, to each their own." Stander and Secrist had such wildly diverse tastes in music that they argued about tunes like an old married couple. Each taking turns giving the other grief, but never with much venom. "And I'll have you know I still have all of my old albums as well. I'll never part with any of those fucking classics. Most of these CDs are ones I bought to replace the cassette tapes I'd picked up back when it started getting hard to find vinyl." Stander and Secrist had warmed up a couple breakfast sandwiches in the tiny microwave they'd brought with them along with a cheap 4-cup coffee maker. With the early morning meal behind them, they were now ready to tear into the project Stander had planned. Getting behind the massive stone fireplace facade he was sure hid something. "What do you want to hear?"

"I don't suppose you have any *Shania Twain* or *Faith Hill* CDs, do you?"

"Jesus, do you enjoy music with your eyes or your ears?" Stander smirked as he flipped past several heavy metal CDs with names like *Disturbed*, *Mudvayne*, and *Enuff Z'Nuff* before finally sliding one out from the protective sleeves. "Ah... here we go! Except for *Bob Seger*, this might be one of the few groups we both can enjoy." He held up a silver disc with the name *Survivor* stamped across it. "This soft enough for you, old man?"

Secrist rolled his eyes though, inside, he was actually relieved he wouldn't be subjected first thing in the morning to Stander's usual barrage of what Secrist considered unintelligible noise. "*Survivor*? As in, *'Eye of the Tiger'* and *'Burning Heart' Survivor*? I'm surprised you have a CD by them."

"Are you kidding? After Rocky 3 came out, *'Eye of the Tiger'* was my favorite song for months. I love that fucking movie!" Stander popped the

CD in the player and pressed play. "Now, hand me that sledgehammer. This is the perfect song to hit and break shit to."

"What do you want me to do while you're swinging for the fences?"

"How about you pry all that trim and flooring out from around the both sides of the fireplace? We'll clear away all the easy stuff first and see if I'm right." Stander placed the handle of the sledgehammer between his legs and pulled a pair of worn leather work gloves out of his back pocket. "I think all this granite and stone was added way after the fireplace was originally built."

"What does that prove? The granite is gorgeous and you're going to bust it all up on a hunch? This home had to be built sometime in the pre-civil war era, damn near everything in it has been replaced or added after the home was first built." Secrist grabbed a claw hammer and dropped to his knees.

"Yeah, I think you are right. I remember my dad saying when he was younger, Madeleine was constantly having work done on the property. But this is the only place with that symbol. The same one Lucas found in France buried so deep underground. Not to mention my ugly fucking birthmark. There has to be a reason Madeleine only had that design in this room." Stander swung the heavy hammer over his shoulder. "Now, watch your eyes, Tommy. Like Mr. T said in Rocky 3," he pointed the end of the sledge at the granite stone covering the wall of the fireplace, "I'm gonna bust you up!"

"I pity the..." But the rest of Secrist's best Mr. T impression was drowned out by the crash of the sledgehammer as Stander slammed it against the wall. Secrist placed his mask over his nose and mouth and sung along under his breath. "And the last lone survivor stalks his prey in the night. And he's watching us all, with the eye of the tiger..."

Two hours later, Stander and Secrist stood side by side. Both were sweating and covered in the dust their demolition of the library wall had produced. Though most of the granite and stone on the massive fireplace remained intact, a five-foot section just to the left of the giant hearth had been stripped clean. Soon after the demo had begun, both men were able to ascertain the portion of wall on one side was completely different than the backing behind the rest of the wall around the fireplace. They'd focused on the promising lead and carefully removed as much as they could around the section, pulling down and disposing of the broken material before daring to explore what was clearly a hollow section built behind it. Now, with the pickaxe and handheld hammers, they pulled out the last of the modern nails and pried apart the wood two-by-fours framing the section.

"This is nuts! Why in god's name would there be a hollow compartment built in the wall? One you can't even get to without pulling down a huge portion of the wall itself?" Secrist had worked construction while in college and seen plenty of strange things in old buildings. But this took the cake. It made no sense.

"Beats the fuck out of me. I think if I hadn't just inherited a butt ton of money, I'd be wondering if my great aunt hid her valuables back in here. But," Stander gave Secrist the side eye, "I know she had all that kind of stuff locked away in safety deposit boxes. This has to be something else."

"I just want you to know, if we find another ancient relict that glows and makes people disappear, I'm going back home to Michigan." Secrist said this seriously, but Stander knew he'd never actually run out on him. "I'm too old for this shit."

"Maybe she trapped another one of those things from the cemetery back here? That might explain why that thing stayed close all those years." But Stander didn't really believe there could be another one of those creatures haunting the walls of his great aunt's old home. "Well, only one way to find out." Stander pulled out what appeared to be the last nail holding the final piece of partition up. The thick nail screamed as he wrenched it loose and let the wood covering drop at his feet.

"What the fuck..." Just beyond the last remaining pieces of broken and shredded wood, a gaping black hole yawned benignly at them. Though not overpowering, a stale, damp breeze billowed out from the unexpected void. Stander pulled his phone out of the back pocket of his jeans and switched the light on. The darkness receded slightly, but there was much more beyond what the tiny phone light could expose. Just past the reach of the light, the black space seemed to turn, and the floor had a downward slope.

"Do you want me to go grab our flashlights?" Secrist pulled his mask down from his nose and mouth. "Maybe, with all we've encountered as of late, my gun too?"

Stander stretched his arm into the black chasm. He turned and nodded at what had caught his eye. Just beyond his reach an old oil lamp hung from a bent and rusty nail. Waiting, it seemed, to be lit. "Tell you what. Let's pull the last of this wood and nails out from around the opening and floor first. But yeah, we'll grab some lights and your gun. Maybe some matches too."

Behind them, Frazier whined softly before turning and exiting the room. Stander and Secrist watched his retreat, then turned and look at each other. "Seems a little ominous, huh?" Stander smirked and Secrist chuckled nervously. Within five minutes, the two men had the rest of the opening cleared and lit up brightly with two flashlights.

Stander stepped first into the cavity they'd exposed. The rubber sole of his boot crunching on chalky pieces of plaster that had come down during their assault of the fireplace. With the interior exposed under their twin beams of light, Secrist followed close behind. Both men squeezed inside the opening together. Their shoulders touching in the previously hidden enclosure. The slight turn and downward slope of the floor they'd first seen took form and crystalized under the glare of the bright halogen flashlights in their hands. The gradual slope bled into steep steps of concrete, which appeared to lead deep underground.

"Is this even happening right now?" Secrist whispered before realizing the ridiculousness of his tone. He spoke normally again when he continued. "This is right out of some old haunted house movie, Stander. Where do you think it leads?" Stander shrugged once before turning his attention to the oil lamp hanging along the wall. It took several matches before he could finally ignite the old steel and glass lamp. A small plume of black smoke briefly caused them both to turn away before Stander fiddled with the wick enough to control the wavering flame. Once it began to burn steadily, Stander set the lit lamp down at the top of the newly discovered stairs.

"That should be safe on the concrete ground away from the wood of the wall. Let's leave it here as kind of a marker until we see where this leads." Stander gestured at the receding steps that led deeper under the ground beneath Relict Mansion. "For all we know, this just leads to an old storm or fruit cellar with nothing more interesting than crumbling rhubarb and dried apples."

"Or maybe your great aunt had a hidden wine cellar!"

"That she boarded up? Not likely. Besides, there is a huge one under the kitchen still with some old bottles inside. I suppose," Stander waved his flashlight in the air as he inspected the cramped passageway, "they could have a built some kind of bomb shelter here in the 60's or 70's. I know when the cold war was in full swing a lot of people built underground bunkers and fallout shelters in case of nuclear war."

"And then boarded it all up later?" Secrist's tone reflected the doubt he had. "I was thinking about the Underground Railroad in Illinois. You know, where they smuggled slaves north to live in free states. The time period this home was built would be about right. Illinois dips farther south than most of the other free states did and was bordered by the slave states Missouri and Kentucky. With this home being so close to the Mississippi River, it would have been an ideal junction for the

Underground Railroad system. I know there were documented routes in southern Illinois that led up this way."

Stander nodded. "That makes a lot of sense. I could see my great aunt wanting to honor and refurbish something like that. I know she always hated all the ignorant dipshits obsessed with race."

"Yeah, but if that was true. Why cover it all up and hide everything?" Secrist moved to the top of the crude steps and shined his light down the descending passage. "Hmmm. Can't see very far down. Looks like the staircase curves."

"As much as great Aunt Madeleine disliked bigots, I know she valued her privacy above all else. If she *had* reported the home as being part of the Underground Railroad, there may have been repercussions. You know, limits on what she could do to the property. But, with her re-sources, I suppose she could have hired a contractor and paid him to keep quiet. Covered up the home's role without destroying the property's legacy." Stander stroked his bushy white moustache contemplatively as he briefly swept his light around the enclosed space. The tiny entryway was barely bigger than a closet, unremarkable and unadorned beyond the cramped stairway leading somewhere under the house. "Well, only one way to find out. You ready to see where this goes?"

"Sure. I'll go first. It's so tight in here we have to go single file anyway." Secrist began to move down the steps; Stander just behind him. Their two flashlights bright in the narrow space. Aged and crumbling bricks made up the walls and ceiling of the passageway. In spots, groundwater seeped past cracks that at some point had splintered the descending corridor. A thick mustiness filled the air; the two men's footfalls on the narrow steps the only sound. Periodically, Secrist swiped at low hanging cobwebs blocking the passage. After another minute of careful stepping, they hit the gradual turn. But the staircase continued to lead deeper.

"I have to say, your great aunt sure sounds like she was way ahead of her time. When was she born?" The temperature began to drop lower along with the two men's descent. Their voices echoing strangely in the narrow passage.

"I know she was over a hundred years old when she died in the early eighties. Not that she ever looked that old from what I remember... So, I don't know, she must have been born in 1880 something or other." Stander looked down at his feet as he trailed cautiously behind Secrist. Some of the steps were slick with moisture and, in places, underground water was pooling along the edges.

"Most people born back then had plenty of prejudices. I can remember as a kid hearing old folks saying some of the most embarrassing things at times. How do you think your great aunt avoided all that ignorance?" Secrist never looked up when he spoke. His eyes trained on where his feet landed.

"For starters, she wasn't born here in America. I can't remember where all she lived, but I think living abroad likely expanded her view on things." Stander stopped momentarily. He raised his head and inhaled deeply. "Jesus, Tommy. Did you just shit your pants or something? What is that fucking smell?"

Secrist stopped and turned, about to answer when the foul, sickly smell hit him. He scowled and shook his head no as he slid the mask back over his nose and mouth before continuing his descent. Over his shoulder he said, "Maybe this leads into the home's old sewage drain or septic tank. Or..." He stopped walking down the stairs and Stander stepped down on his heel. "Check it out. A door. Finally!"

Stander looked up as both men's flashlight beams exposed what appeared to be a very old and warped door. Made of dark wood, the door's handle was a circle of rusted iron. The ground in front of the door was no longer concrete, but packed dirt and rock. Both men looked down at their feet. Surprise registering on their faces. Unnoticed until now, several steps behind them, the concrete stairs had slowly given way to stone steps. The bottom-most steps and the ground running up to the aged and wooden door all made of similar rock. Possibly bedrock. Stander and Secrist crept down the last several steps of the stairway and crowded the small landing at the bottom of the passageway. Stander reached a hand out and slid it up and down the rough wood of the aged entryway.

"I'm pretty sure this door was hand-hewn. See these cut marks? No way that was done by an electric or handsaw. This was cut with an axe, or maybe even an adze. A hand-cut door!" Stander's eyebrows were raised as he looked over at Secrist.

"Seriously? That doesn't fit at all with the concrete staircase we just came down." Secrist turned and cast a glance back up the long twisting staircase. Where they now stood did seem to have been dug out long before the concrete steps would have been laid. But, then again, the cement or concrete may have been added at a much later date. Perhaps the original stairs had all rotted away. A cool dampness was pervasive this far underground. From where they stood at the bottom of the stairs, Secrist could just make out the dull glow coming from the lit lamp they'd left at the top of the stairs.

"Well," Stander looked over at Secrist. "Let's see what's behind door number two..." He grasped the iron circle and turned it. The flaking and rusting metal groaned like a tired old man trying to rise from the floor before finally popping loose. The door seemed to swing freely, and Stander gave it a shove. The door opened about two feet before coming to a shuddering stop. The stench they'd begun to smell as they'd neared the bottom of the stairs grew thick. Stander pulled the collar of his t-shirt up over his nose and mouth. "God, what the fuck died in there!"

Though more protected with his industrial quality mask still in place, Secrist could still tell behind the door something reeked terribly. "Ugh! Maybe this is the family crypt? I could imagine a bunch of dead Standers smelling like that. I've followed behind you in a bathroom a time or two..."

"Smells like Frankenstein took a shit." Though both men were struggling to breathe in the pungent air that wafted out from behind the old door, they were chuckling under the cloth pulled across their faces.

Secrist blurted out, "Talk about the Horror of Frankenstein!"

"True terror!" Still in his most professional sounding announcer voice, Stander added. "The Smell of Frankenstein!" His shoulders began to heave, but Stander didn't want to laugh out loud if only to spare himself from having to take any deep breaths. "No wonder the blind guy in the hut immediately lit a match..." He couldn't help himself; Stander began to laugh out loud. "Smoke! Good!" He did his best Frankenstein monster impersonation before dissolving into belly laughter.

As their laughter faded and they became more accustomed to the rank smell, Stander let the collar of his shirt fall. "Come on. Something must have just gotten trapped down here and died right on the other side of the door. Help me push it all the way open." Secrist joined Stander in front of the partially opened door. Both men placed their hands on the wood door and pushed. The bottom of the door ground along the bottom and bowed slightly under the strain. But after a few seconds, it gave completely and the door swung open with a troubled screech.

Stander went in first. The bright beam of his flashlight sweeping back and forth. Secrist stepped in behind, and their combined lights exposed much of what was a dirt floor in an unadorned room barely twenty feet squared. The dirt walls of the smallish chamber were held in place by half-rotted timbers of amazing thickness. The room, like the stairwell they'd just descended, never had electricity run to it. Above their heads the small room's ceiling had once been made of wood planks. However, several had collapsed at some point. Exposing the hard packed dirt and rock the room had been carved out of. At the opposite end from where they entered were two identical doors that matched the one just opened. The entire room, with one exception, was completely barren.

In the center of the chamber stood a single, long table that appeared to be made of wood. Judging by the discoloration of the stained wood, the table was obviously much newer than the wooden beams, planks, and doors that made up the underground structure. The wood stand resembled a kitchen or dining room table manufactured sometime in 20th century. The four legs were ornate and had circular patterns and decorative markings carved in several places around each.

On top lay the unmistakable, shrouded form of a man.

Stander and Secrist had not uttered a word upon entering the smallish cellar. They'd each played their lights about the room and observed there was little to look at beyond what lay atop the single piece of furniture in the chamber. The form was blanketed with a single piece of cloth of an undetermined color. As the light from their handheld torches flashed across the form, the covering appeared grey or silver. But as both men approached the table, the cloth seemed to become more beige or brown. The halogen light, perhaps, leaving the true determination of color unclear. In unison, Stander and Secrist slowly approached the still form on the table.

"Russell. That is a body underneath there. You know that, right?" Secrist, though retired, had been a cop for more than half his life. Much of it spent as a detective serving the people of Michigan. He automatically reverted back to form as the seriousness of the find took hold in him. "We should contact the local police and report this."

"No shit, Sherlock..." Stander reached out one hand and grabbed at the covering. "But just in case this is an old mannequin or doll of some sort, let's take a little peek under here first." He started to tug at the cloth when he let the fabric slide out of his hand. "Feel this stuff. What a weird texture." Together, both men reached out and grasped it. Secrist's eyes opening wide and nodding his head when he felt the thick and strangely interwoven material in his hand.

"Told you. Strange, huh?" In unison, they slowly pulled off the covering and let it fall to the dirt ground at their feet. The stench in the room became nearly unbearable. Growing thick as the nude body of an old man was exposed from where it had lain under the cloth. Stander said out loud what both men were thinking. "What the fuck!"

The dead man was older than Stander and Secrist, but likely not by a whole lot. Outside of some seepage that had pooled down near his groin and up near his head, the body was clean and remarkably well preserved. Folded neatly beside the body was what appeared to be a man's suit. The black jacket draped over a yellowing shirt that likely had once been white. Stander bent over the body to take a closer look when he felt a hand grabbing at his elbow. "Don't get too close. We don't know how he died. Could have been disease. And the body can't be more than a few days old at most. Don't take any chances."

"A few days old?" Stander turned away from the corpse on the table and arched an eyebrow at Secrist. "No one had been in this room for years. Maybe decades. It took both of us to even wedge that door open, it had sat unused for so long."

"What about those two doors?" But as both men turned to contemplate Secrist's possible solution, it was obvious no one had passed through either anytime recently. Both were covered in cobwebs that hung listlessly across the door frames. "Or maybe not..." Secrist admitted as they both trained their lights back on the ghoulish table decoration.

"Wonder how he died?" Stander began to peer closer when a frenzied barking began. Instead, he turned to Secrist. "That's Frazier. There must be someone here. Come on. This stiff ain't going anywhere. Let's get out of this stink hole and get some fresh air. Must be about lunchtime anyway."

"Lunch? How can you think of eating after smelling and seeing this?" Stander waved a dismissive hand back and forth in the air before turning to leave. Frazier's barking seeming to grow more urgent with each passing moment. "What about him? Should we cover him back up?"

"Fuck it. Not like he gives a shit. Grab that blanket, or whatever it is, and bring it upstairs. We'll shut the door behind us. Though I can't imagine anyone getting curious enough to head down here."

Both men exited the room and pulled the stubborn door of the underground room shut behind them. They were met halfway up the staircase by Frazier who'd made his way down to alert them. But by the time they'd made it back into the library and checked outside, there was no sign of whatever Frazier had been barking about. Back on the main level of the house, Frazier seemed to forget whatever had spooked him as well.

After cleaning up, the two men and Frazier piled into Stander's Jeep and headed towards Almore. Stopping to eat at Arlene's Café, the lone restaurant in town, they ate and discussed in hushed tones what their next steps would be. Frazier sitting contently beside Stander in the small cafe's booth.

As they finished off a couple pieces of banana cream pie, and Stander paid the bill, they settled on their course of action. They would continue their inspection of the rooms under the manor. Checking out the two unopened doors before contacting the police and alerting them to their grisly find. Satisfied with the plan, they stood and headed outside just as a truck came roaring up the street. When the driver's side door opened, a man sprayed with what looked like blood stumbled out of the pickup truck. A small crowd of six, including Stander and Secrist, clustered around the newcomer.

"I just saw a monster," the man blurted out. Behind him, back down the road he'd just arrived on, a small swell of black smoke stained the sky. Frazier, unheard, whining softly and huddling at Stander's feet. "It came from the woods..."

CHAPTER ELEVEN
CAIRO, EGYPT - 1962

SAQQARA NECROPOLIS

TIM, STILL LEANING OVER the open sarcophagus and face-to-face with the mummy inside, exclaimed loudly and spun his head around quickly. Shaken by the implausible movements of the aged and shriveled corpse interred deep under the Egyptian sands of Saqqara. Balance lost, Tim slipped and tumbled down to the sandy floor from his perch atop the stone sarcophagus. As a trained medical professional, Dr. Tim Stander thought he'd seen everything. But the resurrection of the figure lying in the tomb believed to be Imhotep's, shattered all the conventional learning he'd ever acquired.

Dead is dead. Isn't it?

Unable to tear his eyes from the shocking scene, Tim slowly backed away from the sarcophagus on shaky legs. He stumbled after the first few backward steps in the thick sand that covered the floor of the chamber. Losing his footing and falling down, yet never taking his eyes from the massive stone coffin as his father rushed to his aid. "Are you alright? What just happened?" Emery reached his hand out, intending to help Tim regain his feet. But Tim merely pointed. His focus never wavering or straying from the aged tomb in the middle of the burial chamber. When Tim didn't take his hand, Emery turned to look as well.

Long bony fingers were grasping at the top of the sarcophagus from the inside. Clutching tentatively until a second hand of floundering digits appeared beside it, also grabbing for a handful of the worked stone. Both hands cracking loudly as they closed around the outer rim of the open tomb. Moments later, behind the disturbing grip, the top of a near hairless head began to emerge out of the limestone-carved grave. The withered skin stretched tight against the hard bone of the skull it barely covered. The flesh on both hands and head the color of burned charcoal; grey and dry with long creases distorting the thin skin in places. When the features of the rising dead began to show themselves in the dim illumination of the flashlight, the Egyptian worker Tata shrieked and ran to one corner of the chamber with the golden rod clutched to his chest as if for protection. He babbled as he sunk to his knees, desperately trying to lose himself in the black shadows of the chamber. The whimpering sounds escaping his lips no different than those of a small trapped animal. Lucy, with Sherry still held in her arms, quickly and wordlessly retreated behind Emery and the prostrate form of her husband. Her eyes also never leaving the resurrection she was witnessing.

Tim felt himself holding onto the ground as if it might suddenly abandon him. His head swam and crazy thoughts of monsters, curses, and a parade of shuffling Hollywood mummies bombarded his thoughts. When Lucy reached down and touched his arm, he screamed out loud until he felt some of the madness escape through his throat. But some things, no matter how loudly you scream or how badly you wish, you can never unsee. Sights can bind you in a moment and never leave.

Sane or mad...

The face of the undead thing was now fully exposed in the dimness of the flashlight. That is, if you could still call it a face. Grotesque, with parts of it lost and no longer visible. The ghastly image like a jigsaw puzzle with multiple missing pieces, obscuring any identity, race, or gender. What was left defied identification. Black lips hung together loosely, both hanging below a pointed and bony chin. A triangular hole where a nose should have been and, on both sides of the head, there were no visible ears. The eyes, though wide open, were like shiny black marbles without focus. Still, the unnatural thing kept rising. Undeterred by the audience and methodically pulling itself up and out of the sarcophagus where it had lain. Taking no notice of the sounds or presence of the shocked onlookers.

When the unclothed form finished pulling itself down and out of the stone grave, it stood on two legs. Appearing sexless, long and lanky, the form teetered unsteadily for several long moments, its chest heaving in and out. When it raised its head, Tata let loose with a torrent of Arabic words. Whether prayers or curses, none of the other onlookers knew. But, either way, the resurrected creature didn't seem to notice. It turned and shambled in the opposite direction. Still either ignorant of the others inside the chamber with it or not caring. When it moved some fifteen feet from where the sarcophagus sat, it suddenly sank to the ground on both knees. Hunched over and nearly on all fours, the ash-colored corpse began to dig. Using its awful hands of scrambling digits to part the sands at a spot barely a yard wide.

"What are we baring witness to?" Emery whispered hoarsely in the dark cavern. "How could this be?" Neither Tim nor Lucy could answer, both as mesmerized and puzzled as the professor. In the far corner, Tata, eyes wide, continued to babble. The long scepter now held in one hand defensively like a club or a sword. Tim wondered if Tata had lost his mind; this vision certainly could be called one of madness. Slowly and tentatively, Tim regained his feet. In the dim light he could not see this modern-day Lazarus very well from where he had fallen earlier.

"What is it searching for? Does it think it can somehow tunnel out of here?" Tim and his dad both shook their heads. Neither able to answer the questions Lucy whispered in the darkness. Abruptly, the undead digger stopped and then seemed to deflate. His shoulders hunched forward as if in defeat or perhaps exhaustion.

"Imhotep." Emery suddenly spoke the name loudly, and it echoed strangely within the stone room with the sand floor and bounty of treasure. Unmistakably, the digger that had climbed out of the sarcophagus recognized the name. For the first time taking note of the others trapped inside the burial chamber with it. Tottering with each movement, it rose slowly back to its feet and turned to face Emery.

"Im-o-tep." The creature replied haltingly and softly. Yet the tone set Tim's teeth on edge. It was a grating sound like a fork being dragged over a stainless-steel sink. Even from across the room, Tata winced. Baby Sherry instantly erupted in a forceful fit of crying.

The discordant sound unnatural.

Tata, looking as if he'd stared the devil in the face, abruptly roared from out of the corner and launched himself at the creature. He swung the golden rod in his hands like a baseball bat. But unbalanced, Tata staggered on his feet as he lashed out. Only managing to strike the undead thing just below one shoulder. The shriveled joint shattered upon contact and fell at the feet of the walking, ashy corpse. The thing yowled and screeched either in pain or anger. A jarring sound that cut to the core and sliced through the air sharper than any blade. In unison, Tim, his father, and Tata grimaced and covered their ears with both hands. Tata letting the golden rod drop at his feet as his hands flew to the sides of his head. Lucy nearly dropped Sherry as she turned away to blunt the debilitating blare; one ear pressed hard against her shoulder as she stumbled towards the opposite wall of the chamber. Trying desperately to put distance between herself and the creature's awful screech.

Tata, eyes now squeezed shut and the gold scepter at his feet where he dropped it, never saw the thing pounce. His eyes only reopening when he'd felt the teeth at his neck. The undead freak savagely tearing at Tata's throat with rows of monstrous teeth that filled its mouth. Pink flesh and red gore were ripped away. Leaving behind an impossible tangle of arteries that spewed blood at an alarming rate. The sand under Tata flooded in red. The gore clumping and pooling together as his blood flowed from the fatal wound.

Tim regained his feet just in time to see Tata take his last breath. The stringy strands at his neck, now just raw and bloody meat, blowing out one final time. Tim lurched to the scene of the attack, dumbfounded by the sudden savagery and terrified by the crimson-streaked creature still looming over Tata with teeth dripping blood. Tim stepped over the leather-like arm of the vile thing and picked up the now bent rod of gold with the Ankh symbol at the top. He twirled it once in his hands, then plunged the tapered end down with all his might. Surprising the undead thing from behind and piercing it through the back before the end of the rod burst out the opposite side and through its chest.

Whoosh!

Instantly, a flash of extreme brightness flooded the room. The blinding flash, a blueish-white light, bursting from the jeweled center of the Ankh symbol like the flare of a lightning bolt. The outburst came and went in an instant. So fast that, as it faded and Tim's eyesight slowly returned, he'd never taken his hands from the golden staff. Underneath him, his vision clearing, the undead thing that had crawled out from the stone sarcophagus had been incinerated. At the end of the golden rod, only a heap of blackened soot and ash. All that was left of the nightmare from the grave was the single arm Tata had knocked off with his clumsy assault. The arm, like the dead body of Tata, motionless in the sand.

"Mother of god!!" Emery remained frozen where he stood. He blinked several times, trying to focus his eyes once more, hoping to understand what he'd just seen. But as his temporary blindness faded, he found the improbable result did not change. The monstrous thing that had skulked from its grave was gone. Somehow destroyed by the golden staff with the strange symbol.

"What happened?" Lucy asked, as she tentatively made her way to Emery's side. Baby Sherry, in her arms, still crying hard between shuddering breaths. "Where did it go?"

"I have no idea…" Tim released his grip on the rod and it fell to the ground. He backed away and turned to his father and wife. "Are you OK? Is Sherry hurt?" Parental concern still his first thought despite the fantastic events he'd just witnessed.

"I think she's fine. It was just that god awful sound of that thing's voice that set her off." Lucy rocked and shushed the little girl. Her cries slowly began to fade as she looked back and forth between her mother and father.

"How about you, dad?"

"You don't need to worry about me." Emery, his paralysis broken, walked over to where Tata's body lay dead on the ground. "Poor soul. Why did he attack it? We could have learned so much from whatever…"

"Learn? Didn't you see what it did to him? He might have just saved our lives." Lucy was shaking her head back and forth in stunned disbelief.

"I think Tim is the one that likely saved our lives." Emery paused and then added, "That was quick thinking, my boy. We didn't have anything to protect ourselves with."

"But what happened? I was just trying to get that thing off of Tata. I had no idea that scepter was some kind of…of… lightning rod!" Tim walked over and stood beside his dad. "Do you have any ideas about this? Did ancient Egyptians have something that harbored or harnessed power like that? I mean, in their stories and myths?"

Emery looked over at his son but said nothing. Instead, he began to make his way over to where the thing from the grave had been digging in the sand. When he reached the spot he bent over, squinting in the limited light. "Oh my…" He turned back to where Tim and Lucy stood beside their lone flashlight. The beam from it still pointing up and doing its best to beat back the black of the underground. "Tim, grab that flashlight and come over here. Lucy, maybe you want to stay where you are."

Tim walked back to retrieve the light before joining his father. He lit up the small, freshly uncovered, earthen pit and what the creature had exposed within. Neither man said anything, merely looking at each other and then back down at the hole in the ground.

"What is it?" Lucy finally asked but began to walk over anyway. "Is it more buried treasure?" When she reached the two men, Tim held up his hand to try and dissuade her from seeing inside. "Don't try to stop me, Tim. I'm a big girl. What is down there?" Tim sighed and let his arm drop, allowing Lucy to stand beside Emery. All three, along with the now silent Sherry in her mother's arms, looked into the small depression in the sand.

There, curled up as if taking a nap, were the badly degraded skeletal remains of an infant child. The tiny fleshless skull nearly identical in size to baby Sherry...

CHAPTER TWELVE

Tim and Emery carried the lifeless body of Tata over to one corner of the chamber. The head lolled awkwardly from the man's torn and ruined neck. Blood dripping and speckling the sand under their feet like the center line on a road to nowhere.

A dead-end highway.

Tim walked back to the sarcophagus and pulled down the lengthy and thickly textured burial shroud where it hung from the corner. The shroud was tightly interwoven, yet sheer enough to see through. In the poor light it appeared bland and near colorless – somehow both grey and beige – and was heavier than Tim expected. He made his way back to the torn remains of Tata with it in hand and laid the shroud reverently across the man's lifeless body. Stopping momentarily to shut his blank eyes with one hand before pulling it completely over Tata's face. The Egyptian worker's twisted features stamped for all eternity in a disturbing grimace of shock and horror like a molded death mask. Tim then gingerly retrieved the leathery arm of Tata's killer and tossed it hurriedly beside the covered body. It landed in between the dead man and the torches they'd discovered earlier. When he looked up a few moments later, his father had rejoined Lucy beside the small hole in the ground of the chamber. The delicate body of the ancient infant was still untouched inside.

"I don't know what was more incredible. Seeing the thing rise out of that sarcophagus or watching it dig up the grave of this child." Lucy looked up at Tim, addressing him directly. "You're the medical doctor.

How do you explain any of this?" Tim merely shook his head back and forth silently. What they'd witnessed defied all rational explanation.

"If I had not seen it myself, I'd doubt our very sanity." Emery coughed loudly twice before leaning over the small earthen pit. "Clearly the resurrected knew right where this body was. Until Tata attacked it, its sole focus was unearthing the child. What was special?"

"Maybe there is something underneath those bones?" Lucy handed Sherry over to Tim before dropping to her knees. "Let's see if there is anything below." She reached down and swatted aside the tiny skeleton, upsetting the form and strewing the remains haphazardly around the shallow pit.

"Lucy!" Tim admonished her as he shifted Sherry between his arms. "Show some respect."

"Oh? Like you did with Mr. Walking Biting Mummy?" Lucy didn't even look up as she rooted around the hole. Pulling handfuls of sand out and tossing them in the air behind her. Tim started to reply, but Emery beat him to the punch.

"Wait, what did you just say?" Emery looked over at his son though his question was for Lucy. Absentmindedly, he reached in his pocket and fished a single cigarette out of the squashed pack in his shirt pocket. "You said, mister mummy. But..." Tim reached over and pulled the unlit cigarette from his dad's hand.

"You aren't really going to light that, are you? We don't know how much breathable air is down here." Emery nodded once and distractedly put the unlit cigarette and pack away.

"Did you notice any genitalia present when that thing was moving around?" Emery looked at Tim, then down at Lucy who continued rooting around inside the burial spot of the long-dead child. "And the mouth, the mouth was so badly malformed. It didn't occur to me in the midst of what we were seeing."

"I didn't notice, dad. It's so dark in here with only that flashlight beam that I'd doubt anything I thought I'd seen with my eyes." Tim paused briefly before adding, "But, now that you bring it up, I don't think it had any ears either."

"There wasn't a penis. Or any breasts either." Lucy stood and stepped away empty-handed from the hole she'd dug down into. "I just thought it had rotted off. Is it still inside that?" She pointed to the massive stone coffin the thing had crawled out of. "Maybe the ears are in there as well."

"Not likely. King Tut was even buried with an erect..." Emery stopped and shook his head. "Anyway, that's not really important. I'm just saying I am not so sure that was a man who crawled out."

"So, you don't think that was Imhotep?" Sherry began to fuss in Tim's arms, and he tried bouncing her playfully up and down as a distraction. "But you saw how it reacted when you spoke his name out loud. It even replied."

"True," Emery admitted. "But no sex? No ears? The misshapen mouth and all those rows of teeth?" He paused, reflecting briefly before adding, "And that horrid sound it made! How could a tone like that have come from a human?"

"What? Now you are saying, not only that it wasn't Imhotep, but it wasn't a man at all? Or even a human being?" Lucy laughed, but the sound was in no way jubilant. "You? The esteemed Emery W. Stander, who spent a lifetime searching for this very tomb, now says he was wrong. Well, stop the presses..."

Lucy reached over suddenly and took the fussing baby from Tim's arms. "Sherry is hungry. I guess there is no reason for her to starve down here like the rest of us. You two can keep talking all you want about this. I'm going to go feed her." With that, Lucy turned and made her way to the opposite side of the sarcophagus, out of sight. There she sat once more on the stone base and unbuttoned her blouse. Sherry instantly silenced as she was held to Lucy's breast.

Emery stood contemplatively. His gaze alternated between the empty sarcophagus and the four stone walls around them. "Tim, my boy," he began, "bring that flashlight and let's take a closer look at these hieroglyphs. That should tell us who," Emery paused and looked over to where Tata's body and the creature's shriveled arm lay, "or what was entombed here."

"How are you going to read them without your glasses?" Tim joined his father as he moved closer to one wall, training the flashlight beam on the images it held. "I know some of the symbolism. But really just a handful of the most basic characters."

"Yes, yes, yes... But you can describe for me the ones you don't recognize. Hopefully, we can cobble together enough of the story written here to explain what we've seen." Emery stood close to the wall, squinting in the meager light, slowly deciphering the images painted low enough that he could make them out. Tim stood at his shoulder, describing the hieroglyphs farther up the side of the wall. Both men painstakingly interpreting the images together, trying to unravel the names of who may have built the tomb in the first place and who had been interred.

Behind them, now in near darkness, Lucy and Sherry huddled together. When Sherry finished and was satisfied, she fell fast asleep in her mother's arms. Lucy cradled her daughter and closed her own eyes. Both mother and daughter dozing in a fitful sleep. The low murmur of the two men's voices oddly comforting in the still of the shadowy burial chamber.

Hours passed uneventfully.

Slowly and methodically, the story imprinted on the Egyptian tomb walls came to life. Many of the hieroglyphs were now faded, distorted, or missing. But the fragments, still legible, told a fantastical tale. It spoke of a time well before most conventional archeologists, like the world-renowned Emery W. Stander, thought Egyptian civilization had even begun. Much less prospered. The bulk of the hieroglyphs centered on the creator god Ptah and his offspring. Ptah, as both scholarly men already knew, was described in other various ancient texts as being 'the creator in heaven and earth who has made all things, the lord of all that is and is not.' Or the 'father of the fathers of the gods' and 'lord of eternity.' Nothing inscribed across the limestone walls of this tomb differed from these other accounts of which most Egyptologists were already aware. If anything, these hieroglyphs only solidified that Ptah was at one time considered the single true creator god by the long-ago people and civilization who had originally built this tomb sometime in the far-reaching past. The burial chamber, and the adjoined temple it likely once bordered, was built as a monument to Ptah and his revered offspring. It spoke glowingly of the one whom the tomb was constructed for.

Nefertem, son of Ptah.

With the bulk of what was still readable enough to be translated behind them, Emery and Tim began to decipher the meaning of the text. Debating the intent of the message so elaborately engraved in stone all around the sarcophagus and hidden tomb.

"It seems that I was indeed wrong about at least one thing for sure," Emery began. "This clearly was not the final resting place of Imhotep. The style of these hieroglyphs differs from those of his time. Not to mention, I now suspect the tomb itself was likely ancient before Imhotep was even born." Emery covered his mouth as he coughed, trying to dull the sound and not awaken Lucy and Sherry still sleeping nearby.

"Well, based on the section written on this portion," Tim gestured at the wall beside Tata's now cold corpse, "I wouldn't argue that. But what about the funerary texts and spells written over here?" Tim slapped his palm on the section of wall closest to where they stood talking. "I thought the phrasing seemed odd."

"I thought the same thing. Since that was the first wall of hieroglyphs we translated, I expected to find a more thorough explanation in one of the other sections. But that 'eternal-life' spell seems to be contained just on this one wall." Emery's breathing was more labored now; his hacking coughs becoming more frequent. The air in the chamber growing thicker the longer they'd been trapped inside. Tim waited until he had stopped before continuing their discussion.

"Should we go back over our translation? Maybe we missed something? Or misinterpreted the message intended by the scribes?" Tim felt the graininess in his own throat as well. According to his ticking watch, they had been underground nearly twelve hours now. Twelve hours since any of them, with the exception of Sherry, had any food or water. The stale, dry air of the tomb not helping their level of comfort. "Don't you think it ties in with what we witnessed?"

"Every ancient Egyptian tomb I've ever seen has plenty of spells inscribed along the walls. The text is meant simply to help the deceased on their journey to the afterlife. Supposed magical incantations that list what the dead must do to achieve eternal life." But, despite his stated misgivings, Emery began to rescan the hieroglyphs. Paraphrasing as he reread the writing first chiseled, and then painted by the tomb artisans of those long-ago days. "It states the occupant of this sarcophagus was Nefertem. Referring to him in various places as 'He Who is Beautiful' and 'Water Lily of the Sun' and the 'Son of Ptah.'

"And you believe Ptah was one of the oldest Egyptian gods, right?" Tim studied the symbols closely and began describing them once again for his father. Straining his eyes in the poor light of their one flashlight.

"It is hard to say with certainty. You have to remember the people, priests, and pharaohs often later went back and changed the writings, art, and sculptures from before their reigns. Defacing script or changing some of the symbols. Toppling statues and replacing them with images of themselves." Emery snorted derisively once. "Literally trying to rewrite history to glorify themselves, their deeds, and their beliefs. But, despite all that confusion, Ptah was certainly one of, if not *the* oldest of the Egyptian gods. And, though there certainly is plenty of academic debate on the subject, Nefertem is widely accepted as his son."

"So this tomb and sarcophagus, at least starting out, was supposedly built for Nefertem." Tim stopped his reexamination of the symbols. "Was he the one that was eternally youthful? Reborn at sunrise each and every day?"

"Yes. He is often depicted as a lotus flower that shuts its blossom each night only to reopen with the rise of the morning sun. A youthful god." Emery and Tim exchanged glances between looks at the withered arm, all that was left of the tomb's original inhabitant, still lying beside Tata's remains.

"I know you are thinking the same thing I am," Tim began. "We just watched the occupant pull itself out of there." He pointed to the massive sarcophagus that dominated the room. "We must be the first ones to discover this tomb. This place, it seems certain now, was Nefertem's final resting place. Nefertem often reflected in ancient writing as one who is constantly reborn."

"There is also this. The writing on the wall here." Pointing, Emery walked a few steps over to one section low enough that he had not needed Tim's help to read the inscriptions. "This spell instructs the reader that eternal life is theirs for the taking. There are prayers and precise tasks that must be carried out. But, according to this, upon completion you will never die. Living eternally through all the ages of man."

"How is this spell supposed to work? What is needed for one to achieve immortality?" Tim couldn't help but smile and chuckle slightly. "This all just seems absurd, dad. But, after what we witnessed, there has to be something unknown going on here." He paused, thankful for a puzzle to help take his mind off the dire circumstances they all were in. "Maybe there is some kind of plant ingested? Or topical ointments mentioned that need researched? Something must have given that thing at least the appearance of life." He barked out a laugh. "I can't believe I'm even entertaining the notion of any of this."

"Well," Emery began, "do you want the Reader's Digest Condensed version?" Despite their limited physical activity, both men were now winded and tired from breathing the oxygen-depleted air of the sealed tomb. Together, they sauntered back over to the base of the sarcophagus and sat down heavily. On the side opposite where they sat, baby Sherry's and Lucy's eyes remained closed. Both now seemingly sleeping peacefully.

"Sure. Let's hear it." Tim sat the flashlight down between them. Both men pretending not to notice or commenting on how much dimmer the yellowish glow from it had become over the last hour. "What did that guy do to be able to pull himself out of his stone grave thousands of years after his death?" Again, Tim chuckled at the ridiculous notion. Wondering if the dwindling air supply was beginning to hinder his normally rational mind.

"According to all this," Emery gestured around him at the hieroglyph-filled walls, "the spell itself only gets you in front of Anubis and Thoth."

"And what then? Anubis weighs your heart and deeds, right? Then Thoth records the results. That sounds pretty typical of what we've learned from writings and in tombs of later periods." Tim leaned back and rested on his elbows, both legs stretched out in front of him in the sand. "That can't be all of it."

"No, no it's not. To get this special, one-time audience with them before your time is up on the mortal plane, you must make a sacrifice. First," Emery continued, "you must kill the one you loved most in this world. Then, eliminate any of your living offspring."

"How morbid..." Tim listened with his eyes half closed.

"Once you have made this commitment and completed the blood sacrifices as instructed, you supposedly will appear before Anubis and

Thoth. If they agree you have taken all the steps and are prepared, you are granted eternal life." Emery coughed and cleared his throat.

"Geez, you mean like that poor slob? Who would want to come back looking like that? Or wake up only to find yourself stuck deep underground in a sealed tomb? Doesn't really make sense..." Tim made a half-hearted gesture towards where the severed arm of the tomb's original occupier still lay. "So that's it? Murder the one you love and kill off all your remaining family? Sounds like a deal with the devil to me."

"As you well know, this writing far predates anything biblical. The popular modern notion of a single god and a single devil as described in the Old and New Testament was dreamed up way after all this." Emery shook his head is the dimming light. "Just like the Egyptian story I'm telling you now, fiction created to help man make sense of what they don't understand at all. But, anyway, to complete the rest of the spell you must anoint that odd Ankh symbol on the end of the gold scepter we found with the blood of your sacrifice. Then place the tip in an opening or hole that must have been drilled in the lid of the sarcophagus." Emery pointed at the broken top of the tomb they'd seen when first entering the chamber. "Of course, since it is now broken..." He trailed off and closed his eyes.

"But what about the baby? Why was that buried in here?" Tim felt a weariness wash over him like a warm blanket. He wanted only to close his eyes.

"Who knows? Maybe that thing killed it. Or tried to do the spell and sacrificed the child." Emery shrugged, sleep calling to him as well.

Both men soon nodded off. Blissfully unaware of Lucy's open eyes. Or the rustling movement starting behind them on the opposite side of the burial chamber.

CHAPTER THIRTEEN
IOWA/ILLINOIS BORDER - 1964

THE QUAD CITIES

After stopping at one of Howard's favorite diners for lunch near the Rock Island Police Department headquarters, both detectives rode together to the alley they'd been called to in the dead of night just days before. The sky was clear in the late springtime day. The sun was warm and the few fluffy clouds in the sky above them white and unthreatening.

They parked their car in the alley itself, both men grimly noting where the splayed body had been found. The thought of the atrocity recently committed there was hard to square with the benign, sunshine-filled alleyway they walked down. Howard pointed out the nearby sewer drainage grates on both sides of the alley – the wide metal, lattice-like openings black and ominous. Jeff followed behind Howard as he made his way around to the front of the building. The warehouse's weathered siding, peeling white paint, and crumbling brickwork right at home among the surrounding businesses and cracked sidewalks. In the air hung the unmistakable smell of the Mississippi River, only blocks away, competing with the few factories still in operation nearby. Their towering smoke stacks belching god knows what into the midwestern skies. The main entrance of the hospital supply warehouse was adorned with a simple sign stenciled Hancock Medical in faded black letters. Unlocked, they called out as they entered the old building. An unoccupied desk, the only thing greeting them.

"Yes, hold on... coming." The disembodied voice of a man answering somewhere unseen. "If this is a delivery, you'll need to drive around to the... Oh!"

"Good afternoon," Howard started as he pulled his badge. "I was hoping to speak with the person in charge, someone who regularly works here at this location." Beside him, Jeff pulled out his badge for inspection as well. "I assume you are aware of what was found the other night in the bordering alley."

"Sure, yes. What a terrible thing. Makes you question what the world is coming to these days." The middle-aged man wore dark blue coveralls that covered the white shirt and tie he wore underneath. He had thick lensed glasses rimmed with a black frame and was clean shaven; his salt and pepper colored hair swept back from his face. He stretched out one hand and shook with both detectives in greeting. The white embroidered tag on his uniform was stamped "Hancock Hospital" with "Rod" in red thread stitched underneath. "Name's Rodney Harris. I'm here most days. What can I answer for you? I'm afraid I didn't know the woman who was found."

"Yes. What a terrible event. We are still investigating her uh... demise. But we actually were hoping you could tell us about a former co-worker of yours, Mr. Elmer Denbrough. We have reason to believe the two deaths could possibly be related." Howard studied the face of the man before him. Watching for any hint of avoidance or deception. But the only emotion shown was one of sorrow. "I understand he worked here before his own untimely passing."

"Sure. Elmer was a great guy. It is hard to imagine anyone ever wanting to do him harm. Much less attack and kill him in that fashion." Rod paused before adding, "You fellas want to come around back with me? There is a Pepsi machine if you want a bottle of soda." The Hancock

Medical warehouse worker turned and pushed his way through a pair of swinging doors. "There is also a place we can sit back here," he added over his shoulder.

Howard and Jeff followed the man past the double-swinging doors before rounding one corner. The back of the warehouse was a wide-open expanse filled with wooden and steel racks stretching as far as they could see. Above their heads, the ceiling was some fifty feet high, and the massive building appeared to all be on ground level. Both Howard and Jeff commented on the variety of medical equipment being stored onsite. Much of it neatly arranged in crates and boxes with piles of crutches, wheeled walkers, canes, and various steel cots and plastic-coated mattresses spilling over the racks holding them. The three men sat in the seats gathered around a small table that likely served as the warehouse's breakroom. The steel legs of their hard plastic chairs scraped noisily along the concrete floor of the building as each man sat in unison. On the wall beside them stood the Pepsi bottle cooler, crying out for their loose change. Opposite from where they sat hung a large chalkboard filled with scribbles. No sound or movement came from the racks behind where they sat.

"Do you work here alone, Rod?" Jeff had his notebook open on the small table, pen in hand to jot down anything important they might learn. "This building is gigantic. How can one man manage?"

"No. Some of our drivers, like Elmer was, work here in between their deliveries. But Hancock is closing this building down at the end of the year. There is new construction happening down by the main hospital campus and when that work is completed, we will be transferring everything over. I'm responsible for all the inventory here until we get things moved to the new place. Right now, I'm trying to count and organize one section at a time. Our drivers are already loading up what is left of the useable medical supplies once I get them packed up. Some days I have a couple fellas helping me out. Some days, like today, I'm all alone."

"Why is Hancock closing this place down?" Howard chimed in with what he hoped was a relaxed question. He always found a little small talk tended to loosen lips. Though Rod already struck him as being relaxed and comfortable. At the very least, he'd invited them in without being defensive or demanding to know the reason. That was a good sign.

"Beats me. I've been working here for almost ten years, but they don't ever really tell me much. I thought I'd be sad to leave this big old building after so long. But, to be honest, with everything that has happened the last couple of years around here, the sooner the better." Rod pulled a grey striped handkerchief out of an inner pocket in his blue coveralls and wiped at his nose. Howard and Jeff shared a raised eyebrow.

"Everything that's happened the last couple of years?" Howard felt his heartbeat quicken. "What do you mean?"

"I suppose this might sound ridiculous, what with you two being po-licemen and all, but it's almost like the personality of this whole building is changing. Getting darker. I hear strange things I never used to. I know some of it is likely just the age of this old place." Rod gestured around himself in a general way. "Things are kind of falling apart, and you know how old buildings can groan and creak. Add in some strong winds, or the whistles and pops of the old boiler in back, and it can feel like the place is alive and watching you sometimes. Silly, I know." Rod smiled grimly as he cast his eyes downward in embarrassment. "If you'd asked me a few years ago, I would have told you I hoped to stay working at this location right up until I retire. But now I'm glad we're moving out."

"Why is that?" Howard asked casually. Hoping to keep the warehouse worker talking and relaxed.

"Oh, it might just be a product of the neighborhood around here all going to hell in a handbasket. But in the last couple of years we've started to have some break-ins and vandalism. Probably just bored kids, but they sure leave behind a mess. They even damaged some of our inventory of anatomical shipments. Seems to be getting worse lately, too. Though I can't imagine what these kids do with what they steal." Rod shook his head back and forth, a troubled expression on his face. He leaned in close to the two detectives as if imparting a secret. "Maybe they are just trying to scare me. But a few times, they even desecrated the cadavers we used to store here before our refrigeration unit blew out. I told my boss he needs to hire a night watchman or have a security guard patrol."

"Probably a good idea. I'm a little surprised they don't have someone watching over the place at night. There must be a lot of valuable equipment stored in here." Howard kept his voice low and agreeable.

"It used to be, if there was any trouble spotted at night, I'd get the phone call. Have to climb out of bed and drive down here. Usually, it would turn out to be nothing. But I told my boss just the other day that I don't want to come down late at night anymore. Or even work here after dark. You'll think I'm just being silly, and maybe now it is just knowing what happened right outside these doors. But I swear over the last couple years if I'm stuck in here working late trying to finish something up, or waiting on a delivery truck running behind schedule, I hear strange sounds. Probably just alley cats yowling, or tussling with the raccoons and possums that get in our garbage out back, but sometimes it really sounds like someone is being pulled apart."

"You mean like the lady found in the alley the other night?" Howard leaned forward. He thought to himself, now they were getting somewhere.

"That poor woman... Is it true she was found all torn up?" Howard and Jeff both nodded somberly. "You think it is that same guy you were looking for before? That Middle Eastern prince or whatever he was?" Rod refolded his handkerchief and tucked it back inside the pocket he'd pulled it from.

"Middle Eastern what? Who told you we were looking for a foreigner in connection with this crime?" Howard was asking the questions, Jeff discreetly writing in his notebook periodically. "Has another officer already been around to question you?"

"Lately? No. But a couple of you boys from the state police sure seemed hot to find him after Elmer was found all butchered like he was. I was asked to go identify his body, seeing as how his wife was dead. Elmer and his wife didn't have any kids and he had no family, you see. Those state fellas tried to downplay what had happened to him. But I could tell, from his sunken chest under the sheet, he had lost all the important parts inside his body." Rod turned and coughed once. "Just like that body dumped in the alley back in '62. I'll never forget stumbling upon that horrible sight... Let me tell you, I threw up every bit of my breakfast that morning." Rod scrunched his face up, clearly recalling what he'd witnessed as he shuddered once.

"I'm sorry," Jeff began. "Did you say there was a body found in the alley here? You mean the same alley where we found the victim earlier this week?" He looked over at Howard, his eyes narrowing. "Sorry, I'm new to both this town and investigation," he said, still speaking to Rod though his eyes were on Howard. "I must have somehow missed that."

Now it was Rod's turn to be surprised. "Well, sure. I thought that was why you showed up here again. I had already told those state police boys everything I knew about Elmer last year. They told me they suspected his murder might be tied to the young woman found here the year before. In '62."

"State?" Jeff asked before Howard could say anything. "Can you remind me which officer that was?"

"I might still have his card lying around here somewhere. But aren't all you fellas working together?" For the first time, the warehouse worker seemed to carefully contemplate his answers. Howard jumped in before Jeff could respond.

"We have had some turnover. Like Jeff here said, we are new to this investigation." When Howard saw Jeff about to reply, he quickly followed up. "Just so we are clear. When you say State, you mean Iowa, correct? You were talking with the detectives working for the Iowa State Police Department?"

"Sure! Elmer, he'd been out on a delivery over in Bettendorf, across the river in Iowa. The policemen I spoke with said the way he'd been found matched the body I discovered the year before. All cut up and missing organs. I started to get nervous. It doesn't take a fancy-pants mystery writer to see since Elmer worked onsite, right here where that young lady's mutilated body was discovered, that those policemen might be suspecting me. But they assured me they'd already known that poor young lady was murdered somewhere else before her body was disposed of here. Something about the evidence, or lack of evidence, proving she'd been all ripped apart some other place. Plus, one of 'em let slip about the governor's niece."

"Governor's niece? Pardon my language, but what the hell!" Jeff was no longer hiding his stare at Howard. If Rod noticed, he didn't show. "What did these Iowa state policemen say about the governor's niece?"

"Oh, come on, you know. It was in all the papers back when she'd been found murdered. How could you not know about..."

"Humor me. I'm from Marquette, Michigan and, like I said, just transferred here. The killing of a politician's niece in one state isn't exactly newsworthy in another state." Jeff was speaking quickly now while Howard sat staring straight ahead silently. "When did this happen?"

"Let's see... Elmer was killed in the fall of 1962. I found the body in the alley earlier in the spring of that same year. Oh! That's right! They said the governor's niece was killed by her foreigner boyfriend after a springtime fundraising ball of some sort held in Davenport by the Governor."

Jeff was writing as fast as he could in his notebook. When he finished, he reread to himself what he'd written before asking another question. "You said foreigner. Earlier you said something about a prince. I take it her boyfriend was from the Middle East and what? A Saudi Arabian or Egyptian diplomat or royalty? When did they catch him?"

"They never did." Howard spoke as he stood. "Thank you for your help, Mr. Harris. If we need to ask some more questions, are you likely to be around the rest of the week? Will you be working here until 5:00 most days?" All three men began walking back to the main entrance of the warehouse building. Jeff walked slowly, clearly wanting to stay and find out more. But choosing to stay silent.

"I'm pretty much always here. I work from eight to four, Monday through Friday." The Hancock Hospital warehouse worker took the business cards offered by both Howard and Jeff. "I hope you find the bastard doing all this."

"One more thing," Jeff turned and spoke directly to the informative warehouse worker. "Did the State police from Iowa say how the two victims, Elmer and the young lady, were tied to the murder of the Governor's niece?"

"The one who let slip about the governor's niece just said she'd been found the same way as the others. Missing all her insides." Rod seemed to shudder involuntarily.

"Did they give you any indication why they had suspected her boyfriend?" Jeff stood at the outside entrance, his foot holding the door open as Howard turned to hear the reply.

"They said he'd only recently arrived in the states and had just began seeing the young woman. But also, that he wasn't Christian-like. Maybe a Pagan of some sort. That he must have used her parts for some devilish ritual. They didn't come right out and say it, but I gathered they thought he must still need more blood sacrifices. That was why he killed the other girl and Elmer. Using their guts as kind of an offering of some sort." Jeff and Howard merely nodded before the door closed behind them. They walked in silence to Howard's car, neither saying a word until they'd climbed in and shut the doors.

"When were you going to share another girl was found in that same hellish alley!" Jeff fairly roared at his new partner. "God dammit, Howard! I guess I bought you not knowing about Susan, the girl found in the river. And that since it was over in Bettendorf, maybe you didn't know about the Elmer guy killing. But there is no way you wouldn't have been the detective called when that woman's body was found here. What the hell is wrong with you? How am I supposed to trust you? We are partners, aren't we?" Jeff was red-faced and panting, his tone aggressive.

"You have no reason to believe me, but I swear I was not involved in the investigation of that young lady's dumped body." Howard looked over at Jeff placidly, his face an unreadable mask.

"Bullshit! How do you expect me to believe that? Where were you?"

Howard was silent for several long seconds before replying. He sighed before starting the car and dropping the transmission into drive. "In the spring of 1962 I was in Zellers, over by Peoria in Illinois. I was off work for about three months, and the department thought it would be better if I stayed some place away from the quad cities while I recuperated."

"What the hell is Zellers?" Jeff's tone was still heated. Only slightly less accusative.

Howard snorted once before pulling into the street. "It was a kind of hell, I suppose." He looked over at his new partner of barely a month. "Zellers is a mental hospital..."

CHAPTER FOURTEEN

Jeff stood over the soiled bed. The sheets soaked and sticking to the thick plastic mattress cover he'd gotten in the habit of encasing his mattress of "fun" inside of. Sweat trickled down from his scalp and tickled one ear. Though he could barely catch his breath, he somehow found the strength to wipe one hand hurriedly across his drenched brow before collapsing onto his back. He looked up at the ceiling of his home's tiny bedroom. His own red face peering back at him from the lofty height. He was nude, and he loved the way his body looked during sex. Glistening with sweat, muscles hard and strained, his hairy chest heaving up and down in the dim light of the corner lamp.

He spread his legs and watched himself stretch over to the colored glass container on his bedside table. He reached inside his mom's old candy dish that once only held her favorite hard candy mints. Jeff grabbed a square package wrapped in foil from out of the dish and brought it to his mouth. He bit down on one corner, tearing the package with his teeth and pulling out its contents before tossing the empty wrapper into the wicker trashcan beside his bed. He gazed admiringly up at his image in the grouping of mirrors he'd installed above the single bed of his spare bedroom. Silently, he thanked the man who was his father. Whoever that guy might be. Jeff understood what a blessing it was to have been born so well-endowed. The only problem was finding rubbers big enough.

Woe is me, he thought to himself as he smiled. Or, as was more often the case than not, *whoa says she.*

"I hope you are ready for this, Emma. I've barely started..." Jeff rolled towards the woman next to him on the bed. She whimpered slightly when he playfully swatted her flabby ass. The red stripes from his early whipping likely still stinging her. Sitting up, he couldn't keep his eyes from traveling to the dark mound between her legs, then down one thick thigh and past her knee splintered with spidery varicose veins. He'd bound her ankles, of course, each of her feet secured tightly to the bedposts. Reaching between his own legs, he struggled to roll the constrictive end of the condom over the bulbous knob as he slowly slid himself down to the end of the bed. When he grabbed the calloused heel of the grey-haired woman tied and gagged, he felt her trying to kick him away.

It was pointless. Unlike the knife he'd left out on the headboard for her to contemplate.

Jeff Plant lifted the pudgy toes to his mouth. Rolling one after another between his teeth, his breath quickening once more. Unable to stop himself, he began to bite down. Chewing, licking, and sucking one toe after another, then one foot after the other, all ten toes in his mouth at times. The calloused flesh and rank smell of the mature secretary's feet leaving him breathless with anticipation of things to come. With her feet in his mouth, Jeff watched the blood dripping from the wounds he'd skillfully carved into her earlier. Some were from his riding crop, some from his blade, and some from his bites. Tethered to the bed, her muffled shouts and desperate little kicks only delighted him more. By the time he was ready to mount her one final time, she lay as still as the dead.

Smeared gore staining his grin as he grunted loudly with each of his frenzied thrusts.

"I think you at least owe me that, don't you think? I want to know anything else you are keeping to yourself. I'm not saying we have to like each other. But if I'm going to put my life in your hands, my partner's hands, we need to trust each other. And right now, my trust in you has been seriously breached."

"What? What do you feel like I am holding back?" Howard reached up with one hand, rubbing his tired eyes and brushing the gritty sleep away from the corners of each. He knew Jeff was staring at him. Howard also knew he was only delaying the inevitable. Yesterday, he'd told Jeff about his time at Zellers. He would have had this conversation with Jeff right then if they hadn't unexpectedly been called in as support when things had gotten out of hand at a local tavern in downtown Rock Island. A group of bored, unemployed men starting a brawl that spilled out in the street. It had taken both he and Jeff, as well as six other officers, to restore order and haul the instigators away.

By the time all the paperwork was completed, they both had been in a hurry to get home. Howard, needing to relieve Gloria, the nurse who helped watched over his wife, and Jeff saying he had an urgent appointment to keep. Even though it had been nearly eight PM by the time they'd wrapped up. Now, the day after their visit to the warehouse where they'd learned two separate women were found butchered just outside its doors, the detectives were having the conversation. Both seated at Howard's desk, any lingering officers in the backroom of the Rock Island police department mostly out of ear shot.

"For starters, how could you not be aware a body had been dumped at that same warehouse previously? Not only that, but with almost identical wounds?" Jeff tossed the file on the gruesome discovery from 1962 on top of Howard's desk. "The pictures of both victims' wounds are virtually the same. Apparently, I am the only one who noticed..." Howard didn't open the file. He'd seen the same startling black and white photos earlier that morning.

"You are right. I should have put those two things together. But," Howard looked up at his new partner, "I told you. I was off on leave when that happened. I did get brought up to speed when I returned. That is true. I guess with so many different things coming at me when I first got back, this just didn't stick." Now Howard picked up the file and flipped past the photos and first pages of the report without really looking at them. He knew, after reviewing the file for the first time that very morning, what it said. "She was a young lady who lived somewhere south of the quad cities in a small farming community. The original investigators knew her body had been dumped and that her death didn't occur at the site. The case was referred to the county, where she lived, and that was the end of it. Until the second body, Mary, our grandma as you keep calling her, there was nothing I would or could have followed up on."

"Oh! So now you admit the two are related and we should follow up?" Jeff shook his head disdainfully. "What about this case involving the Governor of Iowa? His cousin or niece, whatever relation she was."

"It was his niece."

"Whatever. Point being I have to learn about that investigation from Rod, the local warehouse worker? What kind of screwed up investigations do you guys run? Does anybody talk to anybody around here? Aren't we all on the same team?" Jeff grabbed at his paper cup of coffee and downed the last swallow.

"Surely you understand why the state police, and likely the FBI and state department, if the suspect truly was identified as her boyfriend and some kind of nobleman from another country, wouldn't share something like that with us. Between the victim being a relative of a powerful politician and the suspect being an international fugitive, they could give two shakes about us peons here in Illinois. You think they need our help? Get real, Jeffrey."

"And the little girl?"

"No one, except Jim the coroner from hearsay, would have tied what was classified as a boating accident into these brutal killings." Howard leaned forward and began to massage his temples. He needed more coffee. "Her death still may not actually be related to all this."

Jeff sat down hard on the barely padded steel chair at the edge of Howard's desk. A dejected look on his face. "That much I guess I can understand." He paused as he scrunched the cup in his hand into a ball before tossing it in a nearby trash can. "So, what *do* we have? Or know?" He looked up at Howard.

"All I know is that we have a mystery on our hands. We have a total of five deaths spread out over about two years. We have our case, which is clearly a homicide that occurred in our jurisdiction. There was no physical evidence left at what we think is the scene of the crime, the alley next to the Hancock Medical Supply warehouse. We have Elmer, the Hancock employee who worked at the same site where Mary's body was discovered, but his remains were found in a neighboring community."

"Bettendorf, right? Out doing a delivery when he was attacked, or surprised, or whatever you want to classify these murders as." Jeff was frowning. "And no word back yet from the Iowa State Police investigating his murder?"

"Not yet, but we only sent in our request the other day. I'm still hopeful they will cooperate."

"And they are only investigating that killing because of the similarities to the murder of the Iowa governor's niece." Both Jeff's tone and voice were more measured now.

"Which happened in downtown Davenport, not Rock Island or Bettendorf. Or Moline for that matter." Howard listing all four of the towns that made up the Quad City area.

Jeff nodded his agreement before adding, "Right. Plus, we have the little girl Susan Hopper pulled from the Mississippi with the same wounds as the other three."

"Not exactly the same. There was no mention of the Governor's niece having her ankles sliced from behind like the others." Howard paused before continuing. "Of course, until we see the actual report, I guess we can't be sure. The Iowa State Police may have withheld some information from the press."

"Yes, but still missing all her insides like the others, though. Just like the latest potential victim we just stumbled upon. The young lady dumped almost two years ago in the same alley beside that old Hancock warehouse." Jeff leaned back in his squeaking chair contemplatively. "But was likely killed elsewhere. Maybe south of us, you say? She was from a small town south of the quad cities?"

"Yeah, I think her hometown was a little farming community named Almore." Howard shrugged. He'd never actually visited the place before. Why would he?

"So, five deaths, for arguments sake, all disemboweled in nearly the exact same manner. All five murders happening in five different communities and in two different states." Jeff shook his head dejectedly. "Could a case be any more convoluted or messed up than this one is? No wonder we are all spinning our wheels here. Each state, county, or city police department is trying to solve these killings separately without even realizing they are likely tied together. This investigation has been screwed up from the get go! I wonder if the killer realizes how lucky he is right now?"

Howard bent over; his hands clasped together in front of his face. Anyone who didn't know he wasn't a regular church-goer might assume his head was bowed in prayer. "Maybe it isn't luck..."

"What do you mean? This guy is super lucky this isn't happening in just one city but four. Or five if you count the young lady from that small town out in the sticks."

Howard looked up at his new partner. "Maybe he isn't lucky. Maybe he is purposefully using our own police practices, and 'siloed' departments, to his advantage. Thinking he can literally get away with murder all in the same vicinity where he lives simply because he knows how spotty communication between police departments can be." Howard began to talk faster. "Think about it. We just got lucky. If the two coroners working across the river from each other in different counties and different states hadn't been friendly, we wouldn't have suspected anything either."

"If this guy truly planned everything out that well in advance, he must know how territorial cops can be when a case gets hot. We all tend to protect our own little fiefdoms, if only just to catch the culprit ourselves. Garner all the glory so to speak. Maybe he is like a police groupie?" Jeff snorted derisively. "I've heard of guys buying CBs and scanners to listen in on radio chatter and calls. Cop 'wanna be's' we called them up in Michigan."

Howard sat stoically, staring straight ahead. "Or," he began without looking over at his new partner, "the killer is a cop."

Jeff immediately stood and walked the few steps over to his own desk. Without turning back around he said, "Oh, come on, Howard. You need to lose that idea. Sure, I mean every department might have a few rule benders taking advantage of their status. But you are talking about murder. An officer of the law butchering the very people he swore to protect?" Jeff turned back and faced Howard. "We shouldn't jump to conclusions. It might cloud our judgement." He leaned against his desk, "Unless we have some psycho working here with us."

His last statement hung in the air. Unacknowledged by either detective.

Finally, Howard broke the awkward silence. "Maybe you are right. How about we head back down to the warehouse? Some of those old buildings around that area have been there for almost one hundred years. Before we start snooping around our own department, lets be sure we don't overlook the second common denominator of most of these killings. The location."

Both detectives slipped their suit jackets back on. Jeff twisted at his tie until the knot was closer to his chin than his chest. "You mind if we drive separately this time? I need to stop by my apartment and check on something first."

"No problem," was Howard's reply. "I'd like to check in on my wife anyway. She doesn't have anyone staying with her today. It is the nurse's day off, and her mom is off visiting relatives up north in Dubuque. I just want to be sure she doesn't need anything." Both men departed after agreeing on the time they would meet back at the warehouse in downtown Rock Island.

CHAPTER FIFTEEN
CAIRO, EGYPT - 1962

SAQQARA NECROPOLIS

TIM WAKES, UNCERTAIN WHAT has roused him. He groggily rubs at his tired eyes, wiping grit and sand away from the corners as his eyelids flutter. He remains motionless and sucks in a deep, but unsatisfying breath of stale air. His heart thumps, and though he fills his lungs repeatedly, the shortness in his breathing remains. There was a heaviness in each inhale that reminded Tim of when he'd once had pneumonia as a younger man. An unrelenting pressure on his chest refusing to move and help with the most basic of his needs.

Breathing.

A muffled sound catches his attention and he opens his eyes. But the blackness never leaves his sight. Tim reaches up and nearly scratches his own eyeball while trying to verify his eyes are unshielded and open. He finds nothing wrapped around his eyes or face. With his head on a swivel, he pushes himself up from the ground where he laid. Searching unsuccessfully for the soft yellow glow of the flashlight. He reaches over to where his dad had been lying beside him, but, just like his search for breath and light, he finds nothing.

"Uh, hello," Tim starts unconfidently, "what happened to the light? Dad? Do you have the flashlight? Did it finally go out on us?" He sits up now, "Try pulling out the batteries and putting them back in a different order. Sometimes that works for a little bit…" Tim's voice trails off. His ears straining in the pitch black he swam in, but he could neither hear nor see anything. "Dad. Lucy. What are you guys doing?" Wide awake now, Tim stands, but still no reply or light came. "Hey!" Tim raises his voice for the first time, concern and worry obvious in his tone. "Someone answer me!"

No one does.

Like a blind man, Tim tentatively reaches behind him and finds the stone sarcophagus still at his back. The carved limestone was cool to the touch in the unsettling stillness of the tomb. With every passing second, his panic deepens. Why wasn't anyone answering? Tim wished he could hear anything until the exact moment he finally does. The slight sound freezes his thoughts and goosebumps ripple up and down his body. He'd caught a faint noise like something scuttling along the floor, the scratch of something moving discreetly along the sand. "I hear that," Tim tried again. "Are you hurt? Where is Sherry?" A pause. He hated the waver in his voice when he asked, "Is someone here?" Nothing for long seconds. "What is happening?"

Utterly sightless, Tim stretches one arm out in front of him while keeping his opposite hand clenched tightly to the edge of the sarcophagus behind him. He waves his free hand blindly in front of him and takes tentative steps along the side of the tomb's stone base. The complete lack of light, eerie and disturbing. The gloom, like the dwindling oxygen in the weak air he breathed, was suffocating. Panic began to grip his every thought, squeezing until they all died, and replacing them with panic's bosom buddy.

Dread.

"Lucy! Dad! Where are you?" Tim took two more steps and felt the curvature of the right angle at the end of his side of the sarcophagus. He'd now made it halfway around one long side and still came across nothing. When the feeble, scurrying sound came again, it accompanied a most uncomfortable vision. One that popped into his mind's eye without warning. The sound, Tim thought, was just like the scampering of rats hidden in the walls of a decrepit house. Rats the size of a man's hand. Tim couldn't help but think of the resurrected thing that had pulled itself from the stone tomb. How the squirming hand seemingly moved independently of the horrid thing that followed behind. Of course, Tim reminded himself, he'd killed that creature. It was all gone. The blasphemy had fallen entirely to ash when he'd speared it with the gold scepter. Except for its arm. Why hadn't the arm?

Or hand.

Before Tim could vanquish it, his mind raced to show him an absurdity of thoughts and fears. They had all been asleep. Lying low to the ground. Lucy and his dad weren't answering him. His dad, when Tim had awoken, was no longer beside him. And Sherry… Oh god! Tim watched helplessly as his mind taunted him with ridiculous images of the severed arm creeping nearly silent along the ground. Its fingernails going black and peeling off as it pulled itself from the corner where Tata's shroud covered body lay. The shriveled, flailing digits snatching at the throats of his weakened family. Choking them? Pulling them down? Burying them in the sand?

In the soundless, sightless, suffocating stillness, his mind was free to play with any unnatural thought that popped in it. Tim thought of how he'd seen the withered corpse come back to life inside the sarcophagus. The unimaginable horror of the undead thing returning to the physical world. What had sparked its awakening? What if the same thing was happening to Tata? Tim pictured in his mind's eye the blood-soaked remains of the man, his ravaged throat, the sinewy lines at the ruined neck. He imagined Tata rising like a lumbering zombie from the depths of death. The undead corpse of the man feasting on his father too weak to defend himself. His wife Lucy desperately sacrificing herself to somehow save Sherry. Tata savaging her while Sherry lay alone in utter darkness.

The soft crunch of the zombie's teeth as it tore into… Tim felt his rational mind swirling down a dark hole he may never be able to retrieve it from. He felt small and insignificant, swallowed whole by this monster called imagination.

Or the tomb.

Tim fought off these rampant images, and his child-like fear, with the only weapon he had. Logic. *Think, Tim. Think!* The dark he was floundering around in was easy enough to explain. The flashlight batteries had simply died. Clearly, the air of this ancient underground place was stale, and any remaining oxygen was dwindling fast. He was having trouble breathing himself. His father had been a lifelong smoker, and in the last few years became easily winded. Lucy, though undiagnosed, likely suffered from asthma like all her siblings. While Tim, though hardly what anyone would call athletic, with all his daily walking during his recent medical rotations and residency, certainly was in the best shape of them all. Perhaps his father, short of breath and in trouble, had woke before him? In his weakened state he'd fallen, or become confused and wandered away from the sarcophagus before then falling in the soft sand on the floor of the tomb. Were the subtle sounds he heard his father writhing in the sand and gasping for his last breaths? And if Lucy was struggling to get enough oxygen, she may not be conscious. Unable to hear him or rouse herself from sleep. *And Sherry,* thought Tim, *please don't let… I can't even think about her just yet. I've got to wake Lucy and locate my father!*

With purpose renewing his resolve, Tim began to move once more. Continuing to balance on the stone base of the sarcophagus, he stepped around both corners of the narrowest side and began to move along the longer backside where Lucy and Sherry had been sleeping. He called out blindly once more, "I'm coming, honey. Just hold on." But with each step, his renewed confidence began to waver once again. When he reached the next corner without finding Lucy or Sherry, his poise evaporated. *Now what*, he thought. Where could they be? Had Lucy, like his father, woken lightheaded and confused before wandering off? It didn't seem likely.

Tim sank down, squatting in blindness and, perhaps subconsciously, making himself small. His breath labored in the thin air. To his right, subtle sounds continued to reach his ear. In the hollow and echo-filled chamber, where they originated from was impossible to tell. But unlike the previous tentative scratching along the sand, these new sounds were repetitive. A cadence or rhythm to them. Back and forth or in and out like... like breathing! Tim felt a prick of fear raising the hair on the back of his neck. Something was right beside him in the black! Something not responding to his desperate pleas and softly inhaling and exhaling. Oh, so quietly. Before Tim could wrap his head around what he was hearing, there was a soft "pop" right beside his ear. So close he practically felt it!

Startled and screaming, Tim lashed out in fear and surprise with both hands in the direction of the unexpected sound. Both his fists thudding into soft flesh that gave easily under the assault. The hushed cadence broken; Tim heard for the first time since awakening the sound of another's voice. His father's.

But where was he?

Tim pounced on top of what he'd struck. Lashing out blindly and desperately in the dark with his fists. Though he missed several wild swings, a few of his blows miraculously found the mark. He felt one punch bounce high off the head of his attacker, while another seemed to strike what felt like the assaulter's throat. Fighting sightless and thrashing back and forth in the sand, it was impossible for him to be certain. But, after a few more solid punches, Tim no longer felt any resistance or any kind of counterattack. What had crept up to him in the black fell silent and unmoving. Without sight, Tim ran his hands across the prostrate body. Using touch to try and ascertain the identity of what had silently come for him in the dark.

When he pulled what felt like a pack of cigarettes from the top pocket of his assailant, Tim knew instantly it was his father. He groaned as he ran his hands farther up the body until he felt a gag pulled taut across his dad's features. He yanked desperately at it but was unable to free it from his father's mouth. With Emery unmoving, Tim reached for the lighter his dad always kept in the front pocket of his pants. He quickly pulled it out and flicked the striker, the warm flame blooming so brightly that Tim had to briefly look away. When his eyes acclimated to the sudden glare, he found he was correct. His father, bound and gagged, lay unconscious underneath him. Emery was bleeding from a cut near his scalp and one eye was quickly swelling and pink, likely from one of Tim's ill-advised blows. But his father's chest heaved up and down with life.

"Dad! What in god's name is going on?" Tim, one hand holding the lighter, used his other to try and rouse him. He never saw the gold scepter glinting behind him as it sliced through the air. Nor felt the blow when it struck the back of his head. Tim joined his father on the sand floor of the tomb. Knocked unconscious, his face planting itself on his father's chest.

CHAPTER SIXTEEN

WHEN TIM NEXT OPENED his eyes, he was flooded with relief. Only a few feet away, as Tim groggily shook his head back and forth, was his daughter Sherry. The one-year-old cooing contently as she fumbled with the pacifier in her tiny hand. Pulling it repeatedly up to her face as she lay sprawled across the burial shroud laid on top of the sand covered floor of the Egyptian tomb. Beside her, the flashlight lay unlit and switched off. When the initial waves of dizziness passed, and Tim was able to shake the remaining cobwebs from his sore head, he tried to speak to her. But the only sound that came out was a muffled grunt.

"Welcome back to the land of the living." Tim looked up and saw it was Lucy who had spoken. Her face, like Sherry lying on the shroud, bathed in the glow of a flaming torch. The light, coming from one of the three reed torches they'd discovered while searching for an escape out of the tomb, wavered hesitantly in one corner of the chamber. The opposite unlit end buried in the sand beside the gleaming trove of golden treasure. Lucy held a small wooden chest in her hands. It was half-open, and a colorful array of gems peeked out from the inside. "For a little bit anyway..." Lucy let the lid close slowly before setting the box down beside the rest of the ancient Egyptian riches.

Tim looked to his right and saw his father was lying beside him. Both men had their hands tied behind their back and were also bound to each other, though separated by several feet of sand between them. The slim rope Tata had carried finally put to use. Across both Emery's and Tim's mouths were long strands of white cloth ripped from Lucy's blouse. Bare armed now, she'd obviously torn the sleeves off it to gag both men. Tim tried to speak again, his eyes narrowing in anger. The stifled sound that came out was not distinguishable, but the why was obvious enough, anyway.

"I bet you are wondering what is going on," Lucy interrupted. "Why, right? What happened?" She smiled down at him, her expression one of rapture and reward. "It is really quite simple. I heard what you and Emery were talking about earlier. You know, when you thought I was asleep." Lucy giggled lightly. "How the magic spell on the walls down here hold the key to eternal life." Tim grunted loudly and shook his head vigorously back and forth. Disbelief as plain in his features as the question he struggled to ask. She couldn't possibly believe these arcane writings would actually work, could she?

"I know, I know… you are thinking I must be crazy." Lucy matched the shaking of Tim's head with her own. "Or that I have gold-fever! But you know me, I'm actually very practical." She paused and let her eyes linger over the treasure-filled room before stopping at the lit torch stuck in the ground beside her. "The way I see it, we were all going to die down here together. As hard as it already is to catch our breath, probably pretty quickly. And even if there is some small bit of air that keeps us from suffocating, without water we'd last only days at best. So, I figure, if we are all dead anyway, I might as well at least try for immortality." Lucy giggled again, and Tim began to wonder if the lack of oxygen in the air was what made her seem so giddy. At the very least, he thought to himself, she clearly wasn't thinking rationally anymore. Tim again tried speaking, grunting in a tone he hoped would sway her from the path of madness she was traversing.

She ignored his protests.

"Once you two finished deciphering the hieroglyphs and finally fell asleep, I got up. I had already pretty much memorized the layout of the room, so even if the flashlight batteries had died while I waited, I knew I could still retrieve the shroud and wrap Sherry in it. Lucky for me, she stayed asleep the whole time I swaddled and moved her out of the way. After that, I came back for the light." Lucy looked down at Tim's father. "I'm afraid I may have hit Emery over the head with the flashlight a little harder than I had intended. But..." She shrugged as if to say, 'what can you do?' "I knew he'd never agree to say the prayer or spell, whatever it is, unless he had no choice." She glanced once more at the still unconscious Egyptologist with a wistful smile. "By the time he woke, I had him bound and held the sharp end of that Ankh staff to Sherry's chest. You know how he feels about her. He was speaking in tongues in seconds, believe me!" Lucy bent over and grabbed the golden rod at her feet. Like Tim, when he'd dispatched of whatever it was that had risen from the stone grave, Lucy twirled it once in her hand. She held the tapered end out in front of her like a spear.

"I waited to light a torch until after I knocked you out. I figured if you woke up before I was ready, and you did by the way, keeping you blind was my only chance. I have to admit, it was kind of fun hearing you struggle in the dark. So confused and panicked. You sounded and acted just like a scared little boy. I was expecting you to make your way around the sarcophagus, and I had a fifty-fifty chance which way. Too bad you went the route you did. You bumped into Emery first instead of me. Boy, did he pay the price, huh?" Lucy giggled again and the light laughter grated on Tim. It was hard to hear the woman he'd married speak so callously. What they say is true, he thought dimly, love really is blind.

"But everything turned out anyway. Hearing how you reacted and lashed out, I may have been luckier, and safer, staying where I was." While she talked, Tim began to struggle against the binding. Working his wrists to try and loosen the rope. "I really wasn't sure if the torches would still work or not. You know, being so old and all. But I want to save any juice still left in that flashlight."

"Yeah," Lucy noted Tim's frantic efforts to free himself, "you aren't going to loosen that knot. But go ahead and knock yourself out." Lucy turned and walked over to the still unconscious Emery. She placed the tapered and sharp end of the golden rod against his chest, right over the heart. Tim yowled desperately from under his gag, the cloth cutting into the corners of his mouth as he struggled to free himself. "He told me not to tell you. But Emery already had his appointment with that specialist you told him he should go see in Chicago." Lucy looked up and met Tim's eyes. Tears streamed from them and snot ran down his face. "He has cancer, Tim. Lung cancer. They gave him until the end of the year. So this," she looked back down at the esteemed Egyptologist Emery W. Stander, "is mercy."

Grunting, Lucy pushed down with all her might and leaned her weight behind the thrust. The long golden scepter with the strange Ankh symbol on top of it sunk down heavily. Piercing the chest and plunging the gold rod through Tim's father's heart. A wave of crimson blood instantly spurted from the wound, the arterial spray coating the bottom half of the Egyptian artifact and nearly splashing onto Lucy's hands. Emery's eyes never opened, nor did he utter a sound, as the lifeblood flowed out of him. His body convulsed under Lucy several times; the death throes shook the quivering rod but little else. Tim howled and raged from where he sat barely four feet away, still tethered to his father.

Watching him die.

Lucy callously wiggled the rod several times as she pulled it from the dead man's chest. When it was freed, she moved close to Tim and squatted in front of him. She placed the dripping end of the gold staff against his chest. Her face barely a few feet from his own. "I want you to know that this has nothing to do with you. Or him," Lucy nodded in Emery's direction. His body now encircled by the blood still pouring out and pooling under him. "As for Sherry, this will ensure she doesn't suffer either. I couldn't bear the thought of her starving to death." She paused, her eyes drifting, "I bet when I come back, I'll be just like Mr. Walking Biting Mummy. The first thing I'll look for is her tiny body..." Lucy's eyes wavered again, and Tim thought he saw a swell of tears filling them. But the moment passed without any of them spilling.

"Here is what is going to happen. Your dad said the spell or prayer already. In the writings, it was very clear that I must sacrifice any of my offspring and the one I loved most in this world. That was why I killed Emery. He was always so kind to me. I know how he adored Sherry and what you meant to him. In my heart, I know I loved that man. He was a wonderful father-in-law and perfect grandfather." Lucy paused and looked down as if afraid to meet Tim's eyes. "But you, you I'm not so sure. I guess I love you. Or did anyway. It doesn't really matter now. I mean, whether it was you or Emery I loved most. The important thing is to not leave this to chance. You only get one shot at immortality, right?"

The dripping gold scepter loomed over his heart with purposeful intent, and fear leapt into Tim's belly. He understood he was about to die. Following after his father into the next world. He thought to himself, the gag has robbed me of my mouth and all I want to do is scream. He idly wondered if he would live long enough to see his blood and guts spill on the floor...

Tim twisted his head and looked once more over at his baby girl. Sherry was on her back at the far side of the chamber where Lucy had left her. He was saddened he didn't get one last look at his beautiful baby girl's face. But he was grateful she wouldn't witness him being skewered to the floor like a squirming bug pinned to some entomologist's creepy display. Tim turned his head back and looked into Lucy's eyes. But he no longer recognized the woman he'd loved. She was gone now. Somehow seduced and replaced by the madness scrawled along this ancient Egyptian tomb's walls.

Tim closed his eyes.

Tap

Tap

Tim opened his eyes. Somewhere behind his head, back where Tata was laid out, came a series of light taps. Lucy heard it as well. Her eyes reflecting the confusion they both felt.

Tap

Thunk

Thunk

The sounds became louder. A persistent pattern, the noise building and growing closer. As if something was coming. A clatter of sand and small stones came down in the far corner of the chamber just above Tata's corpse. Briefly showering his body in earthen debris.

Lucy looked down at Tim once, then laid the gold rod she was menacing him with at her feet. She walked a few steps closer to the sound. Sandy dust floating in the air around her like a swarm of hungry gnats. She cocked her head to one side, likely never seeing the chunk of limestone that split her skull. It was the size of a cinderblock and fell from near the top of the tomb wall where the crescendo of noise came from. Almost as if in slow-motion, Tim watched the arc of the loose hunk of rock as it fell. Smashing into Lucy's head with a sickening crack. Cleaving half her head and face from her body as it landed in a huff. Tim watched her legs spasm while the soft contents of her skull oozed onto the sandy floor of the tomb. Hard bits of bone mixed with brain matter and blood soaking the sand under what was left of her head. Moments later, more debris came crashing down all around her. Quickly burying her entire body under a mound of growing rock, dirt, and sand. The entire corner of the tomb collapsing inward and hiding both Lucy and Tata under the rubble.

Tim turned his face and body away from the swell of cascading debris. The entire chamber now filling with dust. He rolled desperately toward

Sherry who, still lying on top of the burial shroud, was now crying. The noise and confusion all around scaring her into a series of shuddering wails. There was just enough slack in the rope that bound him to his dead father that Tim was able to reach her. Unable to speak or hold her, his hands still bound behind his back, he snuggled up to Sherry. Protectively curling his body around and over to shield the baby from the growing collapse. In less than a minute, they both were covered in chalky dirt. Father and daughter lying together like two spoons in the dirtiest cutlery drawer ever, both crying and afraid. The flaming torch extinguished in the onslaught of cascading dust falling.

Slowly, the noise and clatter from the far side of the tomb faded. Though it was hard to see past the haze of the floating debris all around him, Tim opened his wet eyes and peeked out. In the opposite corner, where he'd first heard the sounds originate, a huge chasm had opened up. Behind the wall of dust, Tim could see shadowy lights sweeping back and forth. He rolled completely over to face the floating, spectral beams. Though the air was murky, he could smell the freshness it held. Tim hollered as loud as he could from behind his gag. Bellowing for all he was worth. Slowly, a human form came forward out of the debris-filled air. It moved steadily towards him, a handheld flashlight piercing the air. The figure moved close and dropped down on one knee. Fingers reached out and tugged at the gag slicing into the corners of Tim's mouth. Pulling it free.

"Oh... oh, thank god," Tim sputtered in the grainy gloom. "I thought I was dead... thought that was it... Who? How did?" Tim shook his head and more sand fell around him like baby powder. It stuck to the snot and tears still wet on his face. "How did you find us?" He nodded down at Sherry, wailing desperately beside him. "Who are you?"

The figure yanked down the handkerchief that covered her face. Incredibly, Tim recognized his savior. "It's me, Tim. Madeleine. Your Aunt Madeleine." She looked down at Tim's bound hands and bloody head and face. Madeleine turned and barked out orders in a language Tim didn't recognize. Two large men materialized from out of the gloom behind her. They lifted Tim and quickly shed him of the remaining binds. As they worked, Tim watched his Aunt Madeleine carefully wrap the shroud around Sherry and pull the still screaming child into her arms. Tim grew woozy on his feet. The blow to his head, lack of food, water, and exhaustion finally catching up to him. He collapsed into the arms of one of the rescuers. Barely conscious, his last sight in the tomb was Madeleine carrying Sherry in one arm and the long gold staff with the Ankh symbol in the other.

Tim, just like Sherry, was carried up and out of the burial chamber like a baby. As he was pulled from the ground, the sun shined brightly in the overhead sky, and the unspoiled outdoor air was the sweetest smell he thought he'd ever inhaled. On either side of him, Tim could hear the small group of men who'd tunneled down and rescued them, talking. Though he didn't understand the words they spoke, he could just make out his Aunt Madeleine's orders.

"Leave the bodies. We'll tell the local authorities they all died in the collapse. They won't question my word. And don't touch any of the other objects! Leave them buried. We have what we came for." Tim smiled. Miraculously, Madeleine had saved him and Sherry. She had come for them, and that was all his aunt cared about. Thinking to himself, even all the treasures of that tomb mean nothing to her, as he was whisked away and loaded into a canvas covered truck. Tim was out of earshot when she added a moment later, "I've been searching for these forever."

Madeleine held the Ankh-topped scepter up in the air, the shroud folded over her other arm. "I know just how to use them..."

CHAPTER SEVENTEEN

PRESENT DAY

As HE TURNED DOWN the dirt road, Barry could feel the hurried pounding of his heart. His breath quickened in excited anticipation as he drew closer, and he stole a joyful glance at himself in his truck's rearview mirror. He briefly lifted the bill on his St. Louis Cardinal baseball cap and ran a quick hand through his short brown hair. As he did, he noted the hastily rolled joint that he'd tucked behind his ear and hoped to soon be smoking. He spoke gleefully to his reflection even as the rear end of the truck fishtailed in the loose gravel under his tires. "I'm going to get some pussy, I'm going to get some pussy, I'm going to get some pussy..." Barry's cadence was almost musical and his tone cheery and bright. He had arranged to meet the flirtatious and much older Mrs. Williams, the village of Almore's busty townhall clerk, over his lunch hour. With the feeble Mr. Williams gone for the next three days on business, Barry expected this to be just the first of several lunchtime dates this week.

And he couldn't wait!

The gravel road led him to its destined end, and the small rocks that covered it slowly gave way to weedy grass that he crushed beneath his knobby tires. When he saw Mrs. Williams's grey Toyota Prius already parked and waiting, Barry had to reach down and adjust the swollen bulge between his legs before he dared exit. He'd spent the entire morning watching the clock in heated and strained anticipation. His little affair with the seemingly insatiable Mrs. Williams was now in its second month. He knew exactly what was to come, and, he snickered, where exactly he was going to. Mrs. Williams had an oral fixation that Barry was more than happy to oblige every time she called. He'd never known a woman more certain of her wants and needs. *Older women just rock,* Barry thought to himself as he shut off the engine.

Stepping out of his truck, he did a quick survey of the surrounding area. The road behind him was clear except for the small cloud of slowly settling dust his truck wheels had kicked up. On either side of the little side road, tall cornstalks stood stoically and the buzz of insects filled the otherwise peaceful and sunny day with their monotonous drone. A wall of crowded timber met the end of the road, and Barry knew more trees were all that filled the acres beyond. Under the branches of the neighboring foliage, where Mrs. Williams had parked, the shade was pleasantly cool. The end of this road was well secluded and buried deep within the countryside of Almore. Hidden far away from prying eyes among the endless fields of crops.

Rounding the back of the Toyota, Barry found Mrs. Williams had started without him. He saw a yellow dress, obviously hers, tossed casually across the driver's seat of her car as he approached. A pair of black panties with a frilly pink bow hung from the small car's gear shift. On the hood of the car, Mrs. Williams lay completely unclothed, the pink nipples of her full breasts defying gravity. She had one hand between her thighs while the other was under her head lost among her thick, red hair. When Barry strode up beside her, he saw Mrs. Williams's pale skin was blotchy in places and her cheeks were already colored from exertion. Barry opened his mouth in greeting, but never got the chance. Taking her hand from between her legs, Mrs. Williams crammed wet fingers into Barry's open mouth. She smiled up at him mischievously and let her long limbs fall open before turning two of the fingers in his mouth into hooks. Reeling Barry in like a fish, pulling him steadily closer and lower until his entire head was buried at the "Y" between her thighs.

Right where she wanted it.

"Yeah, there you go. Don't be shy now. Right there, Barry. I'm already close. Just... um... um... Oh! Oh, yeah. Use both now, baby... come on..." Mrs. Williams soon grew silent and began bucking her hips up and down urgently. But Barry didn't mind. He knew from their past encounters that Mrs. Williams came often and easily. It was one of the things he liked best about her. He kept at it, using his mouth and alternating hands and fingers. He knew what would follow once he got her off. And he could hardly wait. Moments before he knew she was about to finish, Barry latched onto her clit the way she liked it, rolling the bud softly between his teeth as she ground herself against his face for all she was worth. Her guttural moans and piercing exclamations echoing loudly among the surrounding trees.

When she was done, Mrs. Williams pulled Barry out from between her legs by his hair. Straightening, he popped open the top of his jeans and jerked at them to free himself. Without a word, Mrs. Williams reached down and tugged at him, guiding him up to her face as she rolled onto her side.

She engulfed him completely until her nose was buried in the cropping of dark hair that ran up to his naval. Still stretched out across the hood of her car, Barry let his eyes walk all over the older, busty redhead as he pulled a lighter from his pocket. Flicking it once, he used the tiny flame to light the joint he pulled from behind his ear. He took a deep drag but left the marijuana cigarette hang from his lips. Instead, putting one hand on top of Mrs. Williams's bobbing head while his other groped at her expansive chest. "Hmmmm," he groaned loudly for her benefit. The married woman having confessed in the past how much the male moan turned her on. "Hmmmm, fuck yeah! Swallow every bit..." Barry arched his back and closed his eyes while Mrs. Williams gulped hungrily. Spit dripping down her chin and groaning as she reached between her own thighs once more.

Neither Barry nor Mrs. Williams heard the arrival of Mr. Williams. It wasn't until the cold end of his shotgun was placed between Barry's shoulder blades that the younger man knew anything was amiss. Even then it still took all his willpower to pull himself out of Mrs. Williams who, unaware of the newcomer, complained loudly. "No, baby. Not yet. I love sucking that…"

"Pull your pants up." Barry turned slightly, the lit joint dropping from his mouth as he quickly reached down and refastened the top of his trousers. Mr. Williams, holding a double-barreled shotgun, glared at Barry from behind a pair of wire rimmed glasses. With a nervous flick of the weapon, Mr. Williams motioned where he wanted Barry to move. As the younger man scurried to the far side of Mrs. Williams's vehicle, she sat up and began sputtering excuses.

"Shut up," was all Mr. Williams said as he took Barry's place beside the hood of the car. Despite the rising heat of the day, Mr. Williams wore a pair of dark green coveralls that he'd zipped tightly up to his neck. On both hands he wore a pair of tan work gloves. For the first time Barry noticed a spade and a shovel leaning against the back of a tree at the edge of the forest just beyond the two parked vehicles. Barry felt a cold sweat break out across his forehead and the back of his neck. Clearly Mr. Williams had been waiting on them both.

He'd made plans…

With one eye on Barry, Mr. Williams lowered the end of the gun until it was eye level with the still nude Mrs. Williams, now sitting up on the hood of her car. "Put the end of it in your whore mouth." When she began to shake her head no, Mr. Williams place the black barrel on her chin and pulled both hammers back, cocking the weapon. "That wasn't a request." As full tears began to silently wash down her face, Mrs. Williams complied. Her lips, still dripping with wet slobber, closed over the end of the barrels with eyes both wide and white.

"That feel better, honey? You just can't keep your mouth off any guy with something long and hard, can you?" Mr. Williams's expression hardened and he leaned forward until his wife gagged as more steel filled her mouth. "For ten years I've put up with..."

BOOM!

The discharge of the weapon thundered. The recoil, surprising its holder, nearly jerked the shotgun free of the startled Mr. Williams's grip as he stumbled backwards in shock.

As if in slow motion, Barry felt something wet spray his face in a warm mist. When he looked down at his shirt, he found it was now tinged pink and dripping. With ringing ears and the smell of fresh gunpowder filling his nose, Barry looked across the hood of the car where minutes earlier Mrs. Williams enjoyed her last ever orgasm. The grey paint on the Prius now smeared bright red. He looked on dumbly as her near headless torso skated slowly off the car. Mrs. Williams's tongue was blackened, and it danced in the air like the body of a decapitated snake. Below the writhing, her jaw intact, Barry could see the perfect order of her lower teeth. The top of her head and face – everything above her jawbone – was gone. He watched transfixed as the rest of her body slid gracelessly to the ground, one pale leg getting caught and tangled in the driver's side wheel well. It was easily the most horrible and horrific thing Barry had ever seen in his entire 26 years.

For all of one minute.

Soundlessly, a second nude body joined the fray. Staggering forward out of the dense thicket, the thing came. Its flaccid cock bouncing absurdly from one fleshy thigh to the other with each faltering step. The stumbling man, far taller than Barry or Mr. Williams, had likely once been handsome. But now his pallid face drooped as if he'd suffered a stroke or was afflicted with a palsy. A long flap of bloodless skin hung from his neck, exposing a savaged windpipe that flopped along with his limp dick as he moved closer to the two parked vehicles. The man's eyes, though milky white, still seemed to function as the ghoulish apparition remained doggedly fixated on what was left of Mrs. Williams. It seemed to take no notice of the murdering husband, nor of Barry splashed in the blood of the adulteress wife, as it advanced out of the brush. Like the two faithless lovers, it was consumed only by one thing.

Desire.

In moments, it threw itself to the ground and snatched at the ruined neck of Mrs. Williams. Stunned to silence, the two onlookers watched with disbelieving eyes as the thing from the woods ripped desperately at the torn flesh. Cramming its bony fingers down into the wound and peeling back the skin on her chest. Ripping Mrs. Williams open like the peel of a ripe pomegranate before lowering its awful mouth and burying it deep inside the splayed opening. Using its teeth to pull out chunks of pink tissue and viscera still pulsing with blood. Eating her from the inside out.

Mr. Williams slowly staggered backwards on faltering legs. In the last five minutes, he'd watched the love of his life blowing another man before he, in turn, had accidentally blown her head off. And now he was watching his wife become lunch for a lurching monster that looked like it came straight off the set of *The Walking Dead*. Mr. Williams struggled to catch his breath as searing hot pain exploded across his chest. He pulled the zipper at his neck even as his head filled with stars. When he dropped the shotgun to the ground, it exploded once more. The pellets from the second barrel punching a hole in the fuel tank of Mrs. Williams's Toyota. As gasoline began leaking under the car, Mr. Williams toppled over backwards still clutching the end of the zipper. He knew he was in the middle of his second heart attack and powerless to stop it. He closed his eyes and began praying for a miracle.

The second shotgun blast brought Barry back to his senses. He'd watched the bizarre scene play out in front of him in a stunned paralysis. But now he could smell the gasoline in the air as it mixed with the metallic tang of fresh blood. The sickening combination competing with the rot coming in waves off the monster as it split Mrs. Williams innards open and slowly devoured them. Barry didn't know which was worse, the smell or the sight of the carnage.

He didn't care.

Scrambling to his feet, Barry raced back to his truck. As soon as it was started, Barry threw the transmission in reverse. He slammed his foot down on the accelerator and raced backwards down the gravel road. The front end of the big truck swaying back and forth in the loose rocks as Barry struggled to keep it straight while periodically turning back around to glance out his front windshield at the horror he'd left behind. When he spied a tiny lane normally used only for farm equipment coming and going from the surrounding fields, he spun the steering wheel on his truck. The tires bouncing up and down violently as he quickly turned the vehicle around before once again racing down the dirt lane. Accelerating as he pointed his truck towards the town of Almore just a few miles away.

Mr. Williams couldn't see or hear anything. Barely conscious, his life slipping slowly away. Though deaf and blind from the heart attack, he could still feel. Long minutes later, with no breath to scream with, he sensed the ghoul from the woods pawing at him. The air around him grew heavy as slippery hands crept steadily up Mr. Williams's chest before he felt the dull teeth in his mouth. Then at his tongue. The ghoul from the woods tugging out his tongue with its own teeth. Motionless and silent, tears flowed from Mr. Williams's eyes as the abomination slowly ate him alive. The thing soon pulling at the sinewy and stringy flesh at his neck. Mr. Wiliams felt himself slowly being consumed. Unable to scream or make a sound, he felt the soft crunch of his own flesh being enjoyed. Long strips of his skin torn off and consumed.

Piece by piece.

Full now, an unrecognizable wreck of bloody flesh at its feet, the thing from the woods retreated. Heading back into the brush it originally emerged from. It didn't react when the pooling gasoline met the burning ember of the still smoldering joint Barry had dropped from his mouth earlier. Mrs. Williams's small Toyota Prius instantly enveloped in scorching flames. The deafening explosion hushing the surrounding cacophony of nature's sounds. Black smoke billowed in the air as a second, smaller explosion, disturbed the usual peace and quiet of the cornfield. The smoke becoming visible in Almore just as Barry's truck roared into the small downtown area and came to a screeching halt.

"I just saw a monster," Barry blurted out to a small group gathered near the entrance of Arlene's Café. The plume of dark smoke blemishing the blue sky behind him, back in the direction he'd come from. "It came from the woods..."

Peppered with disbelieving questions, Barry took little notice of the two men he didn't recognize. Stander and Secrist, having just exited Almore's only eating establishment, listened attentively as Barry described what he'd seen. He left out the reason for his clandestine encounter on the outskirts of town, instead focusing on what he'd witnessed. As Barry babbled on, several concerned townspeople raised a cell phone to their ears. Either anxious to get help and dialing 911 or hurriedly calling friends and neighbors with the incredible story. None of them paying attention to the two newcomers and their dog as they casually retreated to Stander's Jeep.

After closing the driver's side door, Stander spoke first. "What are the chances the tall, naked zombie this guy says he saw *isn't* the same naked dude we just discovered below Relict Mansion."

"It would be a hell of a coincidence. And I don't like coincidences." Secrist shook his head before adding, "Better get back to the house ASAP and see if our guy is missing."

"Exactly what I was thinking." Stander put the Jeep in gear and drove casually past the swelling crowd. "As soon as I get out of town, I'll punch it. I don't want to attract any attention until we know more."

Secrist nodded. "What are we going to do if it is the same guy we just found?"

Stander just shook his head slowly back and forth. "Guess we'll play it by ear..."

CHAPTER EIGHTEEN
IOWA/ILLINOIS BORDER – 1962

MISSISSIPPI RIVER

THE CRIES WERE FAINT and, at first, still dreaming, their urgency and persistency only confused Tim. But as the bothersome clatter slowly wormed its way deeper into his consciousness, the familiarity of the bawling baby he was hearing woke him completely.

Tim rolled over with a groan and reached for the glass tumbler on the bedstand next to him. He took two quick sips of the lukewarm water it held, before groggily yanking down the covers on his bed. Next to him, the sheets were cold and empty. Just as they'd been ever since Lucy perished under the collapsed wall deep inside the Egyptian tomb the month before. He stretched one arm across the barren linen as if he might still be able to feel some lingering sense of his wife's presence beside him. Though it disturbed him to admit it, in more ways than one, he felt nothing.

As he sat up, Tim could feel the cotton nightshirt clinging to his back where it was damp. He'd been sweating as he'd slept. The pleasant Midwestern spring nights already warming with summer now just around the corner.

"Hold on, baby girl. I'm coming." Tim rubbed his face with both hands and wiped the grainy sleep from his eyes. He smeared the crusty mucus between his fingers before absentmindedly wiping it on his clammy pajama top. Swinging his legs over the side of the bed, he slipped both feet inside his slippers, stood, and made his way, bleary-eyed, over to the white crib in the far corner of the bedroom. By the time he reached the side of the small slatted bed he was already smiling in anticipation. "Well, there she is. What's the matter, honey? Did you wake up wet, too?"

Tim looked down as he picked up his one-year-old daughter, and Sherry stopped crying as soon as she saw her father over the wood rails. As it did most mornings, the toddler's face resembled a glazed doughnut from the mixture of snot, tears, and dried slobber accumulated during the night. Though, Tim thought to himself proudly, she was still undeniably adorable. Her big blue eyes glimmered in the rays of the morning sun streaming from the nearby window, and her wispy blond hair crowned her head like a crow's nest of tangled twigs. Tim kissed his daughter once on the cheek before lifting her high above his head. He sniffed tentatively at her sagging diaper as her chubby legs kicked fruitlessly back and forth in the air. Thankful to find the diaper was only water-logged and not holding an unpleasant early morning surprise, he walked Sherry over to the changing table and quickly swapped it out for a fresh one. Just as he finished dressing her for the day, a light knock came at his bedroom door.

"Yes. Come on in." The heavy wooden door swung open and Kelly, one of Aunt Madeleine's staff of housekeepers, stepped inside.

"Oh my! Someone got up bright and early today, didn't they?" Kelly, red-haired and pleasantly plump, spoke with an accent more common in the Midwest's northernly states like the Dakotas, Minnesota, and Wisconsin. The slight vowel shifts always made Tim feel like whatever she said was agreeable and friendly. "How about we go get you a nice warm bottle while your daddy gets dressed?" Kelly, wearing the same grey uniform top as all Madeleine's staff, met Tim halfway across the large bedroom and took Sherry in her arms. "And so, tell me. Did you both sleep well?"

"Yes, thank you." Tim nodded as he replied. Kelly, in her fifties and with kids of her own but all long grown and gone, had slowly evolved into Sherry's surrogate mother since they'd arrived back in the states from Egypt. For the last month, she'd been the first to check on the little girl each morning. Often watching over the toddler, preparing her bottles, and helping Sherry make the adjustment from breastmilk to the concentrated formula and soft foods she was transitioning over to. The tragedy of Lucy's unexpected death thrusting the change upon Tim and Sherry. "But the nights sure are getting warm, aren't they? I sweated right through my nightshirt."

"It's the humidity here in the Midwest. I think being so close to the river only makes it worse." Kelly, with Sherry in her arms, made her way towards the door. As she stepped out into the long hallway she added, "Breakfast will be served a little later than usual this morning. Kevin was a bit delayed getting here."

"Our cook have another battle with a flat tire?" Kevin was Madeleine's cook. But, unlike Kelly and the other house and groundskeepers she employed, did not live onsite. "Or was it another late-night battle with the bottle?" Kelly just shrugged with a slight smile as she closed the door behind her.

Tim made his way into the adjoining bathroom and turned the chrome handles on the shower. The hot water filling the stately room with steam as he undressed and tossed his pajamas in the hamper. He knew they'd be freshly laundered, folded, and placed neatly back in the bedroom's dresser long before he'd put them back on tonight. As he showered, dressed, and readied himself for the day, he replayed the circumstances of his arrival at Aunt Madeleine's home on the border of Illinois and Iowa. The blurred, mad rush after his and Sherry's rescue. The long flight aboard Madeleine's private plane back to the states.

The awful moment he'd had to tell Lucy's family what had happened. (Well, Madeleine's account of it anyway, he thought to himself). The "official" version being simply that Lucy and his father Emery, had been killed along with several other workers in an underground collapse while digging in Egypt. The tomb and treasures they'd found, how they'd both been killed, and all the rest left buried under the eternally mystifying and shifting sands of Egypt.

The month since that tragedy happened had felt like one long, bad dream to Tim. The empty-coffined funeral and endless processional of relatives from both sides of his family had worn on him. Tim repeatedly having to spew out vague deceptions and half-lies that, each time, left him with a bad taste in his mouth. But, he knew, Aunt Madeleine had her reasons. Tim's father had shared enough with him in the past that Tim knew he needed to trust her. Still, it was hard to imagine he'd have to lie to Sherry about her own mother's death once she got older and started asking questions. So, Tim had started a journal a few weeks ago to keep everything straight, and to fully explain what actually happened. Maybe one day, once she was an adult, he'd be able to share the truth with Sherry.

All of it.

Tim, dressed casually in a button-down white shirt and blue slacks, closed the heavy wooden bedroom door behind him. He strolled down the mahogany-colored carpet stretching across the long, second-floor hallway where his room was sandwiched between a string of other similarly sized bedrooms. When he reached the first of the dark wood bannisters that ran alongside both sets of the carpeted stairs leading from the foyer to the second floor, he turned and made his way downstairs. Above his head hung a massive chandelier made of brass, crystal, and glass that brightly illuminated the entryway below. Reaching the first floor, the heels of his brown leather shoes clicked noisily along the black and white squares of marble that spread out ahead of him like a giant chessboard.

As always, the floor was highly polished and not a speck of dirt or dust could be seen.

Aunt Madeleine's huge estate and manor was nestled near the Mississippi River on the Illinois side. Though Tim visited and stayed here often, the opulence his aunt surrounded herself in was always a startling adjustment. As a world-renowned scholar and much sought after Egyptologist, his father, Emery, had certainly been wealthy. But owning loads of property in and around the Chicago area, including his own stately home near Lake Michigan, was a far cry from Madeleine's regal tastes. Her spacious manor was a constantly shifting sea of breath-taking art, tailor-made furniture, and tasteful décor. The spacious rooms and interior more closely resembling the grand hotels of New York, Paris, or London. The bustling, uniformed staff she employed only added to the surreal feeling. Especially since the closest community, Almore, was only a small farming community with a population of less than a thousand.

"Good morning," Tim greeted his aunt cheerily with a light peck on her slightly wrinkled and tanned cheek. Though Madeleine was now in her eighties, she still exuded a disarming vitality and had retained much of her youthful beauty. Her longish white hair still thick and full, her mouth perfectly modeled with high cheekbones below eyes bright with life. When she smiled, her face glowed around two rows of even teeth that were all still her own. Madeleine had an unmistakable air of imposing elegance that intimidated most who met her for the first time.

The irony of her well-maintained beauty and high sophistication were the stenciled images abundant across the old woman's flesh. His aunt was, outside of clandestine taverns and rowdy carnival tents, still the only woman Tim had ever seen with tattoos. Madeleine had a series of colorful images high on her shoulders and across much of her back. He also knew, from sneaking astonished peeks at her when he was a boy, that she also had symbols inked near her pubis and on her lower back, just above the two hand drawn flowers imprinted on each of her cheeks. His

Aunt Madeleine who still to this day, unabashedly sunbathed nude as often as possible. Her skin tone, a deep rich bronze, the exact opposite of Emery, her brother and Tim's dad, who'd remained pasty and white despite all his time under the unrelenting sun of Egypt.

Indeed, her appearance, demeanor, and mannerisms were so different from Emery that most were shocked to find they'd been siblings. Of course, Tim reminded himself, Madeleine had been 20 years Emery's senior and was raised in the Middle East by her mother. Emery and Madeleine shared a biological father but little else until she'd officially immigrated to America right before Tim had been born. Madeleine was the product of a tryst Tim's grandfather supposedly had while traveling in that part of the world as a young man. Madeleine had seamlessly inserted herself within her estranged family in the states over the years. Eventually, her generosity and endless funds paving the way, becoming the unquestioned matriarch of the family.

This morning, Madeleine had already been served and had eaten and was now merely sipping from a steaming cup of tea. As Tim took a seat beside her at the lengthy, dark wood table in the expansive dining room, he was immediately approached by Cindy, who swiftly emerged from the adjoining kitchen with a small bowl of fresh fruit. "How did you sleep, Aunt Madeleine? The nights seem to be getting quite warm now, don't you think?"

"Yes, but as you know, I like it warm. Summer can't arrive soon enough here for my tastes." Madeleine smiled pleasantly from behind her fine china teacup. She wore a silk dress the color of honey, and her attractive, aristocratic face was topped by a mane of lush white hair that hung, like the dress, casually around her shoulders. "But Aloysius said there are some storms brewing nearby that will likely result in heavy rains for us. So, it seems, we aren't done with spring yet."

"Where is Aloysius?" Tim gestured at his empty chair as a Cindy, a bit mousey in both appearance and mannerisms, returned from the kitchen with a plate of eggs, bacon, and toast that she placed in front of him. He thanked Cindy as she poured him a glass of freshly squeezed orange juice. "Has he already eaten?" Tim finished his fruit, savoring the ripe strawberry he'd saved for last.

"Yes, you just missed him. I believe he is in the kitchen speaking with Kevin regarding his tardiness. You know how fastidious Aloysius can be." Tim simply nodded as he pierced the yolk on his over-easy eggs with the corner of his toast.

Aloysius, his aunt's third husband that she'd met in France around the time of the Second World War, was notoriously meticulous. At sixty some years of age, he was nearly twenty years younger than Madeleine, and towered above most men at nearly six and a half feet tall. Though Tim and his father had always found Aloysius a bit arrogant, he was slavishly devoted to Madeleine. His family lineage stretched back at least to medieval times, and he claimed to be of French nobility. Tim always felt the man was a bit too entitled for his taste. But, then again, Madeleine likely needed someone like that as a partner. Tim's dad always said no one ever seemed to be her equal, but at least Aloysius Leroux fit the part.

"Ma'am?" Cindy interrupting timidly as she approached the table. "The contractor you mentioned was coming this morning has arrived. Shall I show him to your sitting room?" Nodding, Madeleine excused herself. Teacup now emptied; she trailed after Cindy while Tim finished his breakfast alone. Somewhere in one of the neighboring rooms he could hear Sherry giggling as Cindy returned with a cup of coffee for him.

Tim didn't need to ask why his aunt had yet another meeting with a contractor. Her massive home was always in constant flux. If something new wasn't being erected somewhere on the grounds, something old was being torn down or being replaced. This despite its seclusion and out-of-the-way location. The acreage the grand house sat on was heavily wooded on all four sides, and included a nearby lake within walking distance of the house. Beyond the endless trees, on three sides anyway, vast fields of planted corn and beans further isolated the house and property from the rest of civilization.

And any neighbors.

The nearest town, Almore, was about eight miles away, and five miles west of the property the mighty Mississippi River rolled endlessly along like a natural border. The only civilization of consequence was what's known in the Midwest as the Quad Cities, and it was some fifty miles to the north. The collection of four towns, the biggest being Davenport on the Iowa side, was tucked along both sides of the Mississippi and huddled so close together you really couldn't tell any of them apart. Though there were communities between the Quad Cities and where Madeleine lived, with only a small two-lane highway leading to the property, you really had to be invited and know right where it was if you wanted to find it. Most of the locals, except those employed by his aunt, shunned the property and unexpected visits were rare. Though Tim wasn't sure if Madeleine was aware of it (not that she would care, he knew), the property was known locally as Widow Mansion. Or more majestically sounding, Relict Mansion, which had the same meaning. The unoriginal moniker attached decades ago after Madeleine's first two husbands had both died separately on the property in the past.

The house or manor itself was three stories off the ground with several tall spires that stretched up to the heavens. The massive home always seemed to Tim like a hodge-podge of competing building styles. Most likely because some sort of construction was always ongoing. Along with its gothic spires, the rooftop of the house was decorated like something from another time. Very little on the outside of the mansion, or on the inside for that matter, wasn't adorned in some inimitable way. Each room, twenty some at Tim's last count, all with grand windows that invited the sunshine inside. The massive home seeming to have more in common with the grand European estates of England or France. The property visible from those windows was a carefully manicured lawn fenced in naturally on all sides by towering trees and walls of weeds. A single lane driveway of asphalt, flanked on both sides by newly flowering Dogwood trees, split the sea of green grass like a slithering black snake desperate to leave. The beginning or head of the long serpentine driveway caged in by a mammoth metal gate at the end of the drive.

Once Tim finished his coffee, he went in search of Kelly and Sherry. Stepping past the sitting room entryway, he found it unoccupied. Madeleine and the contractor she'd been speaking with both having moved elsewhere. As he crossed the seldom used ballroom to reach the sunroom beyond near the back of the manor – where Kelly often took Sherry to play – he could hear Madeleine and Aloysius speaking in the neighboring library. The door was open and he paused momentarily to look inside, mildly curious what renovations were being cooked up next. The two of them, along with the proposed contractor in white overalls, stood in front of the reading room's enormous fireplace mantle. Aged brickwork, likely from the manor's original build, made up the hearth. Though Tim found the fireplace's façade gorgeous, it seemed Madeleine was looking to have it replaced for some reason.

Aloysius, spying Tim from the corner of his eye, waved him inside. "Good morning, Dr. Stander," Aloysius, ever formal, addressed him with just a hint of a French accent. His thinning salt and pepper hair matching the color of his tweed jacket. "May I solicit your opinion?" Tim nodded once and stepped inside the library, instantly surrounded by rows of leatherbound books. Likely his favorite room in the entire manor, he inhaled deeply as he entered. The lingering aroma of smoke mixed with the unmistakable smell of aged books, usually reserved for antique bookshops, greeted him like an old friend.

"I'm pretty sure I can't dissuade Madeleine if that's what you are after," Tim smiled. "But if she is thinking of removing the library, I'll give it my best shot." The contractor, barely acknowledging Tim's entry, busied himself with measurements as he stretched his tape measure across the fireplace mantle from various angles.

"Nothing of the sort, I assure you." Aloysius gestured towards the fireplace. "Are you familiar with some of the distinct granite patterns found in France? I believe their hue would go splendidly with this room. Would you concur?"

"I'm sorry, Aloysius. I really have no idea what's special about where granite is pulled from the ground. Or, what separates French granite from any other. And I can't match colors to save my soul anyway." Pausing, he smiled before asking, "Does it really matter where it comes from?"

"Perhaps I am being too exacting, but I am partial to French granite. Some of the grandest cathedrals in all of Europe are built with granite from deep within the French countryside. Madeleine owns property where a quarry once produced some of the finest stonework ever pulled from the earth. But I can't seem to convince her to allow us to explore the site..." Aloysius looked sideways at Madeleine. "Sometimes she can be impossible!" Though he said this deferentially, the hint of passive-aggressiveness was plain.

"I told you, Aloysius. The quarry of which you speak is now devoid of the beauty you seek. It would be... unwise of you to bring it up again." Aloysius looked like he was about to open his mouth once more, but at the last moment appeared to think better of it. Instead, pulling a long-chained pocket watch from inside his tweed jacket and making a show of checking the time. Tim was relieved. Aunt Madeleine may be in her eighties now, but she was still not one to be trifled with. Madeleine winked slyly at Tim, though he had no idea why since she was still speaking to Aloysius.

"Don't be an idiot."

CHAPTER NINETEEN

After Tim excused himself from the library, his search for Sherry ended in the sunroom where he found the one-year-old and Kelly digging through a small pile of toys. A humming radio wrapped in rich wood sat on a nearby table. The lone speaker, set between two spinning dials and emblazoned with the manufacture's name, Zenith, cooed softly in the background. *"The lion sleeps tonight,"* a popular new tune, purring out the lyrics. *"Near the village, the quiet village. The lion sleeps tonight. Wee heeheeheehee weeoh aweem"*. Tim sang along to the tune as he played on the floor with his daughter for much of the morning. Freeing Kelly to tend her usual daily tasks. But the reoccurring questions about what he'd witnessed back at Saqqara kept stealing his attention.

As if she'd read his mind from afar, Madeleine soon joined them in the mostly glass enclosure. Taking a seat in one of the comfortable chairs where she often sunbathed. She twirled the pearls hanging around her neck while Sherry repeatedly pulled the string of a barnyard animal See-N-Say. Entertaining herself with assorted duck quacks, cow moos, and pig oinks.

"The gathering clouds appear quite ominous, don't you think?" Madeleine gestured above her where rolling black clouds gathered in a wave. "I think a storm is coming..." She let the question linger in the air, and let Tim ponder if she was really here to discuss the weather. Madeleine rarely spent time on the triviality of small talk.

"I suppose so," Tim replied as he stood and took the cushioned high-back chair next to her. "Maybe it will finally usher in the warm temperatures you crave." Tim had decided earlier that he needed to formally discuss what he'd experienced down in the Egyptian tomb. There were many unanswered questions. So much had required his immediate attention after returning home, that he'd been avoiding the queerness of that day. Since he'd soon be leaving Madeleine's home for the medical practice he'd bought into — partnering with a primary care physician a year from retirement in Kankakee, Illinois — would require all of his focus. Before that happened, he felt like he had to get his head around what transpired in that tomb. The questions — like sores inside his cheek that he couldn't keep his tongue from probing and poking at.

"I trust this time spent healing from the loss of your father and wife have proven beneficial." Tim was relieved to hear his aunt broach the topic first. Though he was now a grown man, licensed doctor, father of one, and responsible for all his late father's holdings, he still felt like a child around Madeleine. Often feeling like an outsider in his own family. Around his aunt, Tim always seemed like the proverbial red-headed stepchild. Tolerated but uninteresting, not really part of his aunt's life. He couldn't recall her ever actually asking how he felt about anything. "I suspect you wonder why I acted as I have. Unsure, perhaps, what should be done about it all."

Tim turned towards her, he hated how weak and unsure his voice sounded in his ear. "Well, now that you mentioned it, yes, exactly. How do I explain to anyone that I saw a corpse thousands of years old come back to life without sounding like a lunatic?"

"The answer is in your question. Could you ever speak of this again without being deemed a madman?" The corners of Madeleine's mouth rose slightly as if holding back a giggle. "So far, you've chosen to spend your life in pursuit of a piece of paper you believe makes you a respectable man. A doctor. You've sired a child which will require even more of your life in the future. Should *what you think* you saw," the icy way she spoke 'what you think' chilled Tim, "ever be mentioned again, you *will* lose both." Again, her tone shifted when she uttered 'will' and all the hairs on the back of his neck rose in unison. "After all, with such little light down in the burial chamber and the thinning air, who's to say what was an oxygen-deprived hallucination and what was real. The important thing, thanks to my timely intervention, is you still will be allowed to pursue a career in medicine and keep Sherry."

"Are you saying I need to just forget what happened? That's easy for you to say. You didn't see what I did." Tim's voice rose, and from across the room Sherry looked over at him. "I saw what I saw. A horrible thing somehow able to pull itself from out of the abyss of death. I watched men die that day, my own wife running my father through in hopes she could do the same. And you want me to just forget? Every time I close my eyes at night it all comes back." Tim felt tears well in his eyes. Though he'd hidden it, staying strong for Sherry, the twin losses had taken a terrible toll on him. Not understanding what he'd seen, and unable to speak with anyone for fear of ridicule, weighed heavily on him.

"Don't be so truculent, dear. I only want what is best for our family." Madeleine's peculiar mannerisms and old-fashioned speech barely shrouded the threat she spoke. "You've said your piece. Let us not speak of this again." Her disapproving tone – the same a parent would use to correct an unreasonable kindergartener. Tim felt very small beside her. Apparently, unworthy of even an explanation.

Tim watched as she rose; the conversation obviously ended in her mind. He wanted to say more, demand an explanation or threaten to inform the authorities. But, as Sherry began to fuss, Tim understood she was right. Should he make a report he'd be laughed right out of any place he could go for help. If he *swore* he'd seen the dead rise, he'd never see another patient. He needed proof of some sort. If only for his own peace of mind. He watched mutely as Madeleine strolled from the sunroom without a backwards glance.

What if he could get his hands on the bizarre Ankh and burial shroud Madeleine had brought back home with her? Have them tested somewhere? Clearly, they were the key to all of this. That could be his proof. Once experts weighed in on the finds and discovered whatever properties they held, they would clamor to know where they came from. The site Madeleine reburied could be unearthed. The exhumed bodies would back up his version of the events.

Who says the dead don't speak?

Tim decided he would hunt for the two objects that very night. Though Relict Mansion was enormous, he'd seen Aloysius stash both in a room at the opposite end of the second-floor hallway where his bedroom was. Once the daytime staff departed and Madeleine and Aloysius retired to their third-floor master suite, he would smuggle the pieces out to his car. The impending storm should help muzzle any noise if he had to break into the room. Since one of his dad's best friends was a curator of Egyptian artifacts at the Chicago Museum, he could drive the couple hours to Chicago, show them to him, and be back the same day. Madeleine would never know. He hoped.

Tim spent the remainder of the day with Sherry. Eating a picnic lunch with her on the patio, swinging with her in his lap on a wood and rope swing that hung from a large oak tree. Pulling her back and forth down the long driveway in a red wagon several times before the sky finally gave in to the clouds and opened up. Doing his best to wear her out in hopes her sleep that night would be a deep one.

After dinner, as the rain dashed steadily against the bay window of the downstairs TV room, he'd laughed through The Beverly Hillbillies alone with Sherry before changing her for bed and tucking his daughter in for the night. Once he was sure she'd fallen asleep, he'd returned to the TV room where he was joined by Aloysius to watch the latest episode of the popular western Bonanza. Madeleine, as was her habit, stayed in the library reading most of the evening. The idiot-box, her name for television, rarely caught her attention outside of the five o'clock news. Tim stayed to watch the ten o'clock news even after Aloysius, in his usual stately manner, bade him fair well for the evening when the Bonanza episode had ended.

Tim didn't retire to his room until the local news program was completely finished. After he made his way upstairs, he didn't bother with undressing. He lay still atop his bed in the welcomed dark, looking up at the ceiling as the clock on his bedstand ticked away the time.

Shortly after eleven thirty PM – the moon and sky still completely covered by dark clouds – Tim crept outside of his bedroom. He discreetly closed his bedroom door and stood listening for any sign of activity within the mansion. Outside, he could tell the wind was really picking up. The trees on either side of the hallway windows thrashing and swaying back and forth. Certain he alone was awake, Tim made his way cautiously down the second-floor hallway. His way lit by the soft yellow plug-in nightlights at either end of the lengthy corridor, and the fall of his feet muffled by the thick carpet under his step. Tim slinked past the first banister and set of stairs, stopping briefly between the two staircases and glancing below. He couldn't hear or see anything moving beyond the storm raging outside. Lightning cracking across the sky and illuminating the empty foyer beneath him.

Turning once more, Tim continued to make his way towards the doorway he'd seen Aloysius carry the shroud and Ankh into. Thunder boomed outside. As he reached for the door, Tim guiltily peeked over his shoulder back the way he'd come. He froze with his fingertips resting on the metal handle. At the opposite end of the hallway, beyond the dual staircases that led to the first floor, it was now completely dark. Though the hallway nightlight near where he stood was still lit, the one back by his own bedroom door had gone out.

Or something was blocking the light.

Motionless, Tim instinctively shrank back against the doorway, blood pounding in his ears. But, looking down at the nightlight plugged into the wall socket across from him, he realized how exposed and visible he was. Tim strained his eyes in the shimmering light and, though he saw no movement, Tim felt certain someone was watching him. Feeling he should play it safe, he began to run possible excuses through his mind as he walked back the way he'd just come. With an explanation perched on the tip of his tongue, Tim marched steadily towards where he knew the nightlight was plugged into the wall socket at his bedroom's end of the corridor.

Reaching the unlit light, Tim saw there was nothing blocking it. Instead, the nightlight had merely come partially unplugged. Sighing quietly, he shook his head disgustedly at all the nonsense his imagination had conjured up. Squatting, he pushed the two prongs back into place and the soft glow of the small yellow bulb instantly sprang back to life. He quickly stood, spun on his heel, and took a single step before the nightlight back where he was headed suddenly went black. Once again, half of the long second floor passageway was blind to him. The unexpected dark pricking his eyes with their tiny daggers of fear.

"What is going on?" Tim whispered to himself, uncertainty again briefly rearing its head. But, feeling it was likely the lightning storm outside wreaking havoc with the mansion's electricity, Tim walked steadily over to the spot on the wall where the light had been plugged in. To his surprise, finding this nightlight was also nearly completely unplugged, hanging tenuously by one prong. He quickly repositioned it and watched the tiny light spring back to life. But, feeling less comfortable by the moment with the unexplained light failures thwarting his plans, Tim began walking backwards down the hallway. His eyes never leaving the flickering illumination of the nightlight he'd just plugged back in.

As he reached the middle of the hallway, between the two sets of stairs, a single scrawny arm slinked out from inside the doorway nearest the nightlight. The arm was withered and shriveled with age, and it swept back and forth blindly along the wall, clearly reaching for the nightlight Tim had just plugged back in. It snaked out from the door barely a foot off the floor, bending at the elbow. Unadorned of rings, the fingernails were neatly clipped and trimmed. Yet there was something profoundly wrong with the herky-jerky movements it made. When the emaciated fingers finally grasped the plug-in light and plunged that end of the hallway in darkness once more, Tim opened his mouth to shriek, but no sound came out. A second hand, this one powerful and confident, slapped across his gaping mouth, aborting Tim's scream before it was born. Tim was yanked from behind by a powerful form much larger than himself. This second arm springing from a cracked hallway door and pulling Tim into the room's utter darkness. He was roughly spun around and nearly lost his balance in the black of the room. The large warm hand never leaving his mouth or allowing him a word.

In his ear, warm and wet, "Shhhh..."

CHAPTER TWENTY
IOWA/ILLINOIS BORDER - 1964

THE QUAD CITIES

The roar of the four engines was relentless. Howard found it hard to even hear himself think as yet another volley of bullets pierced the side of his B-24 bomber plane for the third time. Thick smoke belched from somewhere behind his pilot seat. He tasted the wafting acrid fumes as they billowed into and flooded the entire cockpit. The only reason he was still able to see was because much of the black smoke entering the cockpit immediately got sucked through the blown-out window yawning on his opposite side. The glass in it shattering as he'd watched Andy, his co-pilot, being ripped apart by the high caliber slugs pouring into the aircraft. Somehow, the enemy's deadly projectiles once again missed Howard. The brunt of the aerial attack absorbed by the young schoolteacher from Kansas. Andy's lifeless body shuddering as he'd been raked by the bullets; like a scarecrow caught in the path of the awful twisters he so feared. Tossed about by a deadly force almost unimaginable if not experienced firsthand. As the latest barrage subsided, Howard stole a peek at the schoolteacher.

What was left of him.

Andy's left eye was wide open and, though sightless, his stare beseeched Howard. It begged of what would never come. Andy, like Howard, had enlisted even though the man was likely the least violent person Howard had ever known. Softly waving away any bothersome bugs that often seemed to cluster inside their barracks. Carefully capturing and releasing insects found crawling near him versus smashing their squishy guts out like the rest of their crew did. And now, on only his second flight as Howard's co-pilot, he'd been riddled with the very violence that he abhorred himself.

The four-propeller bomber plane Howard piloted was part of the allied force's air attack on the German's forces defending positions along the shores of Normandy, France. The spacious bomber had a massive payload, but was considered hard to fly with its stiff and heavy controls. The B-24 Liberator was nicknamed 'The Flying Coffin' because of its difficult handling and single exit near the tail. The ponderous escape route almost impossible to reach from the flight deck if you had a parachute on. Ten men made up the flight crew Howard was responsible for. Andy, his copilot, and Chuck from Wisconsin, the radio/radar operator, the only two members of the crew Howard had flown a mission with before. The other seven men, five married and three with children, all came from different walks of life and parts of the United States.

As Howard struggled to keep his big bird aloft, he doubted any of them were still alive.

The Germans had known the Allies were coming of course. Their defenses were formidable and the task of the bombers, like the B-24 Howard flew, was to soften them up. Destroy key areas, cut off their supply lines, and provide cover for the forces attacking by sea. Howard felt his eyes watering and knew it wasn't just the smoke. As he reached up to wipe the tears from his pooling eyes, the big bomber he flew dipped slightly. When he next opened his eyes, Andy had fallen to pieces. The half of his head still intact bowed as if in embarrassment, while what was left of the schoolteacher's brain plopped sloppily to the floor of the aircraft. A moment later the shattered jaw on Andy's face fell into his lap. Coming to rest near his hands that had somehow come together serenely despite the assault. Both palms flat against each other as if in prayer and resting in his lap. His gleaming white teeth were sprinkled around them like small seashells poking out of the sand during low tide.

Howard understood he was already a dead man. His crippled bomber, with its payload still intact and only in the air by some unknown miracle, began to sputter and dip wildly. Below him, he could just make out the lush greenery of a French forest. Dotted among the towering trees were a few quaint farms and small villages. Somehow, in all the confused dog-fighting in the air, they'd flown far inland. Howard resigned himself to his fate, the big bomber hurtling towards a spectacular explosion.

Like a Pagan he began praying, pleading to anything out there that could save him. Or, if not, take him to whatever heaven might be. As Howard blubbered softly, he contemplated for the first time what his paradise might be. Marriage to a beautiful dark-haired woman? A nice house in a quiet town with a steady job he liked. Maybe raising a son? All things he'd never experience and see...

See? The black smoke grew dense once more. Blinding him before beginning to twist into some sort of form or shape. Out of this morphing dark smog a deep voice suddenly rang out. "I am immortal. Existing before time was counted. Known by many names: Koschei, Pazuzu, Draugr, Mithras, Ithaqua, Legion, Hugbui, Lich, Wendigo..." Continuing to name itself on and on and in languages Howard often could not comprehend. The repeating cycle eventually blending in with the drone of the bomber's faltering engines. Or, thought Howard dimly, was it his mind turning the monotony of the propellers into words?

Am I dead?

Howard had no time to contemplate the question. His attention ripped away by a whirling scream of wind rushing out from the blackness. He gaped in utter horror. Something was evolving from deep inside the howling murk. The thrashing mass of blackness writhing as it adopted a new form. A sinuous shape whipping and shuddering within the dense, black smoke. It was a giant of a man, dark-skinned with long flowing black hair.

Nude and hideous, difficult to look upon. Burning red eyes like hot embers of a fire. The form moved fluidly among the thick smoke, dancing and twirling in a queer fashion before dissolving once more. The shape swirling round and round like a whirlwind or a feared tornado born on the desolate plains of Kansas. Advancing on Howard, still strapped to his chair. When it reached him, Howard felt the rank rot of its breath as much as he smelled it. Fearful he was about to be overtaken, he closed his eyes and screamed. Certain the swarming whirlwind of black had come to claim his soul the moment his plane met the earth in the fiery crash it was hurtling towards.

But, when he reopened his eyes, the maddening vision had dissipated. Replaced by Andy looking down on him serenely. Explaining to Howard he no longer needed to worry. That he would get the paradise he always desired. A woman to love, a son to raise, a place to call home... In exchange, he needed only keep the bomber in the air a little longer. That he, Andy, would go back and release the bombs still secured in the cargo hold.

"But... the bombs... we're way off target. They'll hit that small village below us. We'll kill innocent..."

"No bomb from this plane will kill anybody. We're just... moving people... just herding sheep... lambs for a later sacrifice." But it somehow felt all wrong to Howard. What he was seeing, hearing, doing. It all felt very wrong somehow.

As if reading his mind, Andy spoke once more as he backed away, dissolving once more into the black smoke he was birthed from. "When you wake it will all be over. You'll be safe on the ground. On your way to paradise. A fair trade..."

Howard felt the plane rocking back and forth. Although scared at first, the slow rolling motion soon became a comfort. Like the lapping of water on the side of a boat as small waves gently swayed it across a crystal lake. He blinked. His eyes closed but surely, Howard thought, it was just for a moment. Yet when he reopened them, though he could still feel the swaying motion, all around him was clear blue sky as he floated in the air. By the time he'd begun to comprehend what was happening, he was landing on the ground. Above him, a billowing white parachute floated serenely down, covering him in its silky white folds...

Howard woke with a start, ensconced in the silken sheets of his own bed. Just like the silk parachute he'd somehow used to escape his B-24 bomber before it had crashed to the ground in France just a few miles south of a city named Caen. Even now, some twenty years later, Howard still couldn't understand how he'd escaped his doomed craft. How he'd managed to get from the pilot seat to the rear exit of the "Flying Coffin." A getaway worthy of Harry Houdini himself. But, like the famed magician and escape artist, the trick was never revealed. Lucky was all he'd been told.

Howard looked to his right. His wife lay asleep beside him. Howard rubbed groggily at his eyes before casting a glance over at the ticking clock on his nightstand. The white face and black hands mocking him with their command of time. A mere fifteen minutes had passed since he'd crawled into bed next to Gale. When he'd come home to check on her, he had found her fast asleep. Not wanting to wake her, he'd simply laid beside his wife. Dropping himself into dreamland almost immediately. Knowing he was due to meet Jeff back at the Hancock Hospital warehouse within the hour, Howard pushed himself up from the bed. This time Gale heard him, and she rolled over onto her side and rewarded him with a beautiful smile.

"Well, hello there, stranger. What are you doing in my bed? Don't you know I'm married to a policeman?" Though she'd just woken, her demeanor was playful and happy. As always. "I should warn you, he is handsome and dashing. You have no chance with me while he's still alive."

"Is that so?" Howard bent over and kissed his wife full on the lips. Gale reached up and hugged him around his neck, letting her arms linger. "I guess I better skedaddle then. Before he comes back and finds me in his bed." Gale reached up and wiped something off the corner of his eye. He grunted in acknowledgment, "Yeah, looks like I fell asleep there for a little bit." Gale's face grew concerned.

"Are you still not sleeping much at night?" Howard nodded, straightening and turning from the bed before taking a couple steps over to the rectangular mirror above their dresser. His white flattop hair matted down on one side. He licked his hand and wet his hair once before pulling a small black comb out of his back pocket and running it over his crewcut several times. "Still having those awful dreams?"

Howard put his comb back into his pocket and turned to face her. "No," he lied to her. Unwilling to burden Gale with his troubles while she was still adjusting to having both of her feet amputated. She frowned at him, and Howard understood she knew what he was doing.

"Were you back in your old bomber? That same nightmare? Did you see Andy again?" Gale pushed herself up on her elbows, concern etched into her features, her soft black hair falling to her shoulders. She knew all about his insomnia and haunting dreams of flying over France during the Second World War. "You have to stop blaming yourself for living. Those men loved you. There was nothing different you could have done. All this guilt you still carry twenty years later for having miraculously escaped that doomed flight is slowly tearing you apart. You have to let it go."

"I should have died up there. I know that... Oh, let's not talk about this now." Though he knew the time, Howard looked down at his watch dramatically. "Besides," this time telling the truth, "I have to meet my new partner Jeff somewhere. I just stopped in to check on you. I don't like you being here all alone."

Gale frowned; an expression Howard hated seeing corrupt his wife's beauty. She shook her head, knowing that arguing with her husband was rarely productive. She let the topic of his recurring nightmares drop. "I'm fine by myself. I just got tired after watching that new General Hospital soap opera that I like so much. Besides, I won't be alone all day. My monthly diabetic supplies are being delivered this afternoon. If I need anything, I'm sure the delivery driver can help me."

Howard bent down and kissed his wife once more, his signal that he was leaving. "Your wheelchair is right here," he said, pointing at it. "Do you want to get into it now? I can help you." But Gale just shook her head. She reached for her copy of The Fountainhead by Ayn Rand lying at the edge of the bed.

"I think I'll stay here in bed a bit longer and read. You go on now. I'll see you later tonight." She smiled up at Howard and he couldn't help but plant another kiss on her face. As he turned to leave, she shouted after him, "You be sure to wear your seatbelt, Howard!"

When Howard pulled into the alley that ran alongside the Hancock Medical Supply warehouse, he found Jeff was already waiting for him. The two detectives entered the warehouse together once more. After exchanging a few pleasantries with Rod, the warehouse worker they'd spoken with previously, they asked to look around the massive store-house.

"Sure. I'm actually glad you fellas came back down again today," Rod started to say. He led the two cops into the heart of the giant building, passing the small seating area and Pepsi vending machine where they'd spoken together on the last visit. Above their heads, the soaring ceiling was supported by a series of steel girders splashed with maroon paint. Rod walked down one long aisle of the warehouse with both men in tow. Heading towards the back of the long, rectangular-shaped building nearly the size of a football field. On either side, racks towered over them. The shelves ending some fifteen feet in the air, each steel rack and wooden shelf full but neatly organized with various hospital supplies grouped together by category. A long aisle of boxed gauze and various bandages of different sizes and thickness. The next aisle holding clear tubes and tanks of oxygen chained to the steel base of the rack. The aisle after stacked with waterproof mattresses all the exact same size and color.

"After you two left the other day, I was kicking myself for not telling you about what happened next door a few months back." Each lofty rack was roughly forty feet long with five-foot gaps between each row. Every third rack, deeper into the bowels of the warehouse, Rod reached over and flipped a toggle switch. The lights above their heads coming on with a slight buzz, illuminating the next succession of columns as the three men walked deeper into the silent building. The only sound was the click of their heels on the unpainted cement floor.

"Next door?" Jeff looked over at Howard briefly before continuing. "I was told all the surrounding buildings were vacated and no longer in use."

"That is true. But Hancock Hospital owns both buildings on this side of the alley. The last one, at the back of the alley, we lease out. The final business to rent that space was a distiller of some sort. They were converting the place and hoping to start making some local whiskey." Rod stopped walking and Howard nearly crashed into his backside before halting himself. "No, I think it was gin maybe. Anyway, not that it really matters." Rod continued on again, ahead of him a border of cinderblocks that made up the backwall of the old warehouse coming into view as he flipped the next light switch. Three gigantic metal rolling doors, all locked with heavy chains, took up half of the cinderblock wall.

"What matters? What happened over there to the renter or lessee?" Howard continued letting Jeff do the talking. He was busy trying to get a lay of the land and understand the scope of the huge building. Hoping to figure out how the two of them could effectively investigate such a large area.

"That's just it. Nothing. I haven't seen hide nor hair out of either of them for months now." As Rod closed in on the backwall his pace slowed, and he gradually turned around to face the two detectives trailing behind him. "My boss told me not to worry about it. They'd paid a year of rent in advance, so Hancock already has their money. But I used to see or hear from them at least once or twice a week. Friendly fellas, you know? When they first got here, I showed them around and all. Gave them their copies of the keys to the place, showed them how to fire up the old boiler, where the fuse box was, all that jazz." The three men were clustered together; the entrance and little breakroom, where they entered over one hundred yards behind them now. "But now, poof! They are gone."

"Business trip? Out buying equipment or busy looking for financial backers, maybe?" Howard rolled his head back and forth. He'd gotten a little kink in his neck when he'd fallen asleep earlier at home. "Might be a perfectly plausible explanation. Besides, if they were really missing, we'd have heard from their families."

"I suppose you might be right. But, if you catch my drift, those fellas aren't the type to have any family if you know what I mean." Rod held one hand out straight before letting his wrist go limp, the silent and derogatory sign for homosexuals. "Now, I'm no gossiper, and what a man does in his privacy is no business of mine. But I really liked those two guys. That's why I am telling you this." He paused, perhaps to gauge the reaction of his small audience before continuing. "I was just thinking with what happened to Elmer, and those two ladies found outside all torn up, that I should mention it." Rod pulled a handkerchief out of his pocket and blew his nose once before redepositing it back into his coveralls. "Sorry," he apologized, "my allergies get worse back here on account of the opening down in the cellar."

"Cellar? This place has a basement?" Jeff looked down at the concrete floor under their feet. "I thought this was all one long slab of poured cement."

"Mostly is except for the old coal room." Rod stepped away a few strides and clicked another light switch. A single bulb in a saucer-shaped metal holder covered with protective wire came to life. Directly below it, a flight of cement stairs leading someplace below them.

"Once upon a time, this whole building was heated by coal. The chute where they would deliver the coal is in the room at the bottom of the stairs over there." Rod pointed to what the light fixture illuminated before walking over to the steps. "You guys said you wanted to nose around this place. Outside of the main entrance and a couple offices up front, you just walked the entire length of the warehouse. I keep this here door locked – in case anyone ever tried to break in again using the old coal chute. Would you believe we actually had someone trying to pry the outside metal cover off? Damaged it enough that I can't even get it to close properly anymore. Darn kids...anyway, I'll unlock it and show you the room before I leave you to do your thing." Rod started down the small flight of stairs. At the bottom of the steps sat some pooled and stagnant water. Two steps down, the air suddenly became damp and musky. The smell thick like that of a rarely opened storm cellar.

"Here you go. Have a look for yourself." Rod unlocked what appeared to be a seldom used steel door and reached inside to pull a frayed, yellowing piece of string hanging down from a naked lightbulb. The door screeched noisily on hinges slow to move, the bottom of the door so rusted that discolored flakes of metal came off as it opened. The room was small, maybe 20 feet squared, one wall made of packed dirt, the other three a combination of dirt, concrete and crumbling brickwork that had to be part of the original foundation. One end, near the ceiling of the room, a warped piece of thin plywood covered what was obviously once the opening to the old coal chute. On the opposite wall, a heavy iron gate or covering of twisted black metal barely four feet high. The damp and rotting smell they'd suffered coming down the steps grew even more rank. In unison all three men covered their noses.

"Whew! That last bunch of rain must have really done a number down here. It usually doesn't get this swampy." Rod's face was twisted in a mask of disgust. Once again, he pulled his handkerchief out of his pocket, but this time he simply held it over his nose and mouth.

Jeff looked about the room. It was empty, only holding the two openings, any coal it once housed now a distant memory. Howard moved forward and squatted down in front of the iron barred opening. "What is this, Rod? Does it go anywhere?"

"Not really. That opening is basically just a big drain that leads down into the sewers and waterways. I think they installed it to help with drainage. This part of downtown can flood pretty bad when the Mississippi River swells and overflows. But nothing else can get in or out of there. It is bolted shut." Rod paused; his expression slowly evolving into one of uncertainty. "Although, right before I left the other day, I finally got around to measuring this old coal shoot opening." He gestured towards the warped wood covering the turn-of-the-century opening. "It's rotting pretty bad and needs replaced. We are going to get a real nice steel shutter installed that I can roll up and..."

"Neat," Howard stood, interrupting the rambling worker. "So, did you see something that caught your eye? Or looked out of place?"

"I didn't see anything, no, sir. But some kind of animal must have got caught or stuck way back in there. Might have been a possum since they've been getting in our garbage lately. Anyway, it was an awful howling like you wouldn't believe. A real tortured sound. Sent chills up and down my spine." Rod visibly shuddered. "Now that I think about it, I need to remeasure that opening again. When that awful sound started, I got out of here just as fast as..."

"What day was this?" Howard spoke over Rod as the detective squatted back down in front of the iron bars. His interest piqued.

"I don't know, let me think for a…"

"Was it the same night we later found the old lady, Mrs. Fitzgerald, in the alley outside?"

"Come to think of it, yes. Yes, it was!" Rod's eyes grew wide with recognition. "But… but you don't think that yowling had anything to do with what happened to her, do you? That has been sealed shut for as long as I've worked here."

"Do you have any tools on hand we can use to open this?" After a moment, Howard reached out with both hands and gave it a pull. The bolts that once held it securely in place gave easily. Howard quickly stepped aside as the heavy iron gate crashed onto the floor. Leaving behind a squared opening just big enough for a small man, like Howard, to be able to duck into.

"Well, I'll be…" Rod's eyes grew wide. "Did the bolts rust out?"

"How far does this go back?" Howard turned and looked over at Jeff briefly before locking eyes with their warehouse tour guide. "Does this really connect to the sewer and drainage system?"

"Yes, sir. It also connects to the other building. The one I told you the two fellas are renting from Hancock for their new distillery." Rod's face was half covered like a bandit out of an old cowboy movie, only his eyes and forehead visible. "Go back a ways and you can see out into the alley, too. The water from the whole block and alleyway drains down into this same brick conduit and empties into the Mississippi River."

"Any flashlights handy?" Rod nodded, his eyes growing large in his head. "Would you mind grabbing them for us? I'd like to take a look back in there." Howard gestured at the pitch-black opening.

A few minutes later, one large square flashlight and a couple smaller tubular flashlights in their hands, the three men squatted low. Howard went in first with the biggest light held securely in his hand, followed close behind by Rod and then Jeff each carrying their own flashlights. The gaping blackness enveloping them one by one as they disappeared into the opening.

Somewhere ahead of them, the steady drip of water. Behind them, the light from the coal room steadily shrinking.

CHAPTER TWENTY-ONE

"I guess at the turn of the century, when all the sewers were being updated and expanded, the city of Rock Island installed several bigger entrances down into these old waterways like this one." The three men were clustered together as they moved deeper into the manmade drainage system. Much of the walls around them were made of crumbling brickwork that over the years had been hastily patched here and there with wide swaths of cement. Without lighting, only their handheld flashlights lit up the underground channel. Howard, at barely five feet tall, needed only to lean forward slightly as he made his way deeper into the cramped tunnel. But behind him, both Rod and Jeff were bent over awkwardly at the waist as they shuffled along. Jeff banging his head twice on the four feet high ceiling and grumbling about the tight quarters every few yards. At their feet a small stream of trickling water only a few inches wide and deep meandered unhurriedly along with them. In places the water pooling and creating slimy puddles they carefully stepped over in the near darkness. Bits of unreadable newspaper, wrappers, and various bottles and cans littering the filthy water along the pathway.

"Why not just have manholes like every other city?" Howard kept Rod talking if for no other reason than to hear his voice. The splash of their feet echoing eerily in the underground system. Up ahead of them a small sliver of light grew gradually larger and brighter. Though the passageway soon split into two separate channels, he ignored the pitch black one in favor of the one with the expanding source of light. "What is the purpose of these wide entrances?"

"Well," Rod replied. "Like I was saying earlier, I suppose it was on account of the flood waters. There have been plenty of years when the Mississippi over-runs its own banks. I've seen darn near the entire downtown area filled with standing water more than once. I think these wider passages were installed in key areas to help combat the flood waters and help them drain more quickly." Rod paused before adding, "Plus, I think the city workers sometimes use these bigger openings to move and store equipment instead of having to haul it up and down the smaller manhole ladders."

"Is that light up ahead?" Jeff tried to look past Howard and Rod but only succeeded in banging his head once again on the low ceiling. "Ouch!" He stopped walking and ran one hand across the top of his head with a grimace on his face. Wiping the crumbling mortar and brick dust out of his hair.

"Yup," replied Rod, "that would be one of the openings into the alley. When we get there, you can look out and see all the way down to the street."

"What about the passage we just passed? Where does that one lead?" Howard continued to shuffle forward. He stepped across pieces of warped wood, water-logged tree branches, and more clusters of garbage made up of old liquor bottles and degraded pop and beer cans that had washed into the subterranean passageways at some point in the past. The smell, though still horrible, seemed to soften. The grated opening into the alleyway above their heads venting much of the stench while adding a bit of fresh air into the otherwise stagnant passage.

"That one goes back under the neighboring warehouse. I'll let you look out there," Rod shined his light at the bright opening now only fifteen feet away, "and then we can head over to the other side."

"Let's just hurry up," Jeff whined from behind. "All this stooping is killing my back. And this is likely just a waste of our time."

"Maybe. I just want to check out these street-level sewer grate openings while we are down here." The three men finished the tour of the drainage channel in silence. When they reached the opening each man took turns looking out in the alley. Jeff greedily breathing in as much fresh air as he could and saying little. Rod pointed out the various landmarks easily spied out of the slated openings. The direction of the street, the side of the Hancock warehouse building, and across at the opening's twin directly across the alley from them. When Howard stepped up, he stuck his arms past the grates and into the alley. With smaller and skinnier arms than either Jeff or Rod, he found he could easily squeeze the entirety of one arm out into the shaded sunshine. He waved his arm back and forth freely. There was no question if someone wanted, they could surprise a passerby walking near the sewer opening and grab or trip them. Without a word, Howard looked across at Jeff who merely shrugged noncommittally. As he pulled his arm back inside, Jeff exclaimed loudly from behind him.

"What the hell is that! A turtle?" Jeff splashed across the small stream of water running along the bottom of the concrete channel. Pointing as he crowded Howard. Rod in turn shined his light in the direction where Jeff pointed. A miscolored and rounded lump protruding up from the stagnant water.

At first glance, it did resemble the shape of a turtle's back. But there was no shell and the coloring was pale and bloodless. Under the combined glare of the three flashlights, it appeared to be a mass of white and discolored flesh bobbing in a small pool of slightly deeper water. The rank water held in place by some broken pipe and crumbling pieces of rock and concrete that had created a mini dam under the alley. Gingerly, Rod bent down and picked up a small stick clinging to some dead weeds that had likely washed down from the opening into the alleyway near their heads. He advanced on the bulge and gave it a slight shove hoping to turn it over or dislodge it enough so they could see what it was. When the end of the stick made contact with the mass, it suddenly popped and rapidly deflated. The three men looked at each other in confusion momentarily before their faces pinched in pained disgust as a wave of fresh rot swept over them. The horrid smell somehow able to best the stench of the sewer they traversed.

"Look," said Howard simply, one hand over his mouth and nose as the punctured thing flattened and shrunk before lazily twisting over on its side. A mass of grey hair that could have been human coming to the surface of the rank and filthy water it bobbed up and down in. "Oh my god, is that what I think…"

"Just a dead possum. See that long tail?" Rod aimed his light, "It just filled with gasses as the innards decayed. Those damn things get in our garbage all the time." He waved his hand dismissively. "Good riddance." He turned and began making his way back the way they'd come. Heading over to the neighboring passage where the second grated opening looked out on this side of the alleyway. Slowly, both detectives turned and followed as well.

"A turtle? You thought that was a turtle?" Howard snickered slightly.

"Maybe. Could have been a mutated one…" Jeff offered before chuckling as well.

"Wouldn't have surprised me," Rod called back over his shoulder as he led them back down the pitch-black channel. "It has happened before. People flushing little baby turtles they buy as pets down their toilets. Down here in the sewers they can grow to be pretty large in their old age."

"I thought it was alligators that got flushed. Didn't they find full grown alligators or crocodiles down in the sewers of New York City? Supposedly surviving down there for decades?" Howard began to feel more comfortable despite the claustrophobia and terrible smell. He picked up his pace. The swaying of all three flashlights eerily illuminating the constricted tunnel ahead of them.

"I don't know about that," replied Jeff. "But I know sea turtles can get really old." He paused before adding, "I heard they are actually very wise as well. You know, smart like dolphins and whales."

"And I suppose you thought we might have found some wise old turtle down here from the beginning of time? Maybe one who could show us how to find and defeat the depraved monster doing this killing?" Howard chuckled again. The light banter helping him feel better about his new partner. "I wouldn't count on it."

As the three men once again reached the junction where the underground passage split, Jeff spoke up. "What is that?" All three men stopped walking and turned. There, clustered around more debris, several bits of greying matter rimmed the edge of another discolored puddle of water. "Are those dead mice? Or part of another dead animal? Did pieces of that possum float over here?"

Rod offered, "Looks like those might be pieces of its tail..." His voice trailing off before adding, "Or maybe its paws." Jeff stepped over the small stream and squatted down; his light trained on what had caught his eye. Abruptly he stood and, though still hunched over in the tight quarters, turned towards Howard with visible anger flashing across his face. The tone of his voice accusatory.

"What are you trying to pull? Do you think that is funny?" He stepped back across the water and confronted Howard directly. "Why would you do that? And down here in this muck!" Venom flashed in his eyes as they narrowed. "Do you have something you want to say to me?"

Howard was taken aback by his partner's sudden change in demeanor. He stood his ground, confusion clear in his face despite the poor lighting. Next to him, Rod had an equally puzzled expression etched into his features before he turned and stepped across the running water at their feet. Just like Jeff, he squatted down to get a closer look at what the detective had spied.

"What are you talking about? What did you find?" Howard looked around Jeff at where Rod sat on his haunches. "Rod! What is it?" When Howard looked back at Jeff, the expression on his partner's face chilled him. Both men locked eyes as Rod reported what he saw.

"Jesus H. Christ! These are toes! There are three... no! Four!" Rod stood suddenly and banged his head on the brick ceiling. He staggered slightly, one foot inadvertently plunging into the stream of filthy water before he quickly righted himself. "I think I'm going to be sick..." He looked over at Howard. "There are human toes over here," he stated flatly.

Howard's face dropped. His jaw unhinging in clear shock and disbelief plain in his eyes. He looked back up at Jeff who, though his face was still contorted in anger, had witnessed the sincerity in Howard's expression. Without a word Howard moved over to the find, not touching anything, but seeing for himself the bloodless digits. He instantly recognized that Rod and Jeff were correct. Several severed human toes were gathered together in the muck. The three men stood in silence for long moments. Each processing the gruesome scene for themselves.

Howard was the first to speak again. His voice calm and measured, though inside a fury had begun to rise. Before losing her second foot, his wife Gale had several toes removed. Four, to be precise. Did Jeff, or somehow Rod — who worked at the warehouse above them where two bodies had been found — know of his wife's misfortune? Howard had never spoken to either man about Gale's affliction. He had no doubt some of the officers at the Rock Island Police Department knew she battled diabetes. But he had never shared the details of her crippled condition or treatment. Was Jeff messing with him? If so, for what purpose? When Howard spoke next, he found it hard to keep the anger he felt inside from bubbling up.

"We walked past this spot on our way to the first sewer grate. I didn't see these when we hiked down here. Did you?" His eyes first on Rod who shook his head vigorously back and forth no. The warehouse worker still looking like he may heave and lose his lunch at any moment. When Howard turned to Jeff, he merely received a quick, disdainful shake of his head as well.

"If I had seen them, I would have pointed them out." Jeff's face still angry, but slowly returning to normal and softening. "Just like I did now," he added. Howard looked over at Rod who turned away, then glanced once more at Jeff whose features had become unreadable. He took a step closer to Jeff, barely two feet separated them. He looked up at his partner with steely eyes.

"Why did you react that way? Why would you think I saw those earlier and…" Howard grew silent, his mind working. "You think I planted those, don't you? And why?" He tried to make sense of what Jeff had discovered as well as his partner's enraged reaction. "Do you know why I can't leave my wife alone overnight? Or go for very long without checking in with her? Do you?" Howard recognized the tone of his voice was rising. It was all he could do to keep his surging emotions in check. Jeff seemed to sense the climbing rage of his new partner. Involuntarily, he took a step back from Howard as he shook his head no once more. "No? You have no idea that…"

"Your wife is a diabetic." Rod spoke, his words slicing through the heart of the building tension surrounding all three men. He stood apart from the detectives, his voice monotone. "She had toes amputated, didn't she?"

Howard's face broke then. Hearing his biggest secret and worst fear, the one he couldn't face, spoken out loud was worse than any blasphemy his mind could conjure. His head slowly swiveled and, for a moment, it was all he could do to keep from lashing out at the warehouse worker. Hearing him speak about Gale and her… no, their most intimate secret, burned his ears. Though tears pooled and dropped from them, his eyes burned with a rage. Howard took a step toward Rod, unsure if Jeff hadn't grasped his elbow and stopped him, what he might have done to the man. He felt like tearing him apart, ripping his tongue out so he could never speak of Gale again.

Yet, Rod continued talking.

"I'm sorry. It's just... when you gave me your card the other day, I thought I recognized your name. We've done deliveries to your home from here. Back before Elmer was killed, he used to talk about some of the customers. I remember him saying there was a younger woman he sometimes delivered diabetic supplies to. That was unusual because usually by the time a diabetic gets to that point, they are much older. I think that was what stuck out to him and why he mentioned it. I remember him saying her husband was a detective and that..."

Howard didn't hear the last words. His entire body was shaking and quivering with emotion. A roaring filled his ears and he felt himself burning up from the inside. The sound in his head was like the revving of engines, like his plane's rotors springing to life. Howard's eyes filled with stars, nearly blinding him with rage. He lost track of time and when he was next able to process what he was hearing, it was Jeff's voice speaking calmly in his ear.

"...terrible to have someone so close to you suffering. I'm so sorry. Why didn't you tell me?" Dully, Howard turned his head, his vision clearing as he looked up at Jeff who still held his elbow. "No wonder you reacted like that when we found those severed toes down here." Howard nodded but his head was still spinning. "Maybe we should head back up to the warehouse. We need to call in what we have found. You look like you need to sit down anyway." Slowly Howard's senses returned. The explosive rage he'd felt dissipating like a storm that had run out of rain.

"No," Howard finally felt like he could speak without spitting a cascade of obscenities at Rod. "I'm fine. Let's finish what we came down here to see. Those…" Howard couldn't even bring himself to look in the direction of the dismembered digits. "That evidence isn't going anywhere. Besides, there may be more… uh… parts in the second tunnel." Howard nodded in Rod's direction and tried to smile. But the expression was more grimace than grin. Jeff and Rod exchanged looks of concern.

"OK, if you are certain that you are up to it." Howard nodded at Jeff, motioning he would follow as Rod slowly began to once again slog through the accumulated rainwater and floating debris swept up in its wake. The three men walked in silence through the second passageway running under the opposite side of the alleyway above them. The second channel was nearly identical to the first. Dark, damp, heavy with the scent of rot, and with a stream of murky water running down the middle.

Minutes later, the light from the second sewer grate became visible ahead of them. The beam also illuminating yet another dead animal. This scene far more disturbing than the bloated possum that had somehow gotten trapped after being washed into the drainage system by flooding waters. Or the desperate scrambling of hungry rats looking for an easy meal. The animal, as the three men slowly surrounded it, had obviously once been a housecat. A tinkling bell, silent in the murk of the underground tunnel system, hung by a pink collar from the feline's twisted neck. The grey cat, the color of smoke, had been tortured.

Horribly.

A pair of medical grade scissors, most likely having come from the Hancock Medical warehouse above, was coated in blood and grey fur. Obviously, the sadist's instrument of choice. The cat had been strung up by its collar, hooked around a rusting piece of Rebar jutting out from the cement wall roughly half a foot off the floor of the tunnel. Whether all at once, or one appendage at a time wasn't clear. But the poor creature was both limbless and tailless. The terrified look frozen across the dead cat's features, as well as the amount of dried blood surrounding the scene, made it unlikely the amputations were done after the cat had been dead.

"Mother Mary of God," all Rod could manage to choke out.

"No mother or god was down here." Jeff turned and looked over at Howard. "Didn't you say the grandma we found in the alley had a cat?" Howard nodded stoically; he was way ahead of Jeff. They'd obviously just found what had lured Mrs. Fitzgerald down into the darkened alley the night she'd been murdered. One mystery solved.

"Do you think… you think that was what I heard? This poor cat being tortured?" Rod turned away from the grisly scene.

"My guess would be the cat was snagged at some point while it was running around outside during the day. You may have heard it trapped down here. The killer could have left it here alive, howling and howling until Mrs. Fitzgerald came looking for it. Maybe… maybe with all the heavy rain the killer was worried it wouldn't be heard. Used the scissors to make sure it was… uh… vocal."

"That sure would have brought her right here." Jeff took several long strides over to the grate looking out into the alley. He once more peered out from the ground level opening into the deserted alleyway. Opposite from him he could see the sewer grate they'd just peered through before stumbling upon the grisly finds. After a few moments he stepped away, and a now pale looking Rod next pressed his face to the metal slats. Breathing in shuddering gasps of fresh air.

Jeff and Howard stood silently together in the middle of the underground passage, a few yards behind him. Rod looked once to his right then turned to his left. "That's weird. There is some kind of flower laying right in the middle of the alley. That wasn't there when we looked out the other…" Rod never finished his sentence, suddenly jerking and convulsing. Urgently trying to separate himself from the opening. His shrill screeches catching Jeff and Howard by complete surprise.

Both detectives lunged forward before halting dead in their tracks. Stunned. On the top of Rod's head, coming down from the sidewalk above the sewer grate, a piercing claw of a hand laid claim to the crown of his head. Slender fingers, more bone than flesh, dug themselves like daggers deeply into the warehouse worker's scalp. Immobilizing him and keeping Rod's face crammed tightly to the inside of the metal slats of the grate. Rod struggled frantically to pull himself free as a crimson wave of blood began to stream from his hairline. Moments later, his scalp began to slowly peel back from the skull as his agonized cries echoed and reverberated inside the brickwork tunnel.

Pushing past their initial shock and finding their resolve once more, both Jeff and Howard dove at Rod. Trying desperately to separate him from whatever was ripping the flesh from his skull. As they struggled, a second equally disturbing arm and hand snaked down from above. Emaciated and skeletal like the one still grasping his hair; the only difference was what it held. A curved blade flashed once, striking deep into the side of Rod's neck and easily splitting the soft tissue and bone that normally keeps one from losing their head. With a sickening slash, the head was severed from the body.

Still pulling urgently, their own horrified screams matching the echoing of Rod's last agonized pleas, Jeff and Howard tumbled backwards in the filthy drainage water running down the center of the passageway. Howard faltered with the headless body of Rod in both his hands. The diminutive detective's feet slipping and staggering around in a small circle as if dancing the box step with the beheaded warehouse worker. As he fell backwards, he lost his grip on Rod's shoulders, losing his desperate battle of tug of war with Jeff who still clung to what was left of the man.

Jeff fell as well. His body splashing in the accumulated muck at the center of the underground passageway. Flat on his back, Rod's severed neck spewed blood directly onto him. As Jeff struggled to get out from under the weight of the shuddering corpse, long bits of stringy and sinewy flesh flapping around the severed neck landed across his chin and lips. Jeff sputtered and spit the bits of flesh out of his mouth as arterial spray soaked his face, hair, and neck.

Though he found himself unable to tear his gaze from Rod's quivering eyes, Howard sprang to his feet and fumbled with his service revolver. Pulling frantically at his gun now slippery with gore and the grainy sewer water he'd landed in. As he pulled it out, the weapon slipped from his hand and landed at his feet. Still transfixed, he stared at the hovering, detached head before the hideously twisted hand released its grip on the hair it held. As if in slow motion, Howard watched Rod's face of frozen horror drop silently to the ground. The two arms that had grasped and butchered the man quickly vanishing back from where they had first appeared from the sidewalk above them.

The carnage was over in mere moments. Rod's twitching body and rolling head both slowly came to rest. Howard instinctively leapt for the barred grate before stopping himself. If the killer was hovering above the sewer grate, Howard knew he would be a sitting duck just like Rod had been. With no reason to help Rod, he turned his attention to his partner. Jeff was covered in grime, sewer water, blood, and gore. He staggered to his feet, eyes wild and still trying to spit the pieces of grisly viscera out of his mouth. Moments later, retching violently.

The splash of vomit coating his shoes.

CHAPTER TWENTY-TWO
IOWA/ILLINOIS BORDER – 1962

MISSISSIPPI RIVER

"Don't move, Dr. Stander. Or say a word when I remove my hand. Is that clear?" Tim nodded, nerves raw; the form behind him thick and towering. He felt the hand slide tentatively down from his face and he turned, wide-eyed to stare up at his abductor. The faint illumination of the single hallway nightlight just outside the room barely exposing the face. It was Aloysius, his features stern and unsmiling. Eyes narrowed and cutting. Tim started to blurt out an excuse for his actions; his face flushing in the darkness with guilt. Once more, Aloysius quickly covered his mouth. "I know what you are thinking," he murmured faintly, nodding towards the hallway on the other side of the cracked doorway. "You are thinking you wished the storm didn't wake you." Tim nodded mutely, unsure what else to do. "But I'm glad you came out of your room to investigate. You can help me with our intruder."

Tim exhaled slightly in relief. Aloysius clearly thought whatever had brought him down from the third-floor master suite he shared with Madeleine was also the reason Tim had left his own room. He leaned into the deception, tilting his head and whispering back. "I thought I heard something, and then the hallway nightlights kept getting unplugged." Aloysius nodded as if he'd expected as much. Tim felt his rocketing pulse begin to slow until he recalled what he'd seen just before being pulled into the unused bedroom they both now stood in. "I saw it. I mean, I saw an arm pulling the lights loose from the electric outlets."

Aloysius raised his eyebrows but said nothing. In the sliver of dim light spilling into the room, Tim could see Aloysius was wearing a half-opened robe of silk that barely covered his thighs. His legs were bare and he had no slippers on his feet, white chest hair pouring out from the barely sinched robe around him. Tim realized dumbly that the man was likely naked under the robe he wore. Tim shifted uncomfortably on his feet. He hoped Aloysius didn't ask him why he was still wearing his clothes.

"I am going to move down the hallway. Stay close behind me until we reach the end of the entresol." Aloysius pulled a small caliber handgun from out of his robe pocket.

Tim looked up at the man uncomprehending. "Entresol?"

Aloysius muttered more words in French, obviously annoyed. "Oui, entresol... Er... mezzanine." He sighed before adding in a hushed tone, "Just follow me and stop when we get to the stairwell. If he gets past me, don't let him go down. Do you understand?" Tim nodded, but was far from understanding how, if the intruder got past the very fit, six-and half-foot tall Frenchman toting a gun, he would be able to stop him. But, as Aloysius moved down the carpeted corridor, Tim followed and peeled off at the head of the stairs as instructed.

Aloysius crept steadily towards the door Tim had seen the intruder's strange arm creep in and out of. Tim was mesmerized by the scene unfolding in front of him. Astonished by the brazen courage of the older Frenchman. Though Aloysius had a loaded weapon in his hand, it was held casually at his side until he reached the yawning doorway. He paused only a moment before suddenly darting inside the pitch-black room as if propelled by a desperate need. Tim held his breath, both of his hands involuntarily rising to the sides of his head, just waiting to cover his ears when the inevitable gunshot rang out.

Only it was not a gunshot Tim heard. Instead, from inside the room, a bright and comforting light suddenly came streaming into the otherwise darkened hallway. Without prompting, Tim hurried towards the lit and open doorway where moments earlier Aloysius had vanished inside. Peering in, his eyes were immediately drawn to the hurried swing of a door on the right side of the unoccupied bedroom. Without looking elsewhere, he quickly stepped towards it, assuming Aloysius was in hot pursuit of the mansion's prowler and likely needing his assistance. He didn't see the slow wave of thick blood making its way out from under the single bed in the smaller guest bedroom until he slipped on it. Tim pinwheeled his arms wildly to keep his balance as his left foot slid out from under him. He skidded to a stop; one brown shoe now darkened in crimson gore.

Instinctively, his medical training taking over, Tim quickly dropped down on all fours to see where the blood had originated from. The mattress had a lone bedspread covered in frilly white lace. On one side, where the coverlet barely grazed the hardwood floor of the room, the white was slowly turning pink as the low-hanging bedcover soaked up the creeping blood running along the floor. There was no question it was coming from under the bed, though the white coverlet obscured the source.

Tim was acutely aware that he was all alone in the unused guest room. He wanted to call out for Aloysius, but worried his cry might alert the one they were pursuing. Instead, Tim tentatively reached out one hand and slowly grasped the edge of the bedspread hiding the black under the bed. Clinically, he noted the tremendous amount of blood now pooling at what must have been a low spot in the wood flooring beside the bed. Thinking to himself that any wound spewing that much blood needed attending immediately. As he started to raise the pink-stained cloth, Tim grew very afraid. Unable to completely shake the residual fears of his childhood when things slithered with impunity under beds, in cracks of closet doors, and the corners of dank cellars. With an adult detachment, he watched the quivering of his own hand as he slowly raised one side of the bedspread.

Flick!

The room went black, the comfortingly bright overhead light fixture went out just as a long-limbed hand clutched at him from under the bed. Tim screamed in the dark. His legs kicking wildly under him as he propelled himself away from the clingy grasp of the thing from under the bed. Blind in the dark, Tim had nothing to replace what he'd barely glimpsed before the light had gone out. The thing under the bed had rolled towards him, futilely scrambling his way. But as it did, just before the black of the stormy night robbed him of the ability to make sense of it, wet and squishy things had poured out from its insides. Splashing Tim's face in whatever was now dripping from the end of his nose...

Tim bellowed desperately in the black of the room. His shrieks so loud he'd not heard the door click shut behind him. The churning darkness vile and with utter contempt for his childhood fears. White lightning streaked somewhere outside. The brief flash cast twitching shadows and turned the enlarging pool of blood on the floor black as tar. When a second bolt of lightning followed close behind, it was paired with the shuddering thunder of the first. Tim felt the fury of the storm outside. The floor under him trembling slightly from the blast. But the second light splitting the nighttime sky revealed something poking out from under the bed. Though the rest of it was still covered by the long bedspread, a distinctly feminine hand now lay unmoving on top of the pool of blood it rested in.

"Oh, god... oh..." Tim's voice splinters, his throat raw and dry from his screams. Above him, the ceiling light of the room flickers back on. Either electricity restored or the mansion's generator kicking in. Either way, Dr. Tim Stander regains his composure and his medical training kicks in. He scrambles back across the floor on his hands and knees, ignoring the blood he wades into as he pulls at the pale hand from under the bed. He jerks when he hears the sudden retort of a pistol firing somewhere in the house, but otherwise keeps his attention on the shockingly white woman he pulls out from under the bed.

In an instant, he recognizes the face frozen in gaping horror. It was Cindy, the mousy-looking local girl who worked for Madeleine and had served Tim his breakfast that morning. Tim moaned repeatedly as bit by bit he dragged her lifeless body out from under the bed. Startled by the gruesome sight, Tim stood and backed away once Cindy was completely exposed. The marred corpse something no man, trained medically or not, should ever have to witness.

Her flannel nightgown had been split down the middle, exposing everything down her front. The faded bedclothes now heavy and thick with blood and gore. Her chest, like the nightgown, was jagged and torn. Cindy had been opened from her pubis to her neck. What was left inside of her a tangled thicket of stringy veins and bulging strands of slippery innards. Lying on her back, under the harsh overhead light, she looked much like an open and ongoing autopsy. Cindy appeared to have been disemboweled. Much of what had tumbled out of her, Tim thought to himself, must still be under the bed where she'd been. Tim replayed what was likely her last moment, the one he'd watched horrified. The petite girl using the last bit of her strength to reach out for his help. Turning towards him from the darkness even as he'd scuttled away from her in terror. Though his eyes had betrayed him and turned away in shock and horror, his ears had recorded her last movement.

It was the sound of wet meat hitting a butcher's slab.

"There is nothing you can do for her, Tim." He jumped, the voice at his ear so unexpected it seemed to come from the walls of the room itself. He turned to see it was Madeleine who had entered the room and was now speaking to him. Tim had not heard her approach, but with the windows of the room still battered by the rain, it was not surprising.

"But you may still be able to help Aloysius. Please come quickly and see what you can do."

Tim rose mutely; there was no question Cindy was beyond any help. He trailed after his aunt as she glided wordlessly across the second-floor hallway. When they reached the doorway Tim had first left his bedroom to find, the four-paneled door was wide open. Entering, he whiffed gun smoke and tasted the coppery mixture of blood in the air before he saw where it originated from.

Aloysius was turned away from the entrance to the room. His body sprawled awkwardly across a cushioned easy chair that at one time had been a cheery, bright green color. But now was stained darker; the color of moss devouring a dying tree left to rot in a damp and shadowy forest. He'd clearly been surprised from behind. His pistol, two yards from his outstretched hand where it had likely skidded. Just beyond the gun, the oddly decorated Ankh was leaning untouched in the corner of the room. The shroud from the Egyptian tomb lay folded across the empty bed among several boxes bulging with benign contents. The unused bedroom clearly had been used as a large storage closet of sorts. Assorted piles of various holiday decorations with no real value stacked neatly along the walls of the room. Had the intruder, like Tim, been after the artifacts hauled here from half a world away? Perhaps surprised by Tim's earlier wanderings before being chased by Aloysius? Had Cindy merely been in the wrong place at the wrong time?

"What happened?" Tim asked his aunt, the only other person in the room, hoping Madeleine might be able to shed light on Aloysius's injuries. But even as the words left his mouth, Tim realized there was no hope of saving her husband. His throat had been hastily cut and he'd quickly bled out. The covering and spongy material of the chair absorbing much of the gore.

"I don't know. I merely heard the report of his weapon and came down as quickly as I could. I found Aloysius just as you see him now.

I knew you were the only one here who could possibly help him, so I went straightaway to your room before coming across you with Cindy..." Tim thought it strange she didn't ask him about her maid or why both men had been out of their rooms this late in the evening. He supposed Aloysius had alerted Madeleine before he'd left their bedroom. She must have known an intruder had broken in.

"Did you see anyone?" A shake of her head. "No? His killer may still be on the grounds!" Tim stood straight up, ready to search for his aunt's husband's murderer. "You need to call the police!"

"I have already contacted the local constable. He is dispatching the county coroner for me as well. When they arrive, I'd prefer you stay in your room with Sherry. I will handle everything."

"Sherry!" In the swirl of madness since leaving his room he'd not thought of his daughter. With nothing to be done for Aloysius or Cindy, Tim's concern coalesced around the one-year-old.

"Don't be alarmed for her safety. Kelly is tending to her now. Why don't you go relieve her?" Madeleine's voice was calm and collected. As if they'd merely stumbled across a dead mouse caught in a trap. Her cool detachment and control, even in this extreme situation, were hallmarks of his Aunt Madeleine's personality. Yet her seeming indifference to the butchery of Cindy, not to mention the murder of her own husband, was astounding to Tim. How could she remain so relaxed when the killer might still be lurking nearby?

"Are you sure you want me to leave you? At least until the police show up?" Tim walked over to her, he reached out and gave Madeleine an awkward hug that she barely returned.

"Thank you, dear. Aloysius was a wonderful friend and energetic lover. I will miss him. But," she cocked her head to one side, "I do believe the authorities are pulling in now." Madeleine smiled up at Tim. "I'll brew some tea and have Kelly bring you a cup when it's done. Drink it up and let it soothe your racing mind. I guarantee you will get a good night's sleep despite these awful happenings..." She grew serious once more, her eyes narrowing slightly. "Your concern for me is sweet. But, if you really want to help me right now, just stay put in your room. It will only confuse the simpleton sheriff if he knows you were present for these awful happenings. Better to have him in and out of here as quickly as possible."

Tim nodded dumbly. "What about the killer? I mean, what if he comes back?"

Madeleine smiled wanly, "Oh, Tim. He won't be back again. In fact, I'm fairly certain even now the killer is likely looking over his shoulder in a panicked retreat. Justice, I assure you," for the first time Tim caught real emotion in Madeleine's tone, "will be served."

CHAPTER TWENTY-THREE

Tim woke briefly under bright sunshine until languidly rolling onto his side to escape the bothersome rays. Unconcerned with the light, his mind rapidly fell in and out of consciousness as he continued dozing. Strange, seemingly disconnected dreams peppering him with images that somehow were vaguely familiar. It was his dad, Emery, holding an Egyptian Ibis bird statue slowly stirring with life in his hands. Lucy, his dead wife, flipping past pages of colorfully dressed Native American Indians in a glossy Life magazine. Aloysius stumbling around in near darkness. His skin ashen and pale as he neared a cavernous hole. It wasn't until Aloysius fell silently into the abyss that Tim woke fully. The deafening silence roaring at him that something was amiss.

He sprung upright in his bed. The slow arc of the afternoon sun bathing the bedroom in an array of colors streaming from the curtains on both windows. His first thought was the time, unsure how he'd managed to sleep so late into the day. His second thought was of Sherry, and Tim quickly gained his feet. Half staggering over to her crib that he found empty. Panic clutched at him from inside. The tendrils of his greatest fear weaving a tapestry that seemed to bind him tighter in its grip. His heart raced despite the slow machinations in his head.

Where was Sherry? Why was it so bright? And, looking down at the pajamas he'd apparently slept in, where were his bloody clothes from the night before? As Tim moved over to his bedside table to check the time, he found himself struggling with another question. Why was he so incredibly hungry? When he saw it was nearly 3:00 in the afternoon, Tim practically bolted from the room. It wasn't until he noticed Sherry's pink onesie, the one Tim had dressed her in the night before, hanging across the top rail of her crib that he relented. Kelly, Sherry's most attentive sitter, always hung what Sherry slept in that way if it was damp.

Though now slightly less panicked, Tim still exited his bedroom swiftly. Not bothering to change out of the nightclothes he'd slept in, his bare feet cooling under him as he crossed the black and white tiled entryway. Moments later discovering Kelly and Sherry seated together, a colorful and large picture book opened on the older woman's lap.

Tim crossed the sunroom, scooping Sherry up in his arms and nearly smothering her with kisses and hugs. His toddler giggling and squirming in delight. Kelly watched placidly from the soft chair, a pleasant smile on her lips. "I'm glad to see you up and about. Are you feeling alright? Earlier, when I tried to wake you this morning, you barely responded. I left you alone thinking you might be sick." She left the last statement hanging in the air.

Tim shook his head wryly before replying. "No, no, I feel fine." He squatted and let Sherry tumble softly from his arms, the little girl scampering on all fours towards a small pile of her toys. "I guess I do feel a little woozy. I know I was up much later than usual with all the commotion last night. But I never imagined I would sleep the day away. Especially after what happened. Maybe, subconsciously, I was avoiding the start of this day... I still can't believe what happened last night. Two murders! Right under this very roof!" Tim regained his feet and walked a few steps closer to where Kelly sat. "Did the police catch the guy? Why was he in here? Robbery?"

Kelly slowly shook her head. "You'll have to discuss all that with your aunt. She asked us not to speak about what happened."

Tim frowned, a puzzled look on his face. "Even with me?" Kelly merely nodded at the same time she shrugged. "Well, what did the police have to say? Did they question you?"

Again, Kelly stayed mute, shaking her head no. A moment later adding, "Your aunt is in the library waiting for you. I believe she is sketching out a design for the new fireplace mantle and hearth she is having installed. You should go talk with her. I'll watch Sherry until you are done."

Tim frowned, the normally pleasant and talkative housekeeper clearly wasn't willing, or able, to speak on the events of the past night. Though frustrated, Tim reasoned he knew little about the relationships in his Aunt Madeliene's grand manor. Perhaps Kelly was very close with Cindy. Afraid if she started talking about her, she'd dissolve into tears. Or, perhaps the police asked Madeleine to instruct everyone to stay silent until the investigation unfolded and more was learned. Or at least until everyone could properly be interviewed and cleared. He supposed there were several possible reasons for Kelly's silence. He excused himself and headed to the library. Hoping his often-cryptic aunt would be more forthcoming.

He was wrong.

"Tim, please understand this is not Chicago. Or even Cairo, for that matter. Your expectations are beyond the scope of this community's meager resources." Madeleine, appearing annoyed at the interruption, had several large sheets of blank paper spread out on the floor of the library. Several with incredibly detailed dimensions and drawings scratched across. Soft music, Elvis crooning sadly about not being able to stop falling in love, was playing in the background. "Perhaps I should brew you more tea? Maybe a bit stronger this time..." Tim barely took notice of her odd question, frustrated once more by Madeleine's indifference.

"How can you remain so calm? Your home was broken into, for god's sake! Do the police have any leads yet? Where were the bodies taken? Has Aloysius's family been notified? And what did that girl's family say? Aren't they outraged?" Tim paused, his mind whirling with unanswered questions. "I just can't understand how the officials in this backwater place aren't combing the house for evidence! How did the intruder gain entrance? Was it a burglar?"

Madeleine cocked her head as if, for the first time, carefully studying Tim's face. Instead of answering the myriad of questions he'd thrown her way, she said. "Your passion for a resolve to all this surprises me." She continued to stare at Tim. He tried to hold her gaze, but found he was unable. "Was it really you who destroyed that idealistic... that fool you found at the bottom of the sarcophagus? It wasn't Emery who actually did the deed? Or one of the diggers he'd employed?"

"What does that have to do with anything?" Tim threw his arms in the air in exasperation, but Madeleine remained silent. Long seconds passed, his aunt still studying Tim's face until he grew uncomfortable under the weight of her stare. "I already told you what happened," he finally stammered out. "Yes, yes it was definitely me that dispatched of the creature that, by the way, yesterday you tried to convince me I hadn't even seen." Tim tried his best to glower at Madeleine, but she didn't seem to notice. Or care.

"You alone?"

"Yes! I don't know why or what happened. But I grabbed that staff with the Ankh on the end and speared the gruesome thing. When I did, it basically turned to dust. Why is that so..."

"What made you use the... the staff?" Madeleine's unwavering gaze never left his eyes. She almost seemed to smile. "Perhaps there is hope for you yet."

Tim blinked, uncomprehending and feeling somehow lost in the conversation he'd instigated. He tried to move the discussion back to more familiar ground, back to his original line of questioning. "What is going to happen to Aloysius? His body, I mean. Will there be services this weekend? As you know, I was planning to head back to Kankakee with Sherry on Friday. Should I make arrangements to stay longer?"

"The police took both bodies to the morgue where, I imagine, they will be autopsied before being released to the family. Cindy, the girl you came across, you would expect her family to make any arrangements, wouldn't you? Don't you think it is doubtful we would be invited to any services knowing her demise happened on these very grounds?" Though her questions could be taken as simply rhetorical statements, Madeleine seemed to wait for Tim's reply. She didn't continue speaking until he acknowledged what she'd said with a quick nod of his head. When he agreed, she continued.

"And as you know, Aloysius comes from an aristocratic family of French heritage. I'm certain they would be outraged if I tried to inter him over here and not in his birthplace. It is likely his body will be returned home as soon as possible. Any services would be arranged by his family. Considering all this, I suspect there is no need for you to pay your respects personally. Don't you agree?" Again, she paused until Tim indicated he agreed again or at least understood.

"Do you think the intruder is likely to return? Are Sherry and I in danger staying here?" Tim, not feeling he'd learned much, retreated to more familiar and comfortable ground. Fatherhood. "I hope the person who killed Aloysius and Cindy is caught soon. Such a cowardly act! Sneaking around in the dark and murdering a young woman and a senior citizen under the cover of a storm. I'd sure like to see the killer punished."

"You and Sherry are leaving soon. At the present, this may no longer be your concern. But, just to be sure, I'll let you know once I think the police are on the right track. I may even try to help point them in the proper direction." Madeleine looked away briefly, lost in thought, a small smile playing across her lips. "Anyway, when the time comes, I'll be sure to notify you once everything is set. I just need to see a few more things play themselves out first."

Tim nodded, unsure what, if anything, he was agreeing to. His stomach grumbled. He'd not eaten anything since dinner the day before. Astonishingly, that was now nearly twenty-four hours ago! Distracted, Tim barely registered the last line his Aunt Madeleine spoke as she lowered her head back to her drawings. Assuming her comments were not meant for him.

"When the time comes, we'll see. We'll see if I have been mistaken all along. Perhaps the design is a bit ahead of schedule..."

CHAPTER TWENTY-FOUR
IOWA/ILLINOIS BORDER - 1964

THE QUAD CITIES

Howard and Jeff, both veteran policemen, quickly mobilized themselves. Jeff bent to retrieve Howard's gun, turning slightly to wipe the muck off on his pants before pressing the standard, police-issued revolver back in Howard's palm. Though the startling and brutal killing of Rod had shaken both, their years of training helped steel them from the horror just witnessed. The two men worked in near silence to briefly clean themselves of the worst of the filth caked and splashed all over them. When each had regained a certain amount of composure, they grabbed the flashlights dropped during the fray and slinked back down the passage they'd just hiked up with guns in their hands. Slowly putting distance between themselves and the sewer grate opening where Rod had been so viciously attacked. Unsure if the thing they'd seen might be eavesdropping. When they felt comfortable their conversations would be unheard, they both stopped and turned toward each other.

"We have to go after the... the killer. Whatever the hell it was." Jeff was near frantic. Looking to extract a pound of flesh out of the one who had slaughtered Rod and likely the other murder victims they were investigating. "Call this in and get the area sealed off." He started back down the underground channel, splashing angrily in the streaming water he was now soaked in. "I can't believe we were attacked in broad daylight like that. Even if the buildings and alleyway above are deserted."

"Hold on," Howard reached out and stopped Jeff. "If we think that was the same killer who slaughtered that little old grandma from the other night and the others, it stands to reason they know the layout of the warehouses and this sewer systems better than we do."

"So what? We have to catch that thing! And right now, we know exactly where it is. This may be our best chance to catch the killer. Let's move!" Clearly gung-ho, Jeff turned and started back down the passage again before Howard stopped him a second time.

"Would you use your head? That thing is either already long gone or waiting to ambush us when we rush out of here. It has to know exactly where we are. Just like it somehow knew we were searching down here." Howard paused, absorbed in thought. "It must have seen us poking around and peeking out of the sewer grates. That has to be how it got the drop on us. If we go marching out the only entrance leading down here, don't you think it will be waiting on us? Or, worse than that, what if there are more entrances down here that we don't know about. Didn't Rod say the city had installed several big entrances into the sewers of downtown?"

"What does that matter?" Jeff seemed to barely be listening to Howard.

"Look. If I'm right, we'll walk right into a trap in a location we don't know very well at all. We have no idea how much of a maze these warehouses and underground passages are! If that thing has been lurking and killing using these old sewers and water runoffs, it has all the advantages. And if I'm wrong, and it isn't waiting to attack a second time, it could come in behind us and ravage Rod's body like it did the others. Or, maybe worse yet, get in here and move or hide any evidence of what went on down here. Remember what Rod said he overheard the Iowa State Police talking about? The foreigner making blood sacrifices. If that is accurate, there could be a whole cult or even a group of devil worshippers down here. Don't assume we are dealing with one person. Don't assume anything!" Howard spoke fast. His mind buzzing and weighing all the options. Part of him wanted to rush outside with his gun blazing and take his chances just like Jeff was eager to do. But if they were dealing with more than one killer, or if the killer really was some diplomat or prince from another country, they had better have rock solid proof.

"So, what do you suggest then, boss." Jeff finally seemed to be hearing Howard. His hair still dripped blood, and slick gore covered his shirt and pants. Howard was not in much better shape. Splattered with some of the same, and his backside soaked in filth and human waste. Both men looked like something out of a horror movie. Their flashlights illuminating the small area where they stood talking.

"We work fast and stay together. We'll collect those toes and verify these two tunnels don't have secondary openings on the other end. Once we do that, we'll make our way very carefully back the way we came. Afterall, we do have these." Howard lifted the service revolver in his hand.

"Did you..." Jeff started to say before pausing briefly. A second later blurting out, "Did you see the arm? What was holding Rod by his head?" Howard nodded grimly. "Do you think these guns will even work against something like that? I mean, what was that?"

"I don't really know. That's partly why I want us to be cautious. Nothing about these killings, or what we just saw, makes any sense to me." Howard turned both ways, pointing his flashlight down each end of the pitch-black passageway where they stood. The stench of damp rot still hung heavy, filling their noses while someplace nearby water dripped rhythmically like the ticking of a timer. "Come on. We need to hurry. Let's see how far this tunnel goes back. Make sure there isn't another way in or out of here. Then we'll do the same on the other side, gather up the evidence, and call this in." Jeff nodded and both men splashed down the shallow waterway with guns drawn and eyes straining in the yellowish light of their battery-operated torches.

Five minutes later, they found the second entrance Howard had suspected might be at the end of the underground passage. It was bolted and locked securely from the inside. With cobwebs covering the two corners at the top of the metal door, there was no question the old entrance had not been used for a very long time. However, that soon became a secondary concern.

Lying half submerged in the running water, the two cops found a second corpse. Automatically, Howard searched the eviscerated remains for ID. None was found, but inside one pocket he discovered a small wad of water-logged business cards. Though the name was illegible, the embossed title of the business was not: "Quad City Distillers." Obviously, they had discovered one of the two missing businessmen from the rented warehouse at the end of the alley. Rod had been correct to suspect foul play. Too bad, thought Howard, the Hancock employee will never know he was right.

The man's body had clearly lain undiscovered for quite a while. Like the previous victims that had spawned their journey down into the sewer system, it had been torn asunder. Hollowed out, the chest cavity now only filled with wiggling worms and crawling maggots. As they nudged the remains over with their feet, two beady-eyed rats hissed from inside the split ribcage before scampering back the way Howard and Jeff had walked. It was Jeff who first noticed the brutalized body was missing one foot. The other foot hanging by a lone tendon and missing several toes. Based on the chewed nubs, it seemed likely one or more of the rats had made off with them.

"Guess that explains the toes we saw." Howard stood back up after leaning over the body with his light trained on the stumpy foot. "The rats must have gnawed them right off. Maybe that last rainstorm washed the missing toes down where we saw them." He looked over at Jeff as they turned to head back the way they'd just come. Cautiously moving over to the underground passage they'd first walked down. "Can I ask you why you thought I had something to do with the toes? Why were you so accusatory and angry?"

Jeff walked several more steps before stopping. He didn't look at Howard as he began to speak. "Look, I don't want any trouble. My whole life I have wanted to be a police officer." Jeff stopped talking, embarrassment clear in his features despite the darkness of the underground tunnel. He walked a few more steps before turning again to face Howard. "But I guess if we are going to be partners, we need to be honest with each other." Howard nodded encouragingly, unsure what Jeff was struggling to say. Water continued dripping somewhere unseen; the *plop-plop* echoing in the distance. "Remember a few days ago when we were talking about foot fetish weirdos?"

"Sure, I do. I thought you knew about Gale, my wife, and her recent surgeries. That was why I reacted like I did. I'm sorry if I mistook..." But Jeff waved his hand, cutting Howard off.

"No need to apologize. If anything, I should be." Jeff looked up and met Howard's eyes. "See, I... Well, I enjoy and kind of... kind of have a thing for feet." Jeff stammered a bit before quickly adding, "To be clear, just women. I have always had a thing for women's feet. I know that may sound strange to you. But I swear it doesn't affect my work. Some guys like to go to the movies or watch sports like baseball or boxing. Others might get their kicks looking at girls with big boobs in Playboy magazine. But me, see, I like looking at women's feet." Jeff struggled to meet Howard's eyes.

Howard nodded. This conversation making him feel extremely uncomfortable after dealing with his wife's recent amputations. If he was honest, he thought most people's feet were gross. But, he supposed, to each their own. Some guys he'd known in the service had liked women with broad backsides, or redheads, or women with long legs. He guessed he could accept an attraction to feet. A few seconds of silence passed, and Howard could see Jeff was beginning to worry about what he'd just revealed. To encourage the young man, Howard asked the only question that came to mind. "Any idea why? I mean, what started you on feet? Just born that way?"

Jeff laughed, but the sound was far from joyful. "Oh, I think I know exactly why I'm this way. See, when I was a little kid growing up near Marquette, it was just my mom and me. Never knew who my dad was. Anyway, she worked at a little mom and pop restaurant to support us and sometimes had to work nights and weekends. When I was around 11 or 12, she hired one of the local high school girls to start watching me some of the time. After the girl graduated, she sort of became my regular babysitter." Howard and Jeff began walking again, cautiously making their way through the dark tunnel together. Both on high alert.

"And what? You had a crush on your babysitter? An older girl just out of high school? That doesn't seem that unusual." Howard kept his eyes peeled and his legs moving. The conversation helping make the eerie underground environment less intimidating.

"Right but, and I didn't put all this together until I got a lot older, she was kind of a strange one, I guess you'd say." Jeff looked over at Howard, the two men walking on either side of the murky water flowing between them. "One night she made me undress and get in the bathtub before she would let me change into my pajamas. Told me I was dirty and she would help me get cleaned up. Like I said, I was only maybe 11 or 12 at the most, and didn't dare question her. At first it seemed a little awkward, but once the Mr. Bubbles soap got flowing, everything from my waist down was hidden under white suds. No different than when my mom used to help wash my hair when I was a little kid. But, like most boys, by the time I was that age I was popping boners all the time. Once she started washing me, I couldn't help myself. I know now that I am...uh... well-endowed, shall we say? But at that age I had no idea. Anyway, she started cleaning me with a wash rag, and right there in the bathwater, I experienced my first orgasm. I thought I had done something wrong and was super embarrassed. But she wasn't. At the end she was pumping my stuff up and down, even encouraging me to do it again."

"What does that have to do with your obsession with feet?" Both men were now back in the original passageway under the alley they had first walked down with Rod. Cautiously approaching the sewer grate opening they'd peered out of without incident the first time. As they walked past, both detectives eyed the sunshine streaming in with more than a little trepidation. "Were you looking at her bare feet the first time you, well... I mean, when that happened?"

"No. But after that first time, she started wanting to play with my... my stuff all the time when she would babysit me. At first, it was always in the bathtub under the guise of cleaning. But pretty soon she started having me lay down on my bed and telling me not move. Saying we were just playing doctor and warning me that it had to stay our secret. She would touch me all over, and if I ever looked at her while she was doing that, she'd get really angry. Sitting alongside me in my bed while I laid flat, she'd sit with her back to me with my dick in her hands. The first time she bent over and put me in her mouth, I started kind of protesting. I mean, at that age I didn't really understand what was going on. When I began to sit up, she straddled me and held me down with her legs and feet. After the first few times, she started making me kiss her feet, then lick and suck her toes, too. This went on for months before my mom finally caught us one time. By that time my babysitter was routinely cramming her toes in my mouth, my ears, up my nostrils, whatever. I actually lost my virginity to her when she started riding me. She'd climb on top of me, slide my dick inside her and then put both her feet all over my face. It was like she didn't want to see me at all. Just what was between my legs."

"Good grief! And you weren't even in your teens yet? And she was 18?" Howard had heard plenty of stories while he'd been overseas. Bored

G.I.'s bragging about their sexual exploits, their big-breasted wives or girlfriends, or what happened their first time with a woman. Each man's story often more outlandish than the last. But Howard could tell Jeff wasn't bragging. In fact, it seemed as he continued talking that getting the story off his chest was a relief for him. Howard began to see Jeff in a completely different light. Understanding we all are often left victims of situations beyond our control. Howard couldn't help but contemplate the circumstances of his own near fatal plane crash. He hadn't asked for that to happen to him anymore than Jeff being manipulated and raped by his much older babysitter. Both men struggling with what fate had tossed at them.

"Whatever happened to the girl? Your babysitter?" Jeff stopped walking and, after a few steps, Howard did as well. Just ahead of them was the end of the second tunnel. Just like the one on the opposite side, it too was closed off by a metal door and had piles of trash gathered at the foot of it. Clearly that entrance had not been opened for a long time either.

"You promise not to judge me?" The look on Jeff's face had softened. It might have been the jumbled lighting of their flashlights casting shadows, but Howard thought he could still see the small confused boy Jeff had once been. Howard shook his head no and indicated Jeff should continue. "Years later we ran into one another at the local downtown drug store. I was buying rubbers and she saw what I was picking up. She followed me out of the drug store and suggested we go someplace private where we could use the first one in the package together. This would have been about ten years ago when I was maybe 22 or 23. Anyway, after that chance meeting, I started seeing her as often as I could. No one has ever made me more excited, or sick feeling, than she did. By that time, I had been with plenty of other women. So, I knew why she had been so interested in me back then. Even as a little kid. We never actually dated or anything like that. She'd just call me up when she needed a good fucking. But every time it ended up the same. Me practically worshipping her feet while she enjoyed herself. I think she was a half-crazy bitch. But she fucked so good I couldn't help myself."

"Whatever happened to her? She still live in Michigan?"

"Yeah. She married some rich dentist in town. Dr. Tathum was the name of the main dentist in Marquette where we both lived. He was even my dentist if you can believe that. One day, out of nowhere, the two of them suddenly got married. They had a baby boy named James just eight months later. The baby came early was what they said. A miracle they all said." Jeff gave Howard a wry smile and a sly wink. "But here's the thing. I was still seeing her right up until their engagement announcement hit the papers."

"What are you saying?" Howard asked, but understood he already knew the answer.

"I'm just saying I could very well have a 7-year-old son back in Marquette, Michigan named James Tathum. That's all..." And with that, Jeff turned, his story over. "Now, can I ask you something?" Howard nodded. "I just explained why I reacted the way I did when I saw those severed toes. I got the crazy idea that you somehow knew about my secret foot fetish. That you were making fun of me or trying..." Howard opened his mouth to defend himself, but Jeff just waved him off. "I know you weren't. But your reaction was pretty extreme as well. Does that have anything to do with your time over in Peoria? What was the place called again? Zellers?"

"No, that was completely different. It was like Rod said. My wife is a diabetic and has had some toes amputated in the past. I jumped to the same conclusion you did about me. That you had heard about it from one of the officers at the station. Or rumors anyway, since I have never told anyone the extent of her illness. Then, when Rod said he already knew about my wife, my world went a little sideways on me. That's all..." The two detectives began making their way back down the underground channel again. As they approached the spot where the human toes had likely been whisked away and deposited by the recent rainwaters, Howard began looking for a wrapper or bag he could place the evidence inside to carry to the surface.

"I can understand that." Jeff paused; he looked over at his new partner. A burgeoning feeling of camaraderie emboldening him. "Do you want to tell me why you ended up off of work for those couple months? Back in 1962. Why did you end up spending time in an insane asylum?" He saw Howard flinch and stiffen despite the poor lighting. He tried to quickly diffuse the situation by adding, "I mean, I just shared one of my deepest and darkest secrets with you. My new partner."

Howard nodded curtly, then blew a deep breath out of his mouth. "I guess you'll find out one way or another soon enough anyway. I'm surprised no one back at headquarters hasn't already told you."

"I tried to get it out of Henry when he drove me back and forth from downtown the other day. But he stayed tightlipped. Told me to ask you myself." Jeff shrugged.

"Henry is a good man. An honest cop." Howard reached down and pulled a relatively dry piece of newspaper off of the floor of the sewer system. He held it in his hand as he spoke. "I served in the military during the Second World War. I was a pilot and flew bombers as part of the initial invasion at Normandy." Jeff nodded as Howard continued. "My plane, a B-24 bomber, was shot down in France and my entire crew was killed. Somehow, no one could ever figure out how or why, I managed to escape and parachute to safety."

"Say no more. I can only imagine what that might do to a man. It was the guilt, right? Wondering why you escaped when so many others died." Jeff had registered for the draft during the Korean War, but had never actually served. He'd often wondered how different his life might have turned out had his number been called.

"That was part of it, yes. But while I was flying my last mission, the one that resulted in the deaths of all my crew, I had something like a vision.

Or maybe was visited by something. I don't really know what to believe. Everything is still confusing to me all these years later... Anyway, when my plane was hit and we were going down, I cried out. I begged like a coward for my life. Now, according to the doctors and my wife, oxygen deprivation may have been the cause. But I swear something heard me calling out, and, if you will, answered my selfish little prayers. Right in my cockpit, I suddenly started having a conversation with my dead co-pilot, Andy. He told me if I could just fly the bomber a little longer, he would drop the bombs for me and help me escape. He promised me that if I did that for him, he would give me not only my life back, but the life I always wanted."

"Which was what?" Jeff was enthralled by the story. He'd long believed in the afterlife and supernatural. Not the Christian version of heaven and hell. But instead of a true hereafter without the shackles of man's suit of flesh, ever evolving faiths, and corrupt politics that went hand-in-hand with most religious affiliations. "Did you get what you prayed for?"

"You act like this was real," Howard shook his head. "You might be the first one! But, to answer your question, almost. I got the wife I'd always hoped for. I live in the kind of small community I'd always envisioned living in while doing a job I care about."

"Sounds like a fair trade, boss. The war was won by the side you served on, you escaped certain death, and got the woman of your dreams.

"Maybe. But everything feels tainted. That is what set me off a few years ago." Howard looked over at his new partner. "When the doctors outlined the bleak prognosis after my wife was diagnosed, I decided I couldn't take it anymore. Didn't want to watch her suffer and die. So, I tried to kill myself by running my car into a tree." Pausing, he looked down once at his feet before continuing. "The ironic thing is, at the last moment my car somehow swerved and missed. My wife says I must have subconsciously turned the wheel because I didn't really want to die. But it sure felt like something suddenly took control, like it wasn't ready for me to end it all. Anyway, I ended up back on the road and ran head-on into another vehicle. The car I hit turned out to be driven by my previous partner's sister. She died..."

Jeff stayed silent, merely nodding encouragingly as Howard continued. "That was what sent me spiraling down. I just couldn't take it anymore. I lied to everyone about what happened. Said I just lost control of my car. When I went a little bonkers later on, everyone chalked it up to my guilt over what happened in the war with my crew. That killing the woman with my car just finally pushed me over the edge. I spent three months in Zellers, and really only learned I am not nearly as bad off as a lot of other very sick people. But, earlier this year, I got drunk one night and confessed everything to my old partner. That it wasn't an accident. I had purposefully tried to kill myself and in the process had ended the life of his little sister. That man, a good detective named Joe Carrol, pulled a gun on me. When he squeezed the trigger, something happened and the bullet went off in the chamber. It nearly blew his whole hand off. He died in surgery that same day without ever regaining consciousness."

"My god..." At first, all that Jeff could manage before adding. "When I was hired, they just said your previous partner had died in surgery. I had no idea."

"Exactly. It was like *my* god, the one who saved me, keeps retaking everything he promised. I am a pariah now where I work. My beautiful and wonderful wife, who helped me recover after the war ended, is slowly leaving me piece by piece. And the son I always wanted, the one I was promised, has never come. Gale, my wife, she can't have kids. We found that out shortly after we had wed. So, *my* god got whatever it wanted out of me. Why bombs dropped over some tiny villages in France was so important to him I'll never understand. But he made me a deal. I did what was asked and in return all I got was broken remnants of the life I wanted. Sometimes I think I am a ghost just going through the motions of being alive... Or maybe ghosts only haunt minds, not places. Sometimes I think I might have an entire spook house between my ears."

The two men stood together in silence. They'd each bared their dark souls to each other. Neither really expecting the other to understand. Yet the bond between them only blossomed. Each having dealt with more than most. Each, in a small way, either amazingly lucky or horribly damned and cursed. As if mere pawns pushed around by unseen forces.

Howard bent over, ready to retrieve the severed toes from the muck they had been encased in. "I guess now with the two bodies down here and no other entrances we might as well leave these here." He straightened and looked his new partner in the eye. "Guess I should have listened to you after all. By now, that thing has likely hightailed it out of here. What do you say we get out of this sewer drainage system? We'll call all this in and get some back-up. Then, get cleaned up and go after whatever has been doing this killing. We have plenty proving our theory is correct. These murders are all related. Who, what, and why still makes no sense. But at least we have his location."

Hurrying now, both detectives splashed back down the tunnel. Heading back into the Hancock Medical warehouse and the police radio in their car.

CHAPTER TWENTY-FIVE

Weapons drawn, Howard and Jeff moved in tandem. Each covering the other silently as they rapidly made their way back down the underground sewer passage towards the Hancock Medical Supply building. As the dual tunnels merged back into the single corridor that led into the warehouse above, the two detectives braced themselves. Unsure what might be waiting to surprise them when they emerged.

"There is the opening leading back into the building's old coal room," Howard said, speaking in hushed tones. "Do we want to rush out together and hope we overwhelm whatever severed Rod's head from his body? Or go one at a time so that, if we are attacked, one of us has a clear shot?"

"We are sitting ducks coming out of that opening." Jeff waved his gun at the yellowish light streaming inside the entrance they'd first used to enter the sewer system. "If it hasn't already vacated this location, that thing might be waiting to pounce on us from either side," he whispered back. "The opening is too small for both of us to squeeze out at the same time. My size is working against me here. Since you don't have to bend over as much, I think you could dash out a lot quicker than I could." Howard nodded silently in agreement. "Just give me a minute to get set first."

Adrenaline kicking in and heart racing, Howard watched mutely as Jeff readied himself. Much taller than his older partner, Jeff crouched down on one knee so he could see into the room clearly and pointed the end of his gun at the cramped entryway. Both hands on the weapon in classic shooting form. After taking a deep breath, Jeff looked over at Howard and nodded. Giving him the green light to exit. "I got you, boss. Just be ready for anything." Jeff smiled drolly. "I promise I'll shoot before it can get you."

Howard ran one hand across his face, wiping the perspiration from his eyes. He tried not to notice the wavering in his gun hand or the slight tremble in his legs. Usually, during the course of routine policework, everything happens so fast that one's bravery is never considered. But, right now, Howard felt about as steady as a wobbly-legged baby deer getting its first drink at a river. He grits his teeth and clenches both fists tightly. All his muscles tensing.

Sprinting through the opening, his forehead collided with the single lightbulb dangling by its long cord in the middle of the room. Howard looked quickly to his left and right before turning completely. His head on a swivel and eyes darting all around him. The swaying bulb casting waves of darkness that always kept a portion of the room cloaked in shadow. The obscured views pricking Howard's eyes with fear and doubt. The shifting dark in the corner, the impenetrable crack of the half-closed entryway, the black behind the coal shoot, the shadows hastily retreating from the light. The unseen, the very basis of human fear. But nothing lurched for Howard or pounced. A few tense moments later and it was clear the small room was empty.

Relaxing, Howard turned back to the opening where Jeff remained hidden. "All clear. Whatever it was, it looks like that thing must have taken off after all." Howard holstered the gun in his hand.

BANG!

Howard heard the shot first. He tried to call out a warning, but found he suddenly had no breath. Instinctively, he reached for his chest, confusion etched in his pained features. Was he having a heart attack? A wave of ache radiated out from where he felt like he'd been punched. Looking down, his soaked, filthy shirt began to deeply redden. Howard felt his heart pump in his chest at the same time he watched blood spurt onto his collar. His head swam, and he dropped to his knees briefly before toppling onto his back. When he looked down at his shirt a second time, more blood had soaked into it. Gasping, he placed one hand in the crimson flow and felt the warmth. He'd been shot.

"Wow. You really are a nutcase." Jeff emerged from the sewer opening, grimacing slightly as he stood fully upright for the first time since crawling in after Howard and Rod. The gun in his hand trained on his fallen partner. He swiftly crossed the old coal room and relieved Howard of the pistol he'd just tucked away. Jeff deposited the gun in his own holster. "Guess Henry was right when he told me you were on the verge of cracking up. He said everyone at the station has little side bets on how long it will be before you blow your brains out with your own gun." Jeff lifted the gun in his hand.

Seeing a flash of confusion replace the pained look on Howard's face, he continued. "Yeah, I gave you my gun back there after you dropped yours. Since we both carry the same department-issued weapon, I didn't think you'd notice. After all, the only difference between the two is the serial number. I couldn't risk having the bullet come from my gun. That would be a lot harder to explain."

"Wha... what... Why?" Howard struggled to put any words together. He could taste blood in his mouth, and each breath seemed shallower than the last. When he tried to move and sit up, the searing pain in his chest flared.

"When I was hired to replace your dead partner, I was told they were looking for someone with strong leadership. I think the chief said something about wanting to modernize and streamline the department. Told me if I came onboard and played my cards right, that he could see me rising quickly to lead detective. Said there were certain questions about your fitness for the job and he wanted to 'hire for the future' I think is how he phrased it. Well, the future is now seeing as how you just shot yourself." Jeff stretched and twisted his neck back and forth several times before moving to one of the crumbling brick walls and leaning casually against it. A big smile on his face. "Guess who is about to get a nice promotion and raise?"

"Shot?" Howard coughed and watched blood spatter one of the few unsoiled spots on his shirt. "Why would I…" He drew in a raggedy breath before finishing. "Would I shoot myself? In my… my chest?"

"Are you kidding? Why wouldn't you? I'll tell them how distraught you became when you couldn't save Rod. That you blamed yourself for letting him even tag along with us. Especially after I had tried to dissuade you. How you rushed out of this opening before I could stop you," Jeff motioned toward the sewer opening they'd emerged from, "hoping the killer would end it all for you. When that didn't happen, you pointed your gun at yourself. I tried to stop you, and we wrestled briefly. But you pulled the trigger before I could take it away from you."

Howard was weakly shaking his head back and forth. He wanted to call out, tell Jeff his plan was madness. But, even without speaking the words, Jeff understood Howard. "What? You don't think they'll buy that? Even though you are certifiably crazy! They probably have a full file on you back at that insane asylum that'll back up what I say. And, after all, you tried once before and…" Howard's eyes flew open, panic plain in them. "Oh, don't worry," Jeff continued. "I'll be sure everyone knows that you lied about losing control of your car, boss. And why you are responsible for the death of your last partner and his sister. Not to mention the poor bastards under your command back in the war. I'm sure everyone will be moved that you shared all these horrors with me. There will be no doubt what great friends and partners we became in such a short amount of time. That will be important later."

Howard wanted to argue, tell Jeff no one would believe him. But, deep down, he suspected everything Jeff was saying was true. Howard struggled to move, flailing around like a cockroach on its back. When he tried to lift his head to protest Jeff's words, Howard blacked out momentarily. When he next opened his eyes, he saw his shirt was now entirely colored a deep red. Jeff stood over him. A look of rapturous anticipation gleaming in his eyes. Cold, weak, and his head spinning, Howard waited for his approaching death with eyes barely open.

"Oops! Thought we already lost you there, boss." Howard's eyes opened wider, but both were merely slits. "You know," Jeff continued talking as Howard flashed in and out of consciousness, "I wanted to thank you before you go. It felt really wonderful sharing what happened to me as a kid. You know, with my babysitter and all. It felt good to finally talk about that with someone. Kind of unburdened me in a way. So, I want to share one more thing about me that..." Howard lost track of Jeff's voice. He was so tired he only wanted to sleep.

Smack!

"There he is. Hey! Hey!" Jeff slapped Howard across his face a second time until he heard him groan. "Anyway, like I was saying, the only thing I love more than playing with women's feet is seeing that terrified look in their eyes. It gets me so hot when they finally understand the little game they thought we were playing together has real consequences. You might be surprised to hear how easy it is to pick up older women. Especially when you show them a badge. So trusting..." Jeff's eyes drifted, clearly relishing the memories of his past encounters.

"Anyway, I like to cruise downtown dives, taverns, and club lodges near closing time. Showing interest in the stumbling drunks and pathetic barflies so starved for even a hint of affection, they'd agree to about anything if you talk to them the right way. Just act interested, or tell them they're pretty even when deep down they know it's a lie." Though Howard didn't see it, Jeff winked conspiratorially once before continuing. "When I'm finally done, they are usually so ashamed and embarrassed by what I did to them that none of them would ever dare share their story. Or probably even show anyone the marks I leave them with. Inside and out."

Jeff chuckled good-naturedly before continuing. Clearly relishing his kinky admissions. "I mean, what are they going to do? Report me, a cop, to the police? After they came so willingly with me? Submitting to my whims and breathlessly telling me they'd let me do whatever I wanted if I took them home with me. None of them ever imagining how much they'd regret it later." Jeff was staring straight ahead, but seeing only the images he replayed in his mind.

"I love collecting old secretaries, widows, or chubby waitresses working the late-night diners. Insecure, older gals all so desperate for a little affection. You see, for me anyway, older women are like forgotten bottles of vintage wine. And I think a little dust on the bottle, so to speak, only makes it sweeter when they finally open themselves up and give me a little taste. Always intoxicating... take them some place private, get a few more drinks down their throats, fifty- and sixty-year-old sluts all alone and helpless. Submissive to whatever I want whenever I want. Playful tickling, tying them down, letting them think – since they are older – that they are in control. Watching their faces and eyes when they start to understand they are completely at my mercy. Helpless."

Jeff looked down at his dying partner. A sheen of sweat covering Howard's ashen face, but his eyes still alert enough to understand what was being said. "You of all people must get that. What with your wife being so feeble." Jeff looked down at Howard with a knowing smile. Though Howard was still conscious, Jeff slapped him hard across his face again, then pulled him up by his collar until both men's faces were only inches apart. "I want to be sure you hear this, boss. Once I share all your secrets, no one will question what a truly great friendship we have. In fact, as I'll let the chief know, you would definitely have wanted me to be the one to share the news of your suicide with your wife." Howard was too weak to move, unable to speak and barely able to pull in a breath, he could only listen.

"I've seen Gale's pictures on your desk. She is a little younger than I usually like 'em, but boy she is a looker. And helpless? I mean, you can't get more vulnerable than being practically bedridden." Jeff smiled then. His glance drifting up as if watching something float in the air nearby. "Bedridden? I promise she'll be ridden on your bed so, so very hard. She'll be helpless. And just devastated to know how much of a burden she was to you. That she'd helped drive you to kill yourself."

Jeff slapped Howard a third time and then backhanded him a fourth. Howard could no longer move or respond. Nearly the last words he heard Jeff say were the ones he whispered directly into his ear. "She'll cry out for you, of course. But not nearly as hard as I'll make her cry out for me. But I promise you this, when I'm done playing with Gale, I'll be merciful. Not like this whacko slinking around down here in this sewer system. I'll just force her to take a bunch of her medication. She'll go to sleep and never wake up. I have no doubt, since I would have just shared the news of your death with her, that Jim, the coroner, will rule her death a suicide as well. It will be just like Romeo and Juliet. Two tragic lovers' suicides. Both of your deaths will be big news. But, once I catch this killer, people will forget all about you two. They'll be talking about the new lead detective. I'll be a hero!"

On the edge of the final abyss, Howard used the last of his strength to open his eyes. "You mean... all this... You... you aren't, aren't working... the killer?" Everything faded then, Howard not seeing, but hearing Jeff's reply.

"Of course not. You saw that thing the same time I did. Must be somebody really sick." Though Howard was beyond hearing now, Jeff continued unaware. "I've been thinking. Maybe the killer is growing weaker. Seems like he is practically working his way down the food chain, if you will. First attacking and tearing apart stronger, healthier victims like the Governor's niece, the young woman from Almore, and even the Hancock Warehouse worker, Elmer, right in the middle of the day. Before later on having to attack weaker prey like those sissy-boy distiller guys, the little girl, and the grandma we found in the alley. None of the last three would have put up much of a fight. Especially if they'd been hobbled first."

Jeff looked down at his unresponsive partner; he shook and slapped him once more before gently letting his head drop back to the floor of the coal room. Understanding Howard was likely beyond even hearing. "Maybe you were right, boss. This thing might have had to start using the sewer and drainage system to get around unseen. We both saw its withered arms, hard saying what the rest of the thing might look like. And, if it is growing weaker, surprising and slashing at its victims may be the only way it can overpower them."

Jeff stood. He backed away from Howard until his back brushed against the temporary wood covering that partially closed off the old coal chute. He casually leaned against it while pulling his gun back out and wiping it down. As he worked, his mind began to piece together the story he would share. Where he and Howard had stood, how his partner had shot himself, the words of his last confession…Jeff knew it was important his story was rock solid and what he said was unshakeable.

CHAPTER TWENTY-SIX
PRESENT DAY

STANDER DROVE STEADILY THROUGH the streets of Almore, only accelerating when his Jeep was beyond the sight of the gathering townspeople. He sped back to Relict Mansion with Secrist in the passenger seat and Frazier panting contently in the backseat. As they crested the last hill before the turn that led to the long driveway of the grounds, Stander turned to Secrist.

"When we get there, why don't you grab your gun before we head back down those stairs? Even if what that guy back in Almore was babbling about isn't the stiff we found earlier, he must have seen something strange." Stander pointed out the window at the plume of black rising above the trees in the distance. "Where that smoke is coming from isn't even a mile from the house."

"I didn't realize we were that close. Where is that? Down by those fields that border the property to the south?" Secrist strained to see if he could make anything out through the trees, but was unable.

"Looks like it. There isn't much wind today." The Jeep's tires squealed slightly as he turned down the driveway of the grand house, then barked as he shifted and accelerated at the same time. A minute later, Frazier and the two men jumped down from the vehicle after Stander parked just outside the front door. All three headed into the home, but went three different ways. Secrist walked swiftly to his room where he unlocked the case he kept his licensed revolver secured in. Stander walked back towards the library where they'd been working all morning, Frazier at his heel. But when he stepped over the threshold of the grand room, Frazier didn't follow. Sitting on his haunches just beyond the doorway.

"Really? You just gonna stay up here again?" Frazier cocked his head to one side as if to question why Stander would have thought the dog would follow. Behind him, Secrist reached down and petted the brown and white pit bull boxer mix as he stepped past.

Stander handed one of the flashlights they'd used earlier over to Secrist who nodded once. His gun tucked inside the holster at his back. "OK, let's see if our guy is still a homebody." Stander smiled grimly before he and Secrist began making their way back down the long set of clandestine stairs. The darkness, smell, and curvature of the plunging tunnel the same as their previous trip. Stander stooped once to grab the wire handle of the old oil lamp they'd discovered after first opening up the side of the fireplace. As both men descended silently, he casually relit the lamp. By the time they reached the bottom of the staircase, the warm glow of the wick was steady and unwavering.

"Fuck me," Stander whispered hoarsely. Looking through the door into the hidden chamber still standing wide open. "The dude is gone!" He held the lamp in his hand high, the soft light illuminating the small, dirt-floored room. The partially rotted timbers that helped hold up the walls and ceiling still in place, everything inside the tiny room looking exactly the same except for the missing corpse.

Secrist walked over to the wood table where the body had lain. His flashlight trained on the folded pile of clothes still there. "The guy at the diner said the man who attacked them wasn't wearing any clothes. Here they are."

"Looks like our modern-day Lazarus isn't afraid to strut his stuff in the buff." Stander joined Secrist at the table, placing the oil lamp beside the pile of clothes. He was about to say more when both men heard a sound like the distant snapping of twigs. Spinning in tandem, their flashlights lit up one of the two doorways at the opposite end of the room where the noise originated from. The old wooden door, closed and covered with cobwebs when they were last in the room, swung open several inches before drifting back almost closed once more. With both men silently appraising the motion, it happened again. The door opening and then closing a few inches every five seconds or so. Almost as if what lay beyond breathed with life.

When the cracking sound came again, it was louder and followed by a haunting and pained moan. Stander and Secrist exchanged worried glances. Around them everything seemed to blacken and shrink. "Is it my imagination, or is that sound getting closer?" Secrist didn't wait for a reply as he pulled his gun from its holster. "I think I hear something moving in there."

Secrist reached for the door's plain iron handle. The noise, like splintering chicken bones, came a third time. Directly behind him, Stander whispered, "I'll shine my flashlight inside once you open it. You just be ready with that gun." Secrist nodded once in understanding, then flung the door open.

The black beyond seemed to stretch for an eternity. Behind the doorway, a long tunnel extending out in front of them. Stander pointed his flashlight down the chiseled corridor, letting the light bounce off the jagged ceiling and walls. The passageway had been carved right through the earth like a miner's shaft. The battery powered light fading before it touched the other end. For one beat, both men stood and stared in complete silence.

Then the screams started.

Out of the black near their feet, popping up like an awful Jack-in-the-box, lunged a pale-faced man smeared in blood. His scream was blood-curdling and utterly agonizing. It was so close and unexpected, mere feet from him and waist high, that Secrist stumbled backwards into Stander. The light in his hand swinging wildly back and forth, eerily illuminating the rounded shaft ahead of them.

Stander struggled to keep his feet while separating himself from the backpedaling Secrist. Tortured screeches echoing all around as he clamored to see what they were coming from. When he steadied himself, the light from his handheld torch landed briefly on the shrieking face. Bits of it were missing or torn off, including one eyeball wiggling down from a hollow socket where it swayed. The mouth opened and crooked, pain and fear competing for the taxed vocal cords.

The door crashed shut.

"What the hell was that thing?" Secrist shouted, his voice booming in the tight quarters. After slamming it, he leaned against the wooden door, gun still in hand. "Was that our guy? The same one we found on the table?"

"How the fuck should I know, Tommy?" Stander shouted back, the unexpected shock had both men panicked and yelling at each other. Somewhere in the background Frazier was barking urgently. "Was it... was it coming right out of the dirt floor? Why was it so low to the ground? Was it trying to bury itself?"

"Or was it a different one?" Secrist turned and twisted the round iron door handle in his hand. "Shit! Doesn't this thing have a lock?" He turned back and leaned his weight against the hand-hewn wood door. Behind him, the thing's horrible screams had stopped. A slight scuffle and scratching was the only noise coming from the tunnel beyond.

"Another one?" Stander's eyes narrowed. "The guy at the diner sure made it sound like he had seen a freaking zombie. We sure as hell just did." Stander gestured towards the doorway they'd barely opened. Back upstairs, Frazier continued barking. The rising tone and urgency giving Stander pause.

"And it looks like our dead guy wandered away, too. Are we in the middle of a zombie apocalypse?" Secrist met Stander's eyes. "Jesus, what have you dragged me into? Why do I even hang out with you?"

"Frazier!!" Stander turned and yelled in the direction of the stair-stepped passage that led back up to Relict Mansion. "What has gotten into him?"

"Maybe he's letting you know hell is full and the dead are taking over the earth."

Stander frowned. "Are you OK holding that for a second? Maybe I should run up and see what he's freaking out about?"

Secrist nodded and waved him off. "I don't hear or feel anything on the other side of this door now. Run on up and check on him. Just don't be too long." Stander nodded once then turned and ran back up the stairs.

When he saw Frazier at the top of the strange stairs, the dog immediately turned and bolted. Stander silently cursing and following the canine as the dog raced back into the main foyer before stopping. As Stander skidded across the black and white tiles, his shoes sliding on the accumulated dust, an urgent knock came at the front door. Frazier looked up expectantly at his owner as he sat on his haunches.

"Are you fucking kidding me? Now! We get our first ever visitor now." When Stander looked down at Frazier, the dog merely cocked his head once more. "Great. Thanks for letting me know..."

Stander took a deep breath to settle his frayed nerves before unlocking and opening the front door, already thinking of excuses he could use to get rid of whatever neighborly Almore citizen had come calling. But as the door swung open, Stander found himself face-to-face with the law.

"Sorry to show up like this unannounced." The uniformed officer stretched one hand out and Stander shook it, but didn't invite him inside. "Name's Chuck, Chuck Cunningham. I'm the chief of police in Almore. Nice to meet you." Parked beside Stander's Jeep was a silver SUV adorned with extra lights and various law enforcement symbols and phrases.

"Russell Stander, nice to meet you as well. What can I help you with?" Stander placed a plastic smile on his face, his mind whirring. *Now what,* he thought to himself grimly.

The lawman, black haired and likely in his late thirties, seemed slightly put off that Stander didn't move aside or invite him in, his eyes roaming the empty foyer. "I don't know if you spotted the smoke there beyond the tree line," said the local cop gesturing. "But I wanted to see if you, or anyone else you may have with you, had seen anything out of the ordinary today."

"Out of the ordinary?" Stander kept his face a mask of indifference, "Like what?"

"Maybe people you don't recognize hanging around out this way? Or kids horsing around?" The local cop said this casually, but Stander could see both his eyes and mind were working. After a slight pause he added, "Weren't you just in town?"

Stander nodded, then leaned against the doorframe in what he hoped at least looked like a relaxed manner. Inside his heart was racing. "Yeah, we just had lunch at Arlene's and…"

"We?"

"I have a friend helping me in here with some remodeling." He gestured down at his stained and ragged shirt and jeans. "We stopped for a little lunch break," Stander could tell the policeman's ears had perked up. In case he'd seen them, Stander thought it best to share what they'd saw and heard. "When we got ready to leave and come back here, some guy roared up in his truck babbling a bunch of nonsense. Maybe he knows what the deal is with the smoke. He seemed like a guy who is, well, familiar with smoke if you know what I mean…" Stander gave him his best smile, the one he usually only flashed at liquor salesmen when he bartered with them for better pricing back in Marquette at his bar.

"That would be Barry," offered the lawman, sighing. "He does tend to smoke a lot of weed and embellish a bit from time to time."

"Sorry I couldn't be of more help. But, if you'll excuse me, I left my buddy holding a piece of drywall still in need of a few more screws. I should get back to it." Again, Stander gave him a smile and his hand. Though the cop shook it, he clearly wasn't thrilled with being blown off so quickly. He turned to leave, but only made it two steps before spinning back around.

"Are you the new owner of... this house?" Stander was pretty sure the guy was going to say Relict Mansion before catching himself.

"I am. For right now, anyway. My father passed away not long ago, and I inherited it. That's why we are here. I'm just trying to see what kind of shape the old place is in. Decide what to do with it."

"Father? I thought, I mean around here, all I've ever heard is something about a woman being the last person who lived in here. Would that have been your mom?"

"No. My father and I visited here sometimes back when I was a kid, but neither of us ever actually lived here. I imagine the small-town gossip you've heard is about my Great Aunt Madeleine. She lived here before I was even born!" Stander tried to keep his voice friendly. He knew the kinds of things people said about his aunt. He gave the man a little wave and headed back inside before the officer's voice stopped him for a second time.

"It is strange," the lawman began, half turned as if undecided which way to go. Or how much he should say. "A month or so back we had a man and woman disappear from Almore. Rumor was they may have gone off and eloped, but no one has heard from them."

"Sorry, I'm not following." Stander looked down at his hands, flushing. He knew exactly what had happened to them both, though no one would ever believe him.

"No? I thought maybe since you helped Chris Bond move away from here that you'd know where Dennis Reiner was as well. Weren't you guys all friends back in the day?"

"Chris is in rehab," Stander felt his anger rising. Was this guy fucking with him? "Until I showed up back here, no one around Almore ever offered to get him the help he obviously needed."

"Until you showed up," the phrase left hanging in the air until the cop reclaimed it. "And now I'm dealing with some weird ass love triangle, or marital quarrel, that has our local volunteer firemen taking a couple charred corpses over to the morgue. The only witness babbling about some supposed pyromaniac monster that no one else has seen. All of this high strangeness happening right as you and your friend showed up. The first people to stay here at Relict Mansion in over thirty years."

Stander was smart enough to stay quiet. Unbelievably, this time, he did. When the local chief of police turned an eye on him, Stander just shrugged. Finally offering, "If you are wondering if we had anything to do with that, please ask the folks at the diner. We were there for over an hour before your 'babbling pothead' arrived spewing that fantastic tale." Stander made quote marks in the air as he spoke.

"No need, already did," the cop offered with a sheepish smile. He seemed about to turn and head back to his marked SUV before looking back once more. "You know, when I took this job a number of years back, I inherited more than just this badge and gun. See, I also found locked away with some of my predecessor's things a thick file stamped 'Relict Mansion-Open only at the right time.' Sir, can you tell me if this is that time?"

Stander could see the doubt plain on the smalltown officer's face. The only competing expression and emotion was fear. Though both men seemed on the verge of saying more, neither said a word. The cop just nodded once before turning and retreating to his car. He waved out the driver's side window as he pulled away from the front entrance.

When he shut the front door behind him, Stander looked down at Frazier. "That was one weird fucking conversation, huh?" The dog barked once and, turning his head several times to be certain he was being followed, ran back into the library with the hidden stairway. The dog stopped at the head of the stairs as Stander jogged past him. The heavy footfalls of his boots echoing as he descended.

"Hang on, Tommy! I'm coming!"

CHAPTER TWENTY-SEVEN
IOWA/ILLINOIS BORDER - 1964

THE QUAD CITIES

Madeleine moved with almost imperial gravity as she glided down the grand staircase. She wore a well-fitted beige jumpsuit with a colorful ascot knotted at her neck. Her thick white hair pulled back in a ponytail more fitting of women less than half her age. Tim was surprised at her attire and the energetic bounce in her step. When she'd asked him to join her on a trip up to the Quad Cities, he'd assumed she was simply feeling tired and wanted some help getting around. Perhaps expecting Tim to lend her an arm here and there as needed. But as Madeleine joined him in the foyer at the bottom of the two staircases on the first floor of her mansion, it was clear to him that, as usual, she didn't really need his assistance.

"You haven't yet shared why we are taking this little trip. Does this have anything to do with why you asked me to take this particular week off from my practice in Kankakee? Or why you asked me to come for a visit without Sherry this time?" Tim wore casual clothes, as Madeleine had instructed. A pair of blue jeans and tightly laced boots of leather. His shirt long-sleeved despite the climbing temperature outside with summer just around the corner. "You know how much I hate being separated from her."

"This is not a trip suitable for a toddler barely three years old. Where we're going, and what we will be doing, will require all of your attention. Please trust me, these few days away from her will do you both good." Madeleine brushed past Tim and called out for Harold, her new gardener and groundskeeper. Asking him to pull one of her cars around to the front door. When the eager young man disappeared to retrieve the automobile, she continued. "I'm glad your trip back here went off without a hitch. It gives me faith our little destined rendezvous will kick things off as hoped." Madeleine paused, appraising Tim with eyes sparkling with life. "I'm so ready for all this to be over..."

"Are you meeting someone? Anything I should know ahead of time?" In the background, Tim could hear the rumble of her approaching car in the drive. The brakes squeaking slightly right outside the front door.

"To know? I think not. All I would say is truly be yourself and follow your instincts." Madeleine appraised him silently, her eyes roaming from head to toe. "Is there nothing you wish to bring along?"

"Bring? I still don't even know exactly where we are going. Or what we are doing..."

"Do you remember the night Aloysius and that young housekeeper, Cindy, were murdered?" Tim nodded somberly. Though, now nearly two years ago, much of that night and even the few days after were still a blur. But he'd never completely shaken the fear that he had felt that awful night. Or been able to push the image of the butchered young woman from his mind. "Do you remember what I promised you? That when the time came, I would call you back once everything was set. That time is now."

Tim opened his mouth, but shut it again when Harold entered the front door of Madeleine's grand home. Announcing the car was gassed up and waiting in the driveway. Madeleine thanked the young man before turning back to Tim.

"The hands of fate are closing, but the grip is tenuous at best. There is only so much I can do. So, I'll ask you again. Do you see nothing you wish to bring? Perhaps a weapon to... uh... defend yourself with?" Madeleine smiled mischievously, "Or defend your poor old aunt with?" She gestured about the entryway. The walls were decorated in original oil paintings, marble pillars in the far two corners of the room. One with a leafy fern spilling down its sides, the other with a bust of a longhaired woman of exotic ancestry. Hanging above the front entryway was a sword of impressive length with an intricate design stamped on it. "Does nothing compel you? The sword perhaps?" Madeleine stating the obvious.

Tim screwed up his face. "I'm a doctor. I would never raise arms against another. If we expect danger where we are going, we should alert the authorities. Have them meet us there." He walked to the front door and opened it. Madeleine's bronze colored Bentley purring in the drive.

"Very well," Madeleine said with a slight sigh. "I guess that heirloom will end up with the first child of yours that reaches adulthood." She started for the door still held open for her by Tim.

"You mean Sherry? I'm not sure that a girl is going to have any more interest in brandishing that sword than I do." Tim followed behind his aunt, closing the front door behind him before hurrying to open the passenger side door on the grand automobile.

"We'll see, won't we? I'm positive there is much still to be determined as she gets older. Trials and tribulations, isn't that what they say?" Tim nodded, unsure how to reply when a new voice called out from behind. Turning, Tim saw Kelly approaching the car with the golden staff topped with the odd Ankh in hand. Wordlessly, Madeleine motioned to the backseat. Kelly opening the backdoor and laying it across the leather seats before returning inside the house.

"Why are we bringing that? Surely you aren't thinking of selling it." Tim was aghast! The long gold rod was the last Egyptian treasure his father Emery had discovered.

"Don't be ridiculous. This is likely the last time it will ever even leave this place again." Madeleine was frowning. The change in her demeanor since exiting the house was palpable. "I'm just bringing it along for balance. It will likely help me move things along," she said as she sat in the front seat.

"If your balance is going, I wish you'd let me help you." Tim slammed shut the door of the Bentley and made his way around to the front of the car.

"Help me?" Madeleine watched Tim round the hood of her car. "Bringing him is starting to look like a mistake. Why did I ever doubt myself?"

"Did you say something?" Tim asked as he opened his door and sat in the driver's seat. He dropped the car in gear, driving slowly down the long driveway.

"No, nothing. We should just get moving." Then, turning to face her window she sighed, adding under her breath, "Let's just finish this last bit of unpleasantness."

Though only the third time Tim had ever driven her Bentley, he had no trouble navigating the luxurious automobile. Heavy and stable, it practically drove itself. Tim occasionally spun the dial on the grand automobile's radio, pausing at different stations when he heard a song he liked. Sporadically singing along when a song from his new favorite group, The Beatles, came across one of the stations. Their latest, *"Can't Buy Me Love,"* so infectious he even caught Madeleine tapping her feet along to the beat as they rode north together up a two-lane highway for the next hour or so. The road dipped and swerved as it hugged the curvature of the Mississippi River. The route one that Tim had driven many times in the past when he'd visited his aunt.

Occasionally, rocky bluffs topped with thinning trees soared high above their heads on one side of the road. On the opposite side of the meandering highway, fledgling crops of newly sprouted corn and beans. Small family farms with meadows of grazing cattle and endlessly chewing goats dotting the inexhaustible waves of green the asphalt road split. Their towering grain silos, no different than the smokestacks of industry, obscene in the sky. The endless fields interrupted in spots by small clusters of trees huddled tightly together like confused survivors of a shipwreck. Lost and stranded, surrounded by a raging sea of green.

As they closed in on the clustered four towns that was their destination, Madeleine began giving directions. Her instruction ending when they reached the downtown area of Rock Island. Tim parked the eye-catching automobile near a series of dilapidated factories that crowded the river bank.

Madeleine insisted they bring the priceless golden Egyptian scepter with them as they exited the car. She strolled confidently with it in hand as if it were merely a common walking stick as she led Tim past one desolate factory. The empty building surrounded by a chain link fence peppered with "No Trespassing" and "Danger" signs. After crossing a few mostly deserted streets, and one long empty parking lot paved with weeds as much as concrete, they emerged at the head of an alley. It ended at the back of a building sprayed with colorful graffiti. On either side of the alley were aged factories or perhaps warehouses. Devoid of any visible activity inside or outside made it hard to tell what, if anything, the massive buildings once held.

The odd couple only walked a few yards inside the heavily shaded and darkened alley before Madeliene stopped. "Stay here," she commanded Tim, before continuing another fifteen feet or so deeper down the middle of the deserted alleyway. Her back turned to Tim; she pulled a yellow rose from her pocket wrapped protectively in green tissue paper. She tenderly unwrapped the delicate flower and laid it reverently on the ground. Whispering under her breath, "Sorry I had to leave you here, Cindy. It was the only way…"

She spun on her heel and ignored the question plain on Tim's face. "Come with me," she waved him forward. "Let us shelter under that awning by this building's back entrance." Madeleine pointed to a recessed doorway tucked in amongst the black of the alley. "I suspect from there we should have quite the view."

"View of what? It doesn't look like this alley," Tim paused, "or even this entire industrial park has much of anything going on." But Tim did as he was told. Trailing behind Madeleine as she melted into the shadowed opening.

"Stay still and silent as the grave." Madeleine pulled Tim farther into the doorway until the poorly painted steel door touched their backs and they were both well-hidden. "No matter what you see." Above their heads a ratty canvas canopy hung uselessly from its rusty, broken frame.

Long minutes passed uneventfully. The waiting did not seem to bother Madeleine. She leaned nonchalantly against the hard, steel door, the long golden scepter held in hand. Just as Tim was about to complain, she pressed one finger to her lips while pointing with another.

Maybe twenty yards from where they sheltered, only a few feet off the ground, a badly deteriorated metal plate or cover protruded slightly from the side of one of the alley's bordering buildings. Tim recognized the rusted, hinged door near the foundation of the warehouse as having once been a coal chute. Still commonly seen in older buildings but no longer in use, most were now ignored and rarely ever opened in the preceding decades. Yet this one shuddered and began to move, swinging open just wide enough along its bottom for something on the other side to crawl out.

It did.

Tim watched transfixed as two badly emaciated hands and arms tentatively snaked through the smallish opening. Just behind the leathery arms, a shiny head appeared next. Hairless, the features of the face were badly withered, eyes a milky yellow. Taut skin pulled so tight that the ridges of bone making up the skull threatened to rupture the thin tissue covering it. When the thing twisted its bony neck, Tim thought he even spied patches of bare bone erupting from splits along the base of the skull. He cast a quick glance over at Madeleine to make sure she was seeing the same thing and to gauge her reaction. She watched placidly with an expression of slight reproach. Clearly, she had been waiting for this morbid visitor to make an appearance.

The thing moved gracelessly as it pulled itself free of the tight opening. The iron coal chute cap clanking loudly as it closed once more. As the gaunt specter slowly pulled itself to full height – straightening and standing beside the covering it had just emerged from – Tim was shocked by the decomposed state of the creature. Clearly once a man, the skin tone was indiscernible with so much of it missing. Globs of a viscous black oozing and dripping like warm tar from the body. Though clothed in poorly fitting modern garments, it wore no shoes or socks on its skeletal feet, shuffling awkwardly a few steps away from the large building it exited. The black pants it wore were hitched and tied around the waist, the button-down shirt across its shoulders wasn't fastened. Glistening white bone showed through in various places. One missing patch of flesh exposing the clavicle, others revealing ribs with sinewy strands stretched between them. Like the dripping globs, most of the flesh still clinging to the bones was rotting and falling free. Tim noted the smear of black around the edges of the coal chute opening. Obviously, this ghoulish fiend had entered and exited via the opening at least several times in the past. Losing a bit more of itself with each passing.

As Tim and Madeleine watched, hidden and silent from their hiding place, the living corpse began to shuffle towards the alleyway. It wobbled across the cracked sidewalk like a windblown shopping cart with a jammed wheel. Haltingly, but not entirely directionless. A sewer opening directly in front of it, the zombie-like apparition clumsily lowered itself above the metal grate that covered the gutter's opening. There, it paused.

Hovering motionless, waiting. Perhaps listening.

Tim didn't see the blade until it suddenly flashed in the shadowed light of the alley. With surprising swiftness, the fiend grabbed at something underneath the sidewalk. Its shrunken arm and hand twisting past the sewer grate. Whatever it grabbed began to pull and move desperately, the thing seeming barely able to maintain its hold on what it had latched onto. Terrified screams echoed shrilly from somewhere below. Tim barely had time to react before he saw the flash of the blade as it plunged down at whatever the thing held. The hideous ghoul hacking at what it held in its grip.

Terrified, Tim shrank back in the shadows that hid him. His head swirling and the edges of his vision darkening like the edges of an old photograph. The sudden violence, shocking. He was sure he would black out, but somehow, he didn't.

The revolting horror hastily pulled its arm and hand from the sewer grate. The bowed blade, now dripping crimson, gripped tightly in its claw like fingers. Red gore, mixing with the thing's gooey black rot, left splotches of both colors splattered on the sidewalk like melted ice cream dripping down the arm of a child. Its face, slimy and pasty with lips twitching in anticipation, bared teeth surrounded by rotting grey gums. A black tongue lapped at the warm blood running down the blade as the thing lumbered backwards until its back hit the building it first emerged from. Shadows helping mask the disturbing scene.

Tim could hear confused shouting and screams echoing from out of the sewer opening. His mind flashed back to the mummy he'd watched rise and kill back in Cairo two years prior. This blood thirsty creature of rotted flesh nearly its twin and also propelled by an equal ferocity. Tim suddenly felt very small and useless. He'd somehow been able to dismiss his experience back in Egypt. Though deep down knowing what he had witnessed in the bowels of that ancient tomb had somehow been real, he'd denied it in his own way. Rationalizing he'd been weakened and distraught, pushing from his mind the implications. Chalking it up, at best, as some long-forgotten knowledge better left buried and forgotten. Nothing an academic and educated man of medicine could rationalize. But now it was as if everything he'd believed, learned, and lived for was once again swallowed whole by these monsters.

His world turned upside down...

"What are you waiting for?" Madeleine whispering in Tim's ear, "Go end this now. Destroy it."

Tim, unable to tear his eyes from the dead that walked, shook his head no. "This isn't... this can't be real. I don't... I don't want to be here anymore." He slowly sank lower until he was sitting on his haunches like a baseball catcher, never leaving the comfort of the solid wall at his back. "I don't understand any of this." He tore his eyes from the macabre scene and looked up at Madeleine, his voice splintering with fear. "What is happening right now? What does all this mean?"

Madeleine shook her head with a face so outraged it dispatched any semblance of manners. "It means I never should have wavered. Or doubted what I knew," Madeleine's lips twitched with disgust. "You just got lucky in that tomb under the sands of Saqqara. You aren't the one any more than Emery was. And Sherry, your only child, doesn't seem any more likely. Though, it will be years before I will know for sure..." Madeleine paused, her eyes wavering with uncertainty. "I was so sure when I rooted my way up inside this family tree. Am I simply off a generation?" She looked down at Tim who didn't seem to be listening. His eyes once more riveted on the undead in the alley. Madeleine sighed heavily before propelling herself out of the doorway. Stepping out into the shadowed light of the dead-end alleyway, the long golden scepter in hand.

A finality in her step.

Hissing, the undead fiend brandished the curved weapon menacingly at Madeleine as she began to advance. Two steps later an undeniable recognition filled the creature's watery eyes, quickly followed by a look of absolute horror. Slimy like rotting seafood and smelling twice as bad, the thing lunges for the rusted iron coal chute door. Madeleine's footsteps entangling with the banging of the door as it scrabbles for reentry. Desperately crashing through the opening, abject terror clear on its rotting face as it ran from her.

CHAPTER TWENTY-EIGHT

THE CRACK WAS LOUD in the tiny coal room when the plywood split. Though warped and weakened from months of weathering seeping past the temporary wood cover, the screws used to hold it at the top held firm. Jeff felt the sheet of plywood shudder once at his back and turned just in time to see the bowing wood splinter apart and cave inward. The impact sending him sprawling backwards and landing not ten feet from where Howard was laid out. The gun he was cleaning knocked from his hands and skipping across the concrete floor. Stunned, Jeff looked up just in time to see what came through the new opening.

It was a nightmare.

Blood dripped from its chin, and blind fear poured from its eyes. A decomposing corpse sodden in black rot landed on Jeff's chest. The wind knocked out of him by the fall, Jeff was unable to draw a breath, much less use it to scream like his horrified brain commanded. Rank and foul, the monster that rushed from the opening in the wall raged like a desperate beast on top of him. Barely glancing down at Jeff's face before spreading its bloody lips and opening its putrid mouth.

Widely.

Jeff had no time to contemplate the undead ghoul riding his chest. What it was, how it stirred with life, or why it had suddenly crashed into the tiny coal room. Without air in his lungs, Jeff had no time to holler, beg, or cry. With eyes wide and both pupils blown out, he watched as the rotting mouth of grey closed over his own features. He felt the dull teeth at his cheeks as the abomination tore into his face. The rancid mouth covering his own, ripping off both of Jeff's lips and gnashing his gums in one frenzied bite. When he tried to look up at his attacker, he only saw the ends of its two thumbs and blackened nails as they plunged into his eyeballs. Jeff heard as much felt his eyeballs implode inside his head. Darkness rescuing him from the horrid scene of his disfigurement...

Madeleine had been just steps behind when the fetid wraith had thrown itself desperately at the wood barrier. She had bent low and crawled in after the thing, more concerned with keeping her tan jumpsuit clean than the speed of her arrival below. With some effort, she pulled herself from the opening, jumping down the last few feet before reaching back through the opening for her golden scepter. As she casually brushed herself off, she watched her quarry rage on top of one man, while another man lay covered in blood just feet away. A dark hole in his chest.

THUMP!

The end of the long staff struck once on the concrete floor. Madeleine, letting it rise and fall, still clutched in her hand. Behind her, Tim had followed and was now climbing down from the coal chute opening as well. She ignored her nephew, eyes focused on the feasting dead at her feet. It had stopped the frenzied assault when she'd tapped the rod of gold with the Ankh symbol on the floor.

The monstrosity's face broke. The desperation, fear, and viciousness replaced by a look of timid remorse and regret. It pulled out the two thumbs it had jammed deeply inside the eye sockets of the man it straddled. The body under it now ignored as it lay quivering and convulsing in obvious death throes. The eyeless victim's white teeth clacking together in spasm so hard that several broke and splintered until the seizure passed.

And the man.

"Nefertem." Madeleine addressing the thing she'd chased through the coal chute, "son of Ptah. To see you reduced to this gives me no pleasure." Tim, now free of the coal chute he'd climbed down, stood behind his aunt and surveyed the gruesome scene. His first inclination to rush over to the bloody bodies and let his medical training take over. But he was startled and stopped dead in his tracks when he heard the names of Nefertem and Ptah, two figures so prominent in Egyptian mythology, vocalized half a world away. But the rest of the language Madeleine spoke was unrecognizable to him.

"At one time I might have considered you a peer. A rival, even. But now?" Though Tim didn't understand the words being spoken, it was clear the ghoul at her feet did. Sliding off the disfigured dead, clearly submissive as it pulled itself gracelessly along the concrete floor, stopping at Madeleine's feet, head bowed. "Hiding this from me and the others." Madeleine lifting the gold scepter with the odd Ankh-like symbol at the top. "Selfishly claiming the power within for yourself. Tricking religious fanatics like Imhotep into trading places with you for a promised life eternal. The fool not understanding until too late that the eternity you offered would be spent locked in your old body. You left him trapped in your discarded flesh at the bottom of your tomb. His life sacrificed so you can remain here eternally. Untethered of the responsibility Ptah expected of you."

"Yet, even after all that, you could have still been forgiven. But you chose to run through this feeble world like a fire!" Tim could hear the edge in her voice, the tone rising in intensity to match the piercing look in her eyes. "Practically yelling 'Look at me! Look at me! Look at me!' the entire time." Madeleine laughed joylessly. "Masquerading first as Imhotep, pretending to advance these people under the guise of wisdom while playing at being human. Keeping your part of this world locked in eternal combat, sewing seeds of chaos to hide yourself within. Loitering through time like a petulant child rather than doing the actual chores required." She shook her head pitifully. "We are too close now for these games of yours to continue..."

The undead thing groveled at her feet, supplicating itself in gestures and appearing to look for mercy. At first, Tim couldn't understand why it didn't respond vocally until he spied the wiry strings hanging at what was left of its neck. The rotting throat clearly missing any of the tools needed for sound and speech. As Madeleine continued talking in her queer manner, Tim made his way cautiously over to where the blinded and near faceless man had been butchered by the ghoulish creature. Checking if the man was truly beyond help.

"...what has all this resulted in? Once the shroud was removed from the body you imprisoned Imhotep in, your own eternal protection ended as you knew it would. That was why you hid your tomb so well. Hoping no one would ever discover your betrayal and secret. But I never gave up. I may not have known exactly where Ptah intended your history and story to be carved in rock, but I had a pretty good idea. And once the location finally came to light, I stripped away all its true value. Secreting this rod and the shroud back here to my lands where I knew you would have to come for them. I just hope you weren't able to bamboozle any other lost fools with your supposed religion and 'prayers' while hiding yourself away in this place. Tricking another vain man into following the same pathway Imhotep so foolishly stumbled blindly down."

Madelaine switched languages, addressing Tim in English. "I wouldn't bother with that one. He is beyond gone now."

Tim didn't look up as he confirmed the veracity of her statement. "I have to make sure. If there is even a chance I can save him, I have to try."

"Believe me, if you knew who that man was. Or, I guess in your case, who he will turn out to be, I doubt you'd waste even a moment on him." Madeleine, still speaking in English, added, "I believe your efforts will be better suited saving the other man." She gestured toward the much older and smaller man with the gunshot wound. Though his face was nearly as white as the short-cropped hair on his head, Tim crawled over to him on his hands and knees.

"Doubt it. Looks like he's been gone for a while now..." But Tim bent over him just the same. As he ripped the man's shirt open, he heard Madeleine begin speaking once more in the language he didn't recognize.

"You've felt the spoil and rot eating you from the inside. The rapid decay only temporarily sated by the consumption of the same organs that continued to fail you. Of course, I knew this punishment would be severe. But I did not expect that body to fail you so quickly. By the time you broke into my home, just weeks after the shroud was lifted off of Imhotep, I knew this was all going to end badly for you. You traveled to this land under the guise of diplomacy, rubbing shoulders with local politicians before understanding the hunger would ultimately consume you. Once I realized how bad off you were, I tried to point the local law enforcement officials in the right direction. Hoping they would end all this nonsense before I had to become involved. I even left my housekeeper's body, the girl you senselessly slaughtered the night you came for the shroud, right outside the front door of where I knew you hid. Yet, somehow, the clue was overlooked. I started to hope I might have been mistaken about how badly degraded you were becoming. But then the other bodies began to show up. The men in the neighboring building, the little girl you callously enticed into the drainage pipe down by the riverside park, and, more recently, the old woman you surprised under the torrent of a rainstorm. Torturing that poor cat to lure her to you. Only to devour her soft parts raw in a back alley like a feral dog. Indeed, had that garbage truck not shown up when it did, there likely would have been even more bodies after her. But, now that I realize just how far gone you really are, I know the time has come to end all this foolishness."

Tim watched the wretched being out of the corner of his eye as he feverishly worked. Whatever Madeleine was saying clearly being understood. The thing remaining passive and still.

"You have suffered and ate at this rancid trough long enough. Time for you to move along. I'd call this a mercy, if I didn't know your next conversation will be with Ptah." Madeleine grinned slightly as she raised the long golden scepter. "Tell your daddy I said hello…" With that, she plunged the end of the rod through the back of the rotting corpse at her feet. The end of it striking the cement after piercing through. The rod of gold hummed; a deep tone felt as much as heard reverberating throughout the chamber. The waves of sound shaking the rotted flesh as it shuddered convulsively at her feet while a bright, blueish flash began erupting at the same time like a bolt of lightning. When it dissipated, though lifeless and unmoving, the body used by Nefertem, once just a very human high priest named Imhotep, began to rapidly decay. In less than a minute, almost nothing remained. The body dissolving to what it would have if it had been left alone after Imhotep's true death nearly 5,000 years ago.

Nothing.

Tim, stunned, staggered to his feet. "My god! That light! Just like what happened in that tomb in Egypt!" He walked on shaky legs. His head shaking back and forth in disbelief as he joined his Aunt Madeleine. "I don't know what happened. Or any of what was just said. But you somehow tamed that… that mad beast or monster of a man. It seemed to be practically begging for the release you gave it."

"Didn't it?" All Madeleine replied.

"You obviously knew what or who that was. Are you going to share what just happened? Am I ever to understand your ways?" Madeleine looked over at Tim, a slight twinkle in her eyes.

"You? Not yet, at least. Maybe sometime after Sherry grows up a bit more. We'll just have to see, won't we?" Then, as if the thought just popped into her head, she continued. "Maybe what you need is a new wife." Madeleine switched tongues then, briefly speaking to herself in the same dialect as earlier. "And quickly before that faltering manhood of yours gives out completely..."

Tim stammered, "A wife? Oh no, I'm not interested in ever getting married again. Are you kidding? After what happened with Lucy at the end. No thank you!" Tim paused briefly before adding, "Besides, where would I find the time to hunt such elusive quarry?"

"Sometimes the answer is in the question, yes?" Madeleine looked at Tim out of the side of her eye. "Perhaps we should find the nearest hospital where we can anonymously drop this one off." She pointed a finger at the unmoving form of the man with the white crewcut soaked in blood.

"Too late. He is already gone. I checked."

"I believe you are mistaken. I am certain he yet stirs with life. Please double check. He still has much to do..." Tim started to debate, but knew it was useless. He sighed and walked back over just as the man coughed slightly. A small spray of red blood tinging his pale lips.

"My god, did you just bring that man back to life?" Tim bent back over the man, working to help revive the man he'd judged completely gone just minutes before.

"Don't be ridiculous. When a doctor, one of your peers, brings someone back to life on an operating table, is it the doctor? Or the tools and learning acquired over their lifetime?" Madeleine smiled mischievously as she casually tossed her white hair over one shoulder.

Tim looked across at her, then down at the small cluster of ash left behind by the dissolving corpse after Madeleine set it free. He couldn't stop himself from asking the question he blurted out. "Have you ever made a ghoul like that before, Aunt Madeleine?"

"Funny you should ask that just now," she said, winking.

CHAPTER TWENTY-NINE
PRESENT DAY

STANDER STOPPED AT THE long table, the lone piece of furniture in the small underground room deep below Relict Mansion. The burning lamp beside the folded clothes of the vanishing corpse still lit and flickering. Secrist was leaning against the door they'd seen the crawling dead behind. Though his gun was still in hand, it was clear he didn't feel he was in any immediate jeopardy. Nothing seemed to stir from the long passage beyond the closed doorway. "Jesus, what took you so long? Is Frazier alright?"

"Sorry. Would you believe we just had our first visitor? Can you guess who it was?" Stander reached for the clothes and began to separate the different articles of clothing. A white shirt yellowed with age, a dusty suit jacket with matching pants that may at one time have been black. The entire suit, including a vest, faded and creased with age.

"Was it a naked dead guy asking for his clothes back?" Secrist gestured to the table where Stander pawed the outfit. "Seems likely a dead streaker would eventually get cold."

Stander snorted once, half a smile on his lips. "No. It was the local police, just one guy. He asked if I saw the smoke nearby. Questioned if we'd seen anything 'strange' today." Stander gesturing the quotation marks in the air with both hands. "I got rid of him," he added, pulling apart the folded vest. As he did, a long-chained pocket watch tumbled from one pocket, clunking on the table.

"You didn't tell him about mister..."

"Aloysius Leroux." Stander read the name engraved on the back of the pocket watch, then wiped at the expensive looking timepiece with the bottom of his black t-shirt. "Aloysius? Why does that name seem..." Stander visibly blanched, nearly dropping the watch.

"What? Did you know the guy?" Secrist stayed against the door, occasionally placing his ear to the wood at his back. No more sounds came from the passage at his back.

"Aloysius Leroux was the name of my Great Aunt Madeleine's third husband." Stander looked up at Secrist. "I never met him. He died years before I was born."

"Was he one of your great aunt's husbands that died in this house?" Secrist recalling his conversation with Stander when they'd pulled up to Relict Mansion for the first time over a month ago.

"Yeah. All four of her husbands died on these grounds."

"You think that naked dude laid out on the table was him?"

"Couldn't be," said Stander, shaking his head.

"Why?" Secrist asked. "Maybe this hidden staircase we discovered originally led down into a subterranean family crypt."

"He would have died back in the sixties. The guy we saw," Stander met Secrist's eyes, "you said so yourself, looked like he just died."

"Are we really going to continue to pretend we are shocked by any of this craziness circling all around us? Maybe we should just dispatch with all the pretense of normalcy from here on out. It is becoming clear to me that there is way more going on around us than we understand." Secrist tossed a thumb over his shoulder towards the door at his back. "Starting with whatever the hell the thing behind this door is."

Stander let the pocket watch slip from his hand, the dusty chain twirling around his fingers as it slid down. "Agreed. Let's see what answers the slithering thing back there has for us." He left the oil lamp on the table as he picked back up his lit flashlight. "Ready," he added with a nod.

"Alright. Just be sure to point that light down at the ground this time. I don't want anything else rising up out of the earth that I can't see." Secrist stepped back from the doorway, then threw the wooden door wide before putting his free hand over his nose and mouth. "God, what an awful smell!"

Stander, a few feet away and saved from the worst of the stench, pulled his t-shirt up to cover the lower part of his face. "Bet you wish you hadn't taken off your mask when we went to lunch."

"I'll live," came Secrist's abbreviated reply. Both men straining to see down the black of the tunnel as Stander swept the beam of his flashlight across the floor of the passage. It quickly came to rest just feet from the now open door.

"The fuck..." Stander could think of nothing more to say.

What was left of one badly decomposed arm was stretched towards the doorway. The rotting hand writhing like a dying insect before becoming completely still. Stander let the light from his battery-operated torch glide slowly up the arm, both men transfixed by the gruesome appendage. At the shoulder, the arm had mostly separated, only a few strands of rapidly decaying flesh clinging to the joint. Stander's light illuminated the head next, a withered and tortured expression barely visible in the troubled features of the face. Both men drawn to the agonized look.

Secrist was closest, and he squatted next to the rotting thing first, his eyes wide and troubled. "This has to be the same thing that jumped up at us earlier. But now it is literally falling apart." Stander, kneeling beside him, nodded in agreement.

"And what? Did it get splashed in acid or something? How could this thing have been alive and moving?" Stander peered closer, both men now just feet from the putrid face. Bits of it shriveling and coming free, wiggling down like burning wax melting under intense heat. "The flesh is dripping off and soaking into the packed earth of the floor." Stander screwed his face up. The sight and smell both vile and disgusting.

"AAAAAAAHH! AAaaah..." Baring wet teeth, the lower jaw unhinged and fell as the thing's last scream echoed down the dim tunnel like madness running from logic. Both men recoiled as if struck, the stunning outburst from the dissolving body utterly unexpected. Stander fell backwards in shock, his flashlight going dark. Ahead of them, the long passageway seemed to blacken and shrink. Leaving them feeling very vulnerable, mere creatures of insignificance disappearing inch by inch. The encroaching darkness a monster in itself and threatening to swallow both men whole as they scrambled back to the room with the lit oil lamp.

"Fuck, fuck, fuck, fuck, fuck..." Stander paced and shook his arms and hands out. "That might have just scared every last fuck I'd ever say in the future right the fuck out of me!" He began to rub his hands up and down his bare arms trying to calm the prickling goosebumps on them.

"I fucking doubt that." Secrist, only slightly less shaken, seemed to recover first. His decades of police work helping him reclaim the rocketing of his pulse. "But yeah, that... that got me, too."

After a minute of salvaging what was left of their dignity, and jokingly checking they hadn't shit themselves, both men gathered their lights. Stander's flashlight worked just fine. During the hasty retreat after his startled reaction to the scream, he'd clumsily managed to flip off the power switch. This time Secrist held his own flashlight in one hand and the gun in the other.

By the time their courage matched their curiosity, and they headed back into the passage, the body they'd ran from was nearly all bone. Puddles of what appeared to be dissolving flesh pooling in low places along the ground. The decay unrelenting in the darkened silence of the underground tunnel.

"Where is the rest of the body?" Secrist, his eyes trained to spot what was out of place. "I only see one arm, the head, and the ribcage. Where is everything else?" Both men began to widen their search. Gradually drawn deeper into the black abyss, their lights sweeping back and forth along the ground. Both noting the path had a gradual incline. Each step taking them slightly higher in elevation.

"Found something," Stander waved Secrist over with the swing of his light. "Is that a leg bone?" Both men now thirty feet down the passageway.

"Yeah, looks like the femur," Secrist bent over it for a closer look. Bits of rotting flesh still clinging in places to the thigh, pools of puss-like fluid surrounding the bone. He lifted his eyes and light, spying more clustered white bones farther down. Standing, he added, "I think there is more over here. Let's follow this path of body parts and see where it leads."

Stander trailed behind him as Secrist began making his way from one disgusting pile of rotting flesh and bone to the next. Walking slowly up the passage, tracing the path, trying to identify the body parts left behind. The air clearing and becoming more breathable the farther they went. A slight breeze helping flush the stench away from their noses. As each gruesome discovery was made, it became clear the parts were all from one body. And all were what was missing from the thing that had scrabbled at the door at the opposite end of the tunnel. Back where their little underground hike had begun.

"What are we seeing here? Was someone hacking pieces off what was at the door? Was it trying to escape its killer?" Stander had remained uncharacteristically silent during the morbid trek. His thoughts collating around similar experiences he'd had in the past. What he and Secrist had recently experienced together back in Michigan. What had chased he and his friends back when they were kids. One of his best friends slaughtered only miles from Relict Mansion.

"I don't think so." Secrist had slid easily back into his detective role. He may have retired a little early when he'd taken Stander's generous job offer, but, before that, he'd spent his entire career as a cop. Even his adopted father had been a policeman and detective. "There are no gashes on any of the bones or any signs of a chemical solvent strong enough to dissolve meat that quickly."

"Well, what then?" Up ahead of them, he could see a light. Though only a pinprick to begin with, the spot grew bigger and brighter with every step they took. Both moving from dissolving body part to dissolving body part. The farther they went, the smaller the finds.

"Did we decide to stop kidding ourselves that any of this makes sense?" Secrist looked up, acknowledging the light ahead of them that Stander pointed out. It looked like they'd made it to another entrance down into the tunnel. Yellow sunlight streaming in maybe one hundred yards away. The trail of body parts gone cold, they walked towards the light.

"I stopped thinking any of this was real when I heard you use the word 'fucking' after that creeping corpse scared the shit out us." Stander looked over at Secrist with a smirk. "I don't know if I've ever heard you use that word before."

"It is my new job environment. You're a bad influence on me." The smell of fresh air beckoned, and their pace quickened, both wanting to leave the horrid tunnel. "Anyway, from what I can see from the path it took and all it left behind, I think pieces were literally just falling off it. We saw how it rotted right before our eyes, right? I think that started earlier. Maybe our guy from the table..."

"Aloysius. I guess that guy from the table must have been my Great Aunt Madeleine's third husband after all." Stander, dropped his eyes briefly in thought. "He was covered with that weird ass cloth like it was some kind of burial shroud. Maybe I should check that out more closely." He looked back up at Secrist as they walked out the back entrance of the passage that had started under Relict Mansion. "Maybe the answer to how, or what happened, could be discovered with some good old-fashioned science?"

Secrist tucked his gun back into the holster at his belt. Then used that hand to shield his eyes from the afternoon sun breaking through the trees above. They'd exited into a thickly forested area full of singing birds and buzzing bugs. A trickling stream of clear water draining into a small lake several hundred yards away from where they stood. "Maybe. If that's true it could explain what happened. We pulled the shroud, your Great Uncle Aloysius wakes from the dead and rambles down this same tunnel. Probably pretty pissed off when he bumped into that couple. When he tried to return home or whatever, he couldn't make it all the way."

"Fell apart at the seams, so it seems." Stander chuckled briefly before stopping dead in his tracks. He looked up at the blue sky, then down at the nearby lake before his eyes fell to the babbling brook of hurrying water near his feet. The sound peaceful and tranquil. Familiar. He turned and looked back at where they'd exited. The clandestine entrance hidden among the lush greenery and trees of the woods. A slight breeze, cloying, tussled his longish hair... All at once, Stander was hit with an overwhelming sense of déjà vu.

It was the fragrant honeysuckle, still part of the sweetest breaths he'd ever drawn, that reached out and touched him. Touched Stander deep inside the hidden place where he alone tended his secret garden. That gated part inside where the best and worst of each of us is cultivated with tender care until we dare show the rest of the world. His own hidden crop of love and hate, of shame and pride, of accomplishment and regret. His oasis. His hell. Where no one was welcomed. Yet, there he found her once more. It was Izzy, or was it Liz? No, no it was Izzy. He'd not thought of her since... since...

How had he forgotten Izzy!

In an instant, he was filled with a myriad of conflicting memories as a tidal wave of emotions rolled unchecked inside. It was like being grabbed by a rip current, tugging at him and pulling him into deep waters.

"Aw, man, Tommy... Aw, man... I need... I gotta sit down." Stander lurched for a downed tree, hurriedly sitting on a layer of soft green moss, his head spinning.

"Are you going to be sick? Was it something in the air back in that tunnel?" Concern was etched on Secrist's face as he stepped to his friend. "You didn't ingest anything back there, did you?" Stander waved an annoyed hand back and forth in the air. The classic sign for just give me a bit. After a couple minutes, Stander periodically looking around himself at the surrounding wilderness, he met the eyes of his best friend.

"Izzy."

"What?" Secrist bent closer, "Are you dizzy? Going to be sick?"

"Not dizzy. I said Izzy. Izzy was the name of my first real girlfriend. We used to meet pretty much right here. At this lake." Stander pointed to the glorified pond that bordered this side of his great aunt's property. A wide swath of bright green pond scum covering much of the water's surface. Dragonflies, with clear wings and elongated bodies, mixing in the air with the mud dauber wasps hurrying to build their nests. Among the rippling waves, turtle and frog heads occasionally punctured the surface, blinking slowly before diving below the surface again. "We were just kids when we first met. Maybe ten or eleven years of age. We'd swim together, climb trees, and make up little games to play."

"Well, isn't that sweet. We just got the living crap scared out of us, and you want to reminisce about puppy love?" Secrist waved his hand dismissively in the air. "Did she live around here?"

"That's just it. I have no idea where she lived. I don't... I don't think, or remember, ever asking her. Or even talking about her family. Outside of an occasional visit with my dad, I usually only stayed here with my Great Aunt Madeleine once a year during the summertime. Really for just a handful of weeks at most. Anytime I was lonely or bored, I'd come down and swim in that lake. Izzy was usually already here or would come shortly after. But, every time she came and went, it was from right here." Stander gestured back where they'd emerged from the hidden tunnel.

"What happened? Did you lose track of her after everything went down with your friends?" Secrist was careful to omit any mention of the horror and trauma Stander went through when one of his childhood best friends was killed right before his eyes not far from where they now were. "Guess what they say is true. You never forget your first love."

"But I did. I really did completely forget her. I couldn't tell you the last time I ever even thought about Izzy. It's like all this time there's been a shroud pulled over my memories of her. Obscuring everything we did together. Hiding the love or destiny I thought we'd have together..." Stander paused, lost in thought. "I feel like I've just been sleepwalking through my entire adult life. Like the walking dead, but more pathetic because I know the way I've been living is all wrong."

"Oh, come on, Russ. Since when did you become so sentimental? I can't count the number of women you've had in your life just since I've known you. I always thought it was on account of what happened to your wife that you never took any of those relationships seriously. At least as far as you let on." Secrist moved closer, sitting beside Stander on the downed log. "Well, except for Liz. Ever since all that happened with her back in Michigan, I don't think you've even been on a date."

"Liz, yeah see, that has me all fucked up, too. She just waltzed into my life that day. But it was like we'd known each other forever. And she," Stander looked up sheepishly at Secrist. "You're going to think I'm crazy, I know. But I swear, now that I remember Izzy, they had the same eyes."

"Give me a break, Russ. You just said you and this Izzy were like eleven or twelve years old. I highly doubt you really remember much of what she looked like. Much less the color, shape, or expression in her..." Secrist paused, Stander didn't seem to be listening and lost in his own thoughts. "In her eyes. Uh, hello! Earth to Stander." He waved a hand across Stander's face.

"It wasn't... it wasn't just when we were kids." Stander stood and began pacing. Secrist knew him well enough to know Stander's mind was working overtime. "That... that's right. It's like it's all coming back to me now."

Stander stopped walking and looked down at the stream that he knew emptied into the lake. Two memories intertwining until he couldn't tell them apart. He was with Izzy, or maybe it was Liz? They were bent over a stream just like this one. He'd been shy and nervous, but he'd reached playfully for her hand under the cool of the rushing water. An oak leaf had rushed past, twirling and twisting as it glided across the surface of the gurgling creek. He'd been stalling, unsure of the right words to say so he'd watched the leaf catch on a partially submerged stick. It spun around several times before finally dislodging itself, hurrying farther down the water. He'd turned to Izzy then, trying to think of a cool way to say he loved her. That he wanted to be with her. The "BE" spelled out in big cursive lettering like it is in a big, fancy leatherbound copy of a family bible. The kind always left out to be seen but rarely, if ever, opened and really seen. Just a family prop.

Stander remembered he'd been with Izzy for the first time that night. In the biblical sense...

"I'd never tell anyone I was coming here ahead of time, but I did come back here. It was only a three-hour drive from Kankakee down to here. When I turned sixteen and got my license, I would drive over and see Izzy when my dad would be gone at medical conferences, or off completing all those 'continued learning' seminars and classes he was always taking. I had my own car and I'd spend the day here with her. A few times even spending the night, though never at my great aunt's house. We'd just stay in my car all night listening to music and talking. Or, if it was a warm clear night, we'd spend it under the stars together."

"After what had happened with your friends, I'm surprised you weren't too scared to come back here." Secrist was still seated on the felled tree.

"I think Izzy helped me with all that. Like, her love was what helped me conquer all my fears. Helped me believe in myself." Stander stopped pacing and met Secrist's eyes. "I know that sounds corny or whatever. But she helped me get my head on straight. After what had happened to Brian, I had a lot of really dark moments. If she hadn't been here for me, I don't know what I might have done to myself back then."

"What happened to this Izzy? She just, as they say, drift away like leaves in the fall? Or was it you chasing your own river of dreams?"

"I don't know. I'm only just now remembering any of this. Maybe more will come back to me later. But I can tell you this much. I never met any of Izzy's family, not that most of us ever do meet the family of our first ever real girlfriend or boyfriend at that age. And the only place we ever met was here, where we are right now. And she'd always be walking from over that way..." Stander turned and pointed back in the direction of the hidden passageway.

"The underground tunnel that leads directly into the bowels of Relict Mansion itself."

EPILOGUE
IOWA/ILLINOIS BORDER - 1965

THE QUAD CITIES

THE DIGGER GASHED THE earth repeatedly. The rise and fall of his tool in the flickering of the overhead parking lot lights nearly as fevered as the one who yielded it. The lone man ignored his sweat drenched brow as he labored beneath the unflinching eyes of the abandoned factory and warehouse's darkened windows around him. Continuing to widen the hole he'd only just started to dig even as broken chunks of concrete, rebar, and the gravelly soil conspired to make the task as difficult as possible. The work was tedious, but not nearly as wearisome as the entire year of planning it had taken the man to finally reach this goal. *All that lost time,* thought the man as he speared the hole again, *was now no longer of consequence to him.* He alone had been gifted the knowledge of Nefertem, offspring of the creator god himself, Ptah. If all the archaic writings he'd been shown were true, the man would have an eternity to make up for any of the time he'd lost.

He alone, Wesley.

Behind him, the only other living creature in the long-abandoned parking lot of what had once been a John Deere plow making factory, chortled and gurgled contently. The baby, his own son still being breast-fed by his mother, reached out and grasped for the simple toys lying around him on the blanket where he lay. A toy figurine of a Universal Movie monster, The Mummy, soon found itself lodged firmly between the toothless, smiling gums of the child. Slobber began to coat the tiny plastic statue as the child's pudgy fingers tried desperately to hold it in place. When it finally slipped from the infant's feeble grasp, the molded monster figurine landed between son and mother.

The mother, throat slit and bleeding out, lay unmoving in the chamber.

Wesley grunted as he finished the last of his digging. He tossed aside the shovel he'd used to open the earth at his feet, then scrambled hurriedly out from the small empty grave. He panted and mopped hastily at his face, eyes, and damp hairline. Barely taking the time to wipe the sting of sweat from his red rimmed eyes. Struggling to contain his excitement and enthusiasm for what would come next. His recently acquired faith and knowledge, courtesy of the Egyptian spiritual leader he'd met and learned from, was a dream come true. Now, as he trembled in excited anticipation, the time was finally at hand. Eternal life beckoned him as if with warm and inviting arms.

Waiting to embrace only him.

Wesley, once a Catholic priest before a myriad of accusations got him discreetly defrocked, stepped over the body of his wife to gather up his son. He gently wrapped the child in the blanket underneath and lifted the baby to his chest. Holding him close and kissing his forehead once as he smiled down at his softly cooing son. Then, turning around, Wesley somberly walked with his son over to the hole he'd only just finished digging. After softly laying the infant in the shallow pit, he tugged at one corner of the blanket and purposefully covered the child's face with it. The baby began to cry. Terror and confusion growing louder in every wail coming out of the earthen pit. The disgraced priest and father worked on seemingly without recognition. Placing the end of his shovel once more into the rocky dirt he'd only just turned over. Without looking down at the shrouded form wiggling under the blanket, Wesley rapidly dumped one pile after another back into the shallow pit. It was the fourth shovelful that never made it into the hole. Behind him, a commanding voice rang out. Calling to Wesley, the instructions clear.

"Drop that shovel and step away from the child. Turn around slowly, and show me your hands." Wesley froze, then bent slightly at the waist, spearing the bladed end in the pile of overturned earth. His hand went to the sheathed knife hanging from his belt. The one he'd used on his wife still stained with her blood.

Wesley spun, nothing was going to get between him and eternal life! Raising the knife, he was immediately shot three times in quick succession. The bullets riddling his chest; the third one piercing his heart and instantly killing him. He toppled over backwards, the knife falling harmlessly from his hand. At his feet, the infant he'd nearly buried alive cried heartily. The desperate screams splitting the night.

Howard holstered his weapon, then ran to where the bawling baby lay half submerged in the rocky dirt of the premature grave. Though he'd lost much use of one arm after being shot a year ago, he used both to unbury the child. Pulling him from the small burial pit and brushing the dirt away from the teary face. He quickly unwrapped the squealing infant, checking what he found was a boy for any injuries, but found none. He clutched the child to his chest and felt the warmth. The baby, perhaps sensing it was safe, quickly quieted in his arms. Detective Howard Davis, his white crewcut stark under the overhead parking lot lights, moved quickly to the woman nearby. She was pale and her chest was covered in blood from the gash at her neck, but she stirred. Her dim eyes focused on his face, the light of life fading quickly.

"Save my baby. Save..." she gasped weakly.

"I have him. He is safe." Howard tried to reassure her before she left the land of the living.

"Please... take... take this... take this for him. Keep... give it to," the woman coughed then. Blood coating her teeth and dripping down her chin. She struggled for something tucked under her. Howard reached down and gently pulled the small thick book she scrabbled for out from under her. He tried to place it in her hand unsuccessfully. The woman shook her head once weakly, her eyes closing.

"For him. Only for... Give to him..." Her words barely a whisper now, Howard could only make out a few of them at a time. He bent close to hear the dying woman's last words and breath. "My son... give... my son Thomas R. Secrist..."

ALSO BY DM GRITZMACHER

The Relict

The Quarry

The Lingering

The Shroud

Coming Soon!

Gritzmonster.com